La collection

« L'ÈRE NOUVELLE »

est dirigée par

Daniel Gagnon

UN DERNIER CADEAU
POUR CORNÉLIA

©
XYZ ÉDITEUR
C.P. 5247, Succursale C
Montréal (Québec)
H2X 3M4

et

Jean Désy

Dépôt légal, troisième trimestre 1989
Bibliothèque nationale du Canada
Bibliothèque nationale du Québec
ISBN 2-89261-018-4

Distribution en librairie:
Diffusion Lougarou inc.
4657, boul. des Grandes Prairies
Saint-Léonard (Québec)
H1R 1A5
514. 326. 14.31

Conception typographique et montage: Régis Normandeau .
Révision: Claude Sabourin
Illustration de la couverture: Daniel Gagnon, *La Coulée*,
acrylique, 60,96 cm x 101,6 cm, 1981.
Maquette de la couverture: Julie Daviau

JEAN DÉSY

UN
DERNIER
CADEAU
POUR
CORNÉLIA

COLLECTION
« L'ÈRE
NOUVELLE »
3

Une heure dans la vie de quelqu'un

Ils m'ont lancé une jaquette en m'ordonnant de la mettre. Ils souriaient de me voir tout nu. Ils souriaient en regardant mes jambes, trop maigres, et mes bras trop longs, et ma barbe tachée de moutarde. Ils avaient des visages d'enterrement mais pourtant je sais qu'en dedans d'eux-mêmes, ils souriaient. Je ne me regarde jamais dans le miroir; j'aurais trop peur de sourire moi aussi. Je sens la moutarde qui s'est figée dans ma barbe; elle provient de mon dernier sandwich, mangé il y a trois jours.

Ils ont fermé la porte. Ils l'ont barricadée. J'ai entendu le loquet tomber en grinçant. Ça m'a donné la chair de poule.

Il pleuvait dehors tout à l'heure. J'aime la pluie et ses odeurs de vers de terre. Sentir tomber les gouttes une à une sur les joues, puis les laisser descendre dans la bouche : voilà un de ces plaisirs dont je n'aurais pas dû me priver… Je n'avais pas goûté à l'eau de pluie depuis des années. Ils ne m'ont pas laissé en boire autant que j'aurais voulu. «Embarque!» m'a crié un policier en me poussant dans son auto. Quelle rudesse! Mais quelle force!

Peut-être que cette pluie a pu éteindre le feu qui brûlait mon immeuble?

Je les entends chuchoter derrière la porte. «C'est un fou. On l'a trouvé tout nu dans son appartement. Un vrai cadavre. Il sent mauvais.»

Cette chambre est glaciale. Toute blanche. Et le lit est comme mort, boulonné au plancher, sans même un craquement quand je m'assois dessus. Je ne vais pas mettre cette jaquette d'hôpital, même si j'ai froid. J'aime mieux sentir la peau de mes cuisses sous mes mains, et me caresser l'entrecuisse, en attendant... en attendant... j'ai parfois l'impression qu'il y a des siècles que j'attends.

Ils ne savent pas que je les observe du coin de l'œil, par cette vitre qui doit être incassable. Toutes les vitres pour les gens de mon espèce sont incassables. Ils pourraient me regarder eux aussi, s'ils avaient le temps. Mais il n'auront pas le temps, je le sais. Lors de ma dernière visite, il y a un an, ils ne m'ont apporté à manger que cinq heures après mon arrivée. Ils ont reçu une dizaine d'ambulances, toutes sirènes hurlantes, et ils m'ont oublié dans un petit coin, jusqu'à ce que tout le monde ait fini de souffrir ou de mourir... Ils sont tellement drôles quand ils courent avec les civières et qu'ils se lancent des ordres pour sauver toutes les loques qui entrent ici...

Ils me croient fou. Si je leur parlais, peut-être qu'ils changeraient d'idée ? Peut-être pas ? Mais je ne dirai rien, comme la dernière fois. Et ils me garderont quelques jours, je mangerai pour leur faire plaisir, j'obéirai à leurs commandements, puis ils me relâcheront en inscrivant « mutisme complet » sur leur dossier. Je retournerai à mon appartement, ou à un autre s'il a été brûlé complètement. De toute manière, ils n'ont pas de place ici pour me tenir prisonnier très longtemps.

Les pompiers ont été d'une efficacité exemplaire, comme toujours. Je n'ai eu que le temps de mettre le feu dans les poubelles ; des flammes toutes neuves rampaient sur le plancher du perron quand la voisine s'est mise à crier au meurtre. Quelle hystérique !

Et les pompiers sont arrivés, en faisant hurler leurs camions rouges. Une beauté ! C'est un gros bonhomme avec une barbe de capitaine qui est venu me prendre dans ses bras. Il toussait à cause de la fumée qui avait envahi l'appartement. Moi, je ne toussais pas, même si j'en avais envie. J'étais comme Jeanne d'Arc, stoïque, tout nu sur mon bûcher. Il y avait déjà de longues traînées de feu qui léchaient les murs de la cuisine mais je ne bougeais pas, assis bien droit sur ma chaise. Je n'ai pas desserré les dents quand le capitaine des pompiers m'a emporté avec lui. J'étais comme une poupée de chiffon dans les bras de sa mère adoptive. Il brisait mon rêve. Mais j'ai aimé descendre dans la grande échelle ; j'y rêvais aussi depuis longtemps. Un rêve en vaut bien un autre…

La voisine a sûrement raconté à tout le monde que j'avais moi-même allumé l'incendie. C'est une hystérique.

Incapable de se contenir. Une vraie angoissée. La prochaine fois, j'irai verser l'essence sur son perron… peut-être dans son lit, sur sa belle robe de nuit en dentelle mauve. Ça la calmera. Elle est gentille tout de même; elle m'apporte souvent des petits gâteaux au chocolat. Je les donne aux oiseaux quand elle est partie. Elle me dit que je fais pitié, que ma place n'est pas ici, qu'on devrait me trouver un foyer d'accueil ou que je devrais être hospitalisé. Et elle téléphone sans arrêt au propriétaire, aux gens du service social, à la police. Elle fouine partout, fait des « beurk » sordides en touchant la crasse de la table et du réfrigérateur. Elle n'a pourtant jamais le courage de pénétrer dans ma chambre. Elle me dit qu'un cochon ne vivrait pas chez moi. Et elle repart en jacassant comme une perruche. Mais elle revient toujours, à toutes les semaines, avec ses petits gâteaux. Et elle essuie le réfrigérateur. Et elle lance des œillades vers ma chambre…

Tiens! Il y a quelqu'un qui tente d'ouvrir la porte. Je vais jouer à faire le mort; je vais me coucher sur le lit, les mains jointes, la langue pendante. J'espère que je n'aurai pas une érection en pleine simulation de mort…

C'est une infirmière. Elle a ramassé la jaquette que j'avais jetée par terre et elle recouvre mon sexe. Je la vois, à travers mes cils. Ses yeux sont cernés. Elle ne sait pas que je fais semblant d'être mort. Ça n'a pas l'air de la déranger. Elle prend mon pouls. Elle n'est pas nerveuse. Moi, si je devais m'approcher d'un mort, je le serais. Faut croire que dans son métier, on s'habitue à tout. Elle s'est assise sur le bord du lit, à côté de moi. Je la sens toute chaude… elle sent bon. Si elle savait que j'ai déjà voulu étrangler une femme qui avait la même odeur, la même couleur de cheveux, les mêmes petits seins pointus. Mais un mort, ça n'étrangle pas les infirmières. Je garde donc les mains jointes, en paix...

Elle m'a tapoté l'épaule, gentiment. Elle a les mains douces. Elle a probablement compris que je feignais seulement d'être mort. Elle a pris ma température. Elle a dû me tourner sur le côté pour entrer son tube dans mon rectum. Je crois que je ne l'étranglerai pas... Elle est repartie, avec sa chaleur et son parfum français. Je n'ai plus le goût de faire le mort. Je mettrais bien le feu à ce lit et à cette chambre. Mais ils ont pensé à tout: pas d'allumettes ni d'essence. Rien. Que le vide avec ses quatre murs et son lit blanc. Ils ne souhaitent probablement pas que leurs patients se tuent ou foutent le feu à leur baraque... S'ils savaient qu'avec de simples mains, un tout petit cœur, on peut faire beaucoup de choses... un peu à la manière de ma sainte patronne, Jeanne d'Arc.

J'aurais aimé flamber dans mon appartement. Sentir les flammes m'enlacer de leurs longs bras brûlants. Rôtir comme un petit poulet, tourné sur la broche, roussi juste à point. J'avais le goût de changer d'air, de voir autre chose. Le feu purifie, semble-t-il. J'aurais purifié ma vie, et celle des autres, en les débarrassant de ma présence. La voisine aurait pu garder ses gâteaux et sa pitié pour quelqu'un d'autre. J'aurais fait le même voyage que Jeanne D'Arc, l'âme tranquille. Je suis puceau, elle était pucelle, et nous aurions pu nous aimer, quelque part, comme deux anges tombés du ciel...

Je me souviens d'un thérapeute qui m'a dit un jour que j'étais ténébreux à cause du manque de sexe. Je me suis déshabillé et j'ai voulu le violer devant les autres pensionnaires. Il ne m'en a plus jamais reparlé. Un autre hystérique…

Je vis dans un monde bizarre, qui ne ressemble pas beaucoup à celui de tous ces gens en blanc qui se pressent autour de moi. Je les regarde courir et s'agiter et ils me font rire. Mon monde à moi est différent du leur. C'est comme si l'action s'y déroulait par l'intérieur. Et à l'extérieur, il ne se passe rien, ou presque. Un clignement des yeux de temps en temps, un vent, un soupir quand il fait trop froid. Et le frottement d'une allumette, le feulement d'un brasier neuf…

Tiens! Il y a une vieille dame qui vient de chuter sur le plancher. Raide morte, probablement. Sa patate se sera arrêtée d'un coup sec, coupée à la racine. Ils se mettent à trois pour la soulever et l'étendre sur une civière. Il y a un type qui s'agenouille près d'elle et lui enfonce ses poings dans la poitrine. Et un autre qui s'avance avec deux palettes dorées, crie à tout le monde de s'éloigner et hop! casse la vieille dame en deux! Quel monde de fou!

J'ai vu sortir un petit garçon qui tenait son œil dans le creux de sa main. Son père gueulait à fendre l'âme qu'il tuerait un dénommé «Jacques». Un colérique!

J'aperçois deux policiers dans un coin. Ils montrent ma chambre du bout du doigt, et d'autres chambres aussi. Ils sont en conciliabule; ils écrivent sur de longs calepins blancs. Ils préparent peut-être une contravention pour la dernière civière qui passait: excès de vitesse! Quant à moi, je n'ai rien à craindre: je n'ai rien volé. «Voler, c'est pas beau!» Mon père me le disait tout le temps quand il me frappait avec sa barre à clous. Par chance que les policiers sont là pour traquer les voleurs.

Les voilà, ils se dirigent vers moi. Je vais faire le mort, encore une fois. Ils ne pourront peut-être pas déverrouiller la porte...

Ils ont réussi à entrer. Ils dégagent une odeur bovine. Un petit homme en sarrau blanc les a précédés. C'est sûrement le docteur, avec ses poches remplies de papiers, d'ordonnances et d'instruments. Sa chemise est tachée de sang. Il a l'air surmené. Je le serais moi aussi si je devais travailler dans un enfer pareil... Mais je ne travaille pas et je ne travaillerai jamais.

Je garde mes paupières aussi serrées que possible, laissant juste l'espace nécessaire pour entrevoir la face blême du docteur qui se penche vers moi. Il a mauvaise haleine. Il me dit d'arrêter de jouer avec ses nerfs. Il a la voix d'un dépressif.

C'est au tour d'un policier de s'approcher. Sa casquette sent la fumée. Il me pince une joue, très fort. J'ai envie de pleurer. Mais je garde mon calme, comme la pucelle d'Orléans. Si elle a pu tolérer les quolibets des Anglais, je peux probablement endurer la torture. Je sens que quelque chose m'écrase le bras. On veut me faire parler... Je ne dirai rien, rien.

Le docteur a ordonné à l'infirmière de lui amener une seringue, un médicament. Ils veulent me droguer. Il ont lancé des monstres dans ma chambre pour m'éprouver !

Je ne vais pas laisser leurs araignées me piquer. Je vais les écraser et leur sang va gicler sur les murs et tacher leur beau lit immaculé. Puis je vais écrabouiller tous les cancrelats qui ramperont vers moi et voudront me bouffer. Je ne me ferai pas dévorer sans réagir.

Un mille-pattes monte sur le lit. Je le frappe de mon pied, un liquide jaune jaillit de son ventre mais il avance toujours. Il produit de longs sifflements. Il s'apprête à me bouffer à l'aide de ses mandibules aux pinces meurtrières. Je me ratatine contre le mur. Impossible de m'échapper. Des montagnes de mille-pattes bloquent la porte. D'autres monstres grimpent sur mes jambes, courent sur mes flancs, atteignent mes bras pour y enfoncer leurs dards. Je veux hurler, mais je suis paralysé. Toutes ces bêtes féroces vont pouvoir me dévorer maintenant. C'est affreux, affreux !

•

Tout est devenu noir. Il s'est fait un grand silence. J'ai voulu vomir. J'ai ouvert, fermé puis rouvert les yeux. Tous les monstres avaient disparu.

Je suis en nage, solidement attaché à mon lit avec des sangles de cuir. La porte est demeurée ouverte et j'aperçois l'infirmière de tout à l'heure. Elle est assise derrière un long comptoir et elle écrit quelque chose. Des poèmes ? Ou peut-être une lettre de remords. Elle a regretté d'avoir exécuté l'ordre du docteur et elle a fait fuir les monstres. C'est ça ! Elle m'aime ! Mais pourquoi me garde-t-elle attaché ? Si elle me regarde et me sourit, je crois que je lui parlerai.

Pour la première fois depuis très longtemps, je trouverai le courage de lui dire que je veux souvent mourir tellement je me sens seul. Je réfléchirai à chacune de mes paroles, je laisserai venir dans ma bouche et sur ma langue des syllabes chaudes qui formeront la plus belle phrase du monde : « Je vous aime, madame. Je vous aime autant que vous ne le saviez pas. » Et après cet aveu, conquise entièrement, elle s'approchera de moi, me caressera les cheveux et les tempes. Son affection sera mon bonheur et je serai le roi d'un monde n'appartenant qu'à moi. Puis je toucherai ses lèvres avec mes doigts jaunis, mes ongles longs et sales. Loin d'être dégoûtée, elle me demandera de lui fredonner d'autres « je t'aime ». Ses paroles seront comme des baisers et mes doigts redeviendront soudain blancs et propres, sentant la menthe et le café. Elle me sourira et ce simple sourire saura me guérir à tout jamais.

Mais l'infirmière continue d'écrire derrière son pupitre. Elle bâille un peu, relève la tête, regarde une horloge. Elle n'ose pas jeter un coup d'œil dans ma direction. Sa nuque est celle d'un merle, tendre et lisse, et quelques mèches de cheveux qui tombent de son chignon sont des caresses que je lui offrirais volontiers.

Ah ! elle se lève maintenant, se dirige vers ma cellule. Elle garde la tête basse comme si elle réfléchissait. Je vais m'évanouir tellement je suis heureux. Je me réfugie dans le noir, les yeux clos, sans bouger d'un poil.

J'imagine son regard posé sur moi. Je perçois son souffle tout frais. Elle touche mon bras droit. Mon cœur va s'arrêter de courir dans mes veines.

J'ouvre les yeux. Elle fait une moue exquise. Elle dénoue les courroies de cuir, elle brise tous mes liens. Elle m'aime, je le sais ! Je vais lui parler...

Le son rauque qui jaillit soudain de ma gorge la fait sursauter. Elle est blême, son chignon se défait lorsqu'elle projette sa tête vers l'arrière et ses longs cheveux tombés sur ses épaules lui donnent un air de Madeleine affolée. Elle crie de toutes ses forces et son cri ressemble à celui de la haine.

Elle doit se taire. Je lui saute à la gorge et je serre, aussi fort qu'elle a crié. Elle chute brusquement sur le plancher, les yeux révulsés, comme une petite poupée de chiffon qu'on malmène. Elle a perdu un soulier de cuir blanc; je le ramasse et je me sauve.

Devant moi, rien que des corridors et des malades. Des patients par dizaines qui pleurent, engueulent ou prient, tenant parfois dans leurs mains des guenilles malpropres aux odeurs de sang frais. Je bouscule une madame les bras remplis d'enfants la morve au nez qui s'agrippent à une poussette de bébé. Un marmot, les dents cassées et le menton éraflé, se pend aux jupes d'une autre madame comme un singe à son arbre. Il y a des cris stridents tout autour de moi, des chaises qui basculent, des bruits de bottes et les visages écarquillés de tous ces gens qui n'attendaient pas autre chose de leur après-midi qu'un mince soulagement de leurs misères. Mais en ce moment ils doivent me laisser passer.

J'étranglerai le premier qui voudra m'arrêter. Toutes ces portes vitrées et ces murs de briques ne seront jamais des obstacles à ma liberté.

Je fonce. Tête baissée. Il y a du verre partout sur le plancher et mon corps à travers la porte et ma jaquette arrachée, mes mains et mes bras criblés d'éclats coupants et mon front qui bat au rythme affolé de mon cœur.

Mais tout au bout de ce tunnel de vitres fracassées, il y a l'autre monde, sans monstres et avec des plantes à qui se confier, avec de grands arbres centenaires et le soleil.

Les autos caracolent et se tamponnent. Les coups de klaxon de ces bêtes métalliques me font penser aux bêlements d'effroi des infirmières qu'on tue.

Je me dirige vers ces grands ormes, là-bas. Collé à leur écorce, confondu à leur feuillage, je pourrai panser mes blessures et m'enfoncer avec leurs racines jusque dans les tréfonds de la terre chaude.

Mais qui sont tous ces gens qui me courent après ? Des policiers ? Conduits par le petit docteur à l'haleine empoisonnée ? Ils hurlent et gesticulent. Ils me poursuivent avec des matraques et des yeux fous.

Je dois m'enfuir. Nulle part et partout à la fois. Car je ne leur parlerai jamais.

Un autobus. Qui charge. Tel un éléphant. Je m'élance vers ses pneus. L'esprit libre de crier au monde entier que personne ne sera jamais intéressé à écouter les facéties d'un fou.

Vraiment, oui vraiment, qui voudrait bien se préoccuper de la vie de quelqu'un pendant toute une heure ?

La fleur que tu m'avais jetée...

Carmen Campion n'avait jamais beaucoup aimé son mari. Elle le trouvait grossier, particulièrement en public, et très laid, notamment en privé. Pourtant, elle l'avait épousé dans un élan d'innocente naïveté — elle considérait que la beauté physique n'avait pas beaucoup d'importance et croyait que le temps affinerait sa personnalité — et en subissait maintenant les conséquences. Bref, Carmen Campion était malheureuse.

Quand Jean-Paul Campion rentra à la maison ce soir-là, il n'était pas de très belle humeur. Abandonnant ses claques sur le parquet propre de la cuisine, laissant tomber son imperméable sur le dossier d'une chaise, il se dirigea droit vers le salon, ses pantoufles et son journal, n'entendant même pas le « bonsoir » de sa femme qui préparait le souper.

— Bonsoir ! répéta-t-elle.

Jean-Paul ne répondit rien. La routine du retour à la maison l'avait toujours enquiquiné et ces imparables «bonsoirs» n'avaient jamais rien arrangé. Il plongea dans son journal et n'accepta d'en ressortir qu'au «viens souper!». Pesamment, il se leva de son fauteuil et se traîna vers la cuisine. La table était déjà mise et son napperon garni de tout l'arsenal pour mari-affamé-revenant-de-guerre.

«Dure journée?» lui demanda sa femme tout en lui servant une assiettée de spaghettis.

Jean-Paul n'ouvrit la bouche que pour engouffrer les pâtes blanchâtres, tentant d'amadouer son estomac et du même coup de faire taire toutes les vicissitudes de son existence. Carmen s'assit à sa place, bien sagement. Elle songea que son père à elle, alors qu'elle était toute petite, prenait plaisir à lui raconter des histoires drôles pendant les repas.

Bien qu'il fût occupé à avaler ses spaghettis à grand renfort de lichettes, Jean-Paul remarqua un livre déposé sur le coin de la table. Un livre plutôt mince, à la couverture bizarre. Son assiette terminée, il demanda :

— C'est quoi, ça ?

— Un livre. Un recueil de nouvelles... Tu veux le lire ?

— Un livre ! Un livre ! lança-t-il, tout à coup enflammé par la réponse pourtant anodine de sa femme. T'as rien que ça à faire, lire, pendant que moi, je me défonce à te faire vivre ! Dans le fond, t'es bien, toi, à brasser tes nouilles !

Un rictus involontaire vint tirer la joue de Carmen, lui provoquant un chatouillement plaisant à la base du cou. Jean-Paul ne s'aperçut de rien, abattant sa grosse patte sur la couverture du livre. Il le feuilleta en l'abîmant de sauce tomate, y cherchant des illustrations.

— L'auteur s'appelle Claude Mathieu, dit Carmen avec des fleurs dans la voix.

— Mathieu, Mathieu! C'est qui ça? Pas un joueur des Expos en tout cas!

Ce soir-là, Carmen toléra avec infiniment plus de difficulté que d'habitude les sarcasmes de son mari. Elle songea au bonheur simple de son enfance, alors qu'elle s'amusait dans le jardin avec son père. Elle pensa à la joie merveilleuse de se laisser balancer pendant des heures, de jouer à la cachette derrière les pins, de grimper sur son dos en s'imaginant être une grande écuyère...

Soudain, elle entendit la voix doucereuse de Jean-Paul.

— Tu devrais lire des histoires d'amour, roucoula-t-il, du miel dans les prunelles. Des histoires d'amour pour faire des gros mamours à ton Jean-Paul en or.

Le glas venait de sonner, et beaucoup plus tôt que prévu. Carmen ne comprendrait jamais quelles pulsions contradictoires s'ébrouaient dans les profondeurs de la cervelle de Jean-Paul. En effet, celui-ci avait toujours eu la manie de sauter du coq à l'âne, autant dans ses conversations que dans ses humeurs. Sans avoir eu le temps de proposer le dessert, elle fut donc transportée vers le tapis du salon, à peu près comme une feuille morte est emportée par un tourbillon d'automne. L'exubérance libidineuse de son mari, probablement émoustillée par un éclat de lumière, la sauce tomate ou quelque autre stimulus, s'exprimait en débordements de caresses humides, de mots sucrés et de soupirs agonisants. À plat ventre sur sa dulcinée, il l'embrassait avec de grands coups de langue. Tout fut consommé en criant coucou et Carmen, encore étourdie, remit ses bas, replaça sa jupe et s'en fut nettoyer la cuisine. Jean-Paul, repu, rampa jusqu'à son fauteuil et s'abandonna à la fantasmagorie de son journal.

Carmen achevait de ranger les ustensiles dans le lave-vaisselle quand elle entendit un tonitruant: «On est bien, ensemble, hein, ma pitoune!»

Elle jeta un coup d'œil vers le livre sur le coin de la table et eut un sourire énigmatique.

—Tu sais, Jean-Paul, qu'il y a une nouvelle assez extraordinaire dans le livre? «La mort exquise»...

Son mari ne répondit pas, toutes ses énergies intellectuelles se trouvant à nouveau canalisées vers la rubrique des sports.

Le lendemain matin, Carmen fut éveillée par les jurons de son mari:

—Quand une femme aime son homme, elle se lève avant lui et prépare son déjeuner! ronchonna-t-il. Tout le monde n'a pas la chance de lire des livres stupides pendant toute la journée ! hurla-t-il en claquant la porte.

Carmen se leva vers dix heures. Sans même déjeuner, elle prit l'autobus, entraînée par un désir incontrôlable. Telle une automate, elle se laissa conduire par une puissance étrangère. Elle descendit dans la ville basse, marcha quelques centaines de mètres et se retrouva devant la façade d'une boutique située au fond d'une ruelle délabrée, en retrait de la rue principale. Toute la devanture de verre ambré était prise d'assaut par une véritable jungle où pendaient des lianes, où se mouvaient d'immenses lichens qui évoquaient des barbes de vieillards.

Carmen entra et fut immédiatement assaillie par une odeur de terre pourrie. Une bruine collante rendait l'atmosphère surréelle.

Elle toussota deux ou trois fois, tout autant pour se donner confiance que pour alerter un éventuel vendeur: rien. Un chuintement bizarre émanait de plusieurs plantes grasses. Leur feuillage ondoyait au ralenti dans un ballet féerique. Bien qu'elle fût toute seule sur le seuil de la porte, Carmen avait la nette impression d'être regardée par des milliers d'yeux, d'être entourée par des centaines de bras, de jambes et de pieds.

Religieusement, un peu apeurée par la bizarrerie de l'échoppe, Carmen s'avança vers le centre de la pièce, enivrée par tout ce capharnaüm de verdure. Enlevant un gant, elle tendit la main vers une fleur vermeille.

— N'y touchez pas !

Le cri la glaça, l'annulaire figé à quelques centimètres des pétales qui viraient au mauve puis au violet. Carmen se retourna vers un petit homme qui avait émergé d'un taillis d'hibiscus en fleurs et trottinait vers elle. Instinctivement, elle recula. « On ne touche pas aux plantes de ce magasin. C'est clair ! Qu'est-ce que vous voulez ? »

Carmen regardait avec un mélange de crainte et d'émerveillement ce nain à barbichette rousse qui la semonçait. Un sécateur à la main, une ceinture en bandoulière remplie de sachets de graines et de bouts de cordes de chanvre, il lui faisait penser à un Rambo lilliputien, protecteur de l'intégrité d'un jardin botanique d'État.

— Vous voyez cette fleur que vous alliez toucher, continua-t-il. Il s'agit d'un trille rouge que j'ai nourri à ma façon, fertilisé avec des engrais que j'ai développés moi-même… Je l'ai dressé, comme un petit chien…

— Et il passe du rouge au violet quand on lui fait peur ? risqua Carmen avec un courage qui la surprit elle-même.

— C'est en plein ça, petite madame, dit le nain en se radoucissant.

Celui-ci approcha alors un morceau de papier mouchoir des pétales violets du trille. Il s'en dégagea aussitôt une fumée rosâtre, à l'odeur aromatique. Le papier fut désintégré sur-le-champ et la fleur reprit sa couleur vermeille.

—Extraordinaire ! J'espère qu'on peut en acheter ? laissa échapper Carmen, éblouie.

—Bien… Ça dépend des clients… Vous savez, tout ceci — et le nain montrait de ses petits bras grands ouverts la véritable forêt qui s'étalait autour de lui — est plus qu'un gagne-pain. C'est une passion, un art…

—Ah bon… mâchonna Carmen, à la fois ravie et troublée, contemplant les volutes de gaz qui s'échappaient encore de la fleur.

—Mais dites-moi donc ce que vous cherchez, petite madame ?

—C'est que, c'est que… je me demandais si vous cultiviez des plantes carnivores…

—Mais certainement !

Carmen se sentit soudainement très à l'aise. Elle déboutonna son manteau et fit un pas en direction du nain.

—Vous n'auriez pas une plante appelée *Carnivora Breitmannia* ?

Le vendeur sourit et, sans dire un mot, prit la main de Carmen en l'attirant vers l'arrière du magasin. Celle-ci se laissa conduire, entièrement conquise. Derrière un muret, il farfouilla dans une marée de pots de grès pour finalement en ressortir une petite plante un peu terne.

—Je ne connais pas de *Carnivora Breitmannia*, dit-il en tenant le pot à bout de bras, tel un trophée. Vous savez, je me spécialise dans les plantes nordiques. La *Carnivora Breitmannia* est probablement une espèce tropicale. C'est d'ailleurs la première fois que j'entends ce nom. Mais j'ai ici pour vous, et pour vous seule, petite madame, parce que vous m'êtes très, très sympathique, une plante exceptionnelle, oui, très exceptionnelle. Il s'agit de la *Sarracenia purpurea*, communément appelée la Sarracénie pourpre : la tigresse de nos tourbières, la carnivore des forêts, la déchiqueteuse par excellence !

Carmen frissonna. Elle tendit ses mains ouvertes vers la plante, mais le nain la fit reculer d'un geste brusque. « Faites très attention. *Sarracenia purpurea* est dangereuse. On ne l'approche pas impunément, à moins d'une grande habitude et de beaucoup d'affection. Regardez bien ceci... »

Il déposa le pot sur une petite tablette accrochée au mur. Un rayon de lumière l'éclaira alors directement, ce qui permit à Carmen, adossée au mur opposé, de l'admirer à loisir. Seule dans son petit pot, elle se dressait, souveraine, ses quatre feuilles en forme de trompette, veinées de pourpre, irradiant d'une tige solide surmontée d'une unique fleur rouge sang. Chacune de ces feuilles semblait tendue dans l'air, prête à mordre, happer, broyer et avaler, les opercules de leurs sommets ressemblant à s'y méprendre à des gueules entrouvertes.

Subjuguée, Carmen ne vit pas le nain plonger une main dans un sac de toile et en faire surgir une libellule aux deux paires d'ailes transparentes, presque aussi longues que ses propres doigts. « Et maintenant, dit-il d'un ton solennel, vous allez être témoin d'un prodige. Reculez-vous. Il pourrait y avoir du danger pour tout ce qui bouge. »

À ces mots, il laissa échapper la libellule qui voleta dans deux ou trois directions puis, s'élevant avec un léger vrombissement, se dirigea tout droit vers *Sarracenia purpurea*. Elle n'était pas à vingt centimètres du pot qu'une feuille se déploya vers l'avant, ouvrant bien grand son opercule et découvrant une longue rangée de dents pointues. Cette gueule saisit la libellule par le thorax, se referma dans un claquement sec et reprit immédiatement sa place. Seul un léger ondoiement de la plante vint rappeler à la spectatrice ébahie qu'un insecte volait dans la pièce quelques secondes auparavant.

Carmen, à la fois effrayée et émerveillée, se tourna vers le nain qui battait des mains et trépignait de joie. « Vous avez vu les dents de ma *Sarracenia* ! Fabuleux, n'est-ce pas ? Un crocodile ! Un lion ! Un requin ! »

Il fouilla à nouveau dans son sac et en retira cette fois un minuscule colibri à gorge rubis, aux ailes d'un vert lustré. « Vous voulez sûrement une autre démonstration », dit-il, tout excité.

Et avant même que Carmen ait pu répondre, il relâcha l'oiseau-mouche. Quelques zigzags, deux ou trois vrilles et celui-ci se retrouva à la portée de la terrible *Sarracenia* qui s'agita brusquement alors qu'une deuxième feuille s'élançait vers l'oiseau, découvrant deux rangées de crocs acérés qui mordirent l'air plusieurs fois, cherchant à attraper cette proie qui virevoltait dans tous les sens. Le colibri fit un mauvais soubresaut vers l'avant et sa tête fut arrachée d'un seul coup par la *Sarracenia*. Le reste du corps s'écrasa sur le plancher. Une autre feuille s'allongea démesurément vers le sol et saisit la poitrine encore palpitante de l'oiseau.

Le nain jubilait. Présentant son sac à Carmen, il lui proposa une nouvelle démonstration.

—Non, non, ça va! répondit-elle, pleinement satisfaite. C'est incroyable! Je ne pensais pas que de telles choses existaient...

—Ce n'est pas une «chose», réagit le nain rendu écarlate par l'excitation. J'ai dorloté *Sarracenia* avec amour, je lui ai prodigué mes soins les plus raffinés. Elle m'obéit comme une enfant...

—Je ne savais pas qu'une plante, même carnivore, pouvait attraper un insecte au vol. Quant à l'oiseau...

Carmen se tut, se remémorant l'attaque sanglante et le minuscule corps décapité, affalé sur le sol, les ailes brisées... Elle en eut un frisson de contentement qui, parti de ses joues, l'électrisa de la tête aux pieds.

—Vous avez raison, la sarracénie est une chasseresse passive dans son milieu naturel. Elle attend normalement qu'un insecte malheureux tombe dans son piège avant de le digérer à l'aide d'une diastase puissante. Ses armes ne sont que des petits poils raides qui empêchent ses victimes de s'échapper. Mais grâce à mes soins amoureux, les dons de *Sarracenia purpurea* se sont développés. Elle a maintenant du nerf et de la combativité, à l'instar de n'importe quel autre prédateur. Oui, madame, j'ai conçu là une plante infiniment agressive et j'en suis fier.

Le visage du nain, exalté, était secoué de tics. Après une pause, il prit avec précaution le pot entre ses mains, murmura quelques mots inintelligibles, ses lèvres allant même jusqu'à frôler la fleur, et le déposa dans l'arrière-boutique.

Le voyant disparaître, Carmen cria: « Je vous l'achète ! Votre prix sera le mien. »

Réapparaissant aussitôt, le nain dit d'une voix lasse:

— C'est que... je me suis beaucoup attaché... avec le temps...

— Je vous donne cinquante dollars !

— Elle est devenue un peu comme ma petite fille...

— Cent dollars !

— Ça n'a presque pas de prix...

— Deux cents dollars ! C'est tout ce que j'ai, cria Carmen, exaspérée par la mine mercantile du nain qui frottait copieusement ses mains.

—Marché conclu ! Vous faites l'affaire de votre vie ! clama le vendeur qui sautilla sur place avant de retourner dans l'arrière-boutique.

Il en revint après avoir déposé la plante carnivore dans une boîte de fer grillagée munie d'une poignée de cuir.

—Faites très attention. *Sarracenia* ne vous connaît pas encore. Tant qu'elle sera dans sa cage, vous ne risquez rien. Mais si vous ouvrez la porte ou si vous la sortez, assurez-vous qu'elle a été bien nourrie et surtout, qu'elle vous aime. Vous devrez lui donner de l'affection, exactement comme si vous possédiez un animal familier... un chacal ou un vautour par exemple ! ricana le nain.

—Je suis certaine que nous allons bien nous entendre, dit Carmen en prenant la boîte.

—Une dernière chose, dit le nain qui ouvrait déjà la porte.

—Oui ?

—Pas de remboursement...

•

Ce soir-là, Jean-Paul était plus bougon que jamais, ressentant un oppressant mal de vivre.

Quand il aperçut Carmen, éblouissante dans une nouvelle robe bourgogne, il ne put se retenir et leurs deux corps roulèrent jusque sur le tapis du salon.

— Oh, ma belle pitoune ! Regarde-moi la grosse, grosse envie d'amour de ton Jean-Paul en chocolat !

Et Carmen subit ce nouvel enfer de lubricité sans mot dire.

•

Le lendemain matin, alors que Jean-Paul s'apprêtait à dévorer un muffin aux bleuets, il aperçut la cage de fer suspensue au-dessus de la table de cuisine. *Sarracenia purpurea* semblait y dormir tellement elle était paisible, toute menue dans son petit pot de grès, sa fleur pourpre courbée vers l'avant comme dans une génuflexion.

— Tu veux m'expliquer qu'est-ce que cette chose-là fait dans ma maison ?

— C'est une plante, mon chéri...

— Une plante dans une cage ? J'aurai tout vu !

— C'est une plante carnivore, très spéciale. J'ai d'ailleurs commencé à la dresser.

Pour la première fois en trois mille matins, Jean-Paul ne put s'empêcher de rire.

— Tu vas la faire sauter dans un cerceau de feu, j'imagine ?

— Non, mais je vais lui apprendre quelques petits trucs...

—Ah... Bon, je te laisse à ton dressage. Moi, j'ai d'autres chats à fouetter!

Et Jean-Paul sortit en riant, tout fier de sa blague.

Carmen ne put s'empêcher d'ouvrir la porte de la cage. *Sarracenia purpurea* resplendissait sous la lumière drue du soleil qui emplissait la cuisine et le cœur de sa propriétaire.

Carmen déballa un énorme morceau de bœuf saignant et le tendit vers la cage à l'aide d'un bâton. Les quatre feuilles se déployèrent en même temps, cherchant à se faufiler par la porte entrouverte, se mêlant les unes aux autres et exposant une dentelure nacrée dégoulinante de salive rose.

Carmen n'eut que le temps de retirer son bâton; déjà claquaient dans l'air quatre paires de mandibules affamées qui se partageaient leur déjeuner. Les feuilles mastiquèrent longtemps la viande. Ce n'est que lorsqu'elle fut certaine d'avoir rassasié *Sarracenia* que Carmen osa approcher délicatement la main à l'intérieur de la cage. Émue, la gorge serrée, elle frôla une feuille puis descendit ses doigts le long de la tige, comme dans un attouchement. Rien n'arriva. Carmen en éprouva un plaisir étourdissant.

Les jours passèrent, Carmen apprivoisant sa bête sauvage, la rendant de moins en moins bête mais de plus en plus sauvage, moyennant des quantités importantes de viande rouge. Un soir, après un nouvel accès de mal de vivre, Jean-Paul devint hargneux et décida que cette plante prenait trop de place dans la cuisine et l'empêchait même d'avaler ses spaghettis avec tout le plaisir auquel il avait droit.

—Carmen! Ta bebitte me dérange! Tu pourrais pas la pendre ailleurs... dans la cave par exemple. On dirait tout le temps qu'elle me regarde.

—Mais voyons chéri, ce n'est qu'une plante.

Ce simple «chéri» vint tout arranger. Jean-Paul dédaigna les quelques pâtes rougies qui restaient dans le fond de son assiette et se précipita sur sa femme. Sans même la transporter dans le salon cette fois-là, il décida de lui montrer son affection directement dans la cuisine. Nu comme un ver, il allait se coucher sur elle quand il sentit tout à coup la peau de son dos arrachée. Il hurla en roulant sur le côté. Une feuille mâchait lentement un lardon d'entrecôte; la tige était passée par la porte de la cage laissée ouverte par mégarde.

Carmen ne put s'empêcher de sourire, son cœur battant la chamade, malgré son mari qui geignait en tentant de porter une main à son dos labouré par deux rangées de crocs. Pâle comme la mort, il ne put se relever.

Ce n'est que dans l'ambulance qu'il trouva la force de demander à sa femme ce qui s'était passé.

—Je ne sais pas... Probablement que tu t'es frotté au rebord d'acier de la table.

Il fallut deux greffes de peau et un mois de convalescence pour guérir Jean-Paul de la plaie qui le torturait. Il fallut un mois de soins attentifs pour guérir Carmen du contentement qui l'enivrait.

Carmen feignait de veiller sur son mari alité, constamment couché sur le ventre. Elle ne cessait de dorloter *Sarracenia*, de lui prodiguer les soins les plus délicats et de lui donner l'affection la plus émouvante. Quand son mari parvenait à s'endormir, elle la sortait de sa cage, jouant avec elle pendant des heures entières, lui faisant bouffer des morceaux de saucissons qu'elle envoyait en l'air et que *Sarracenia* attrapait au vol. Très souvent, celle-ci allait même jusqu'à mordiller les joues et les bras de sa maîtresse en guise de remerciement.

Le bonheur de Carmen aurait été total si son mari n'avait pas fini par se rétablir et redevenir l'intolérable brute qu'elle avait connue.

Un soir qu'il rentrait du bureau aussi rembruni et détestable qu'à l'accoutumée, il s'attarda dans la cuisine au lieu de se précipiter dans le salon. Changement majeur dans ses habitudes : peut-être son mal de vivre chamboulait-il complètement sa raison ? Après avoir tapoté les fesses de sa femme, il se dirigea vers la plante, toujours suspendue au-dessus de la table. Mal lui en prit de la taquiner en passant deux doigts à travers les barreaux. En un éclair, deux feuilles s'ouvrirent d'un même élan pour lui dépecer les phalanges. Jean-Paul s'effondra, sous le choc d'une douleur suraiguë.

Dès qu'il sortit de l'hôpital, Carmen eut droit à la plus terrifiante des colères. Le vin venait de tourner au vinaigre; il avait tout compris — de la bonne humeur de sa femme qui durait depuis des mois jusqu'au supposé accident de la table de cuisine — et il explosa. Il la roua de coups. Longuement. Savamment. Avec ses poings et ses pieds. La traînant par les cheveux dans toute la maison.

Puis, fou de rage, il arracha la cage du plafond, prenant bien garde de laisser sa main valide sur la poignée de cuir, hors de portée de *Sarracenia*. Il sortit dehors et la projeta à bout de bras sur le parterre du voisin. La cage fit plusieurs bonds avant de s'immobiliser, de guingois. Agrippant une pelle ronde, Jean-Paul frappa et frappa, écrabouillant la plante sans pitié.

Lorsqu'il rentra, Carmen gisait, inconsciente, les vêtements déchirés, les membres tuméfiés. Il enjamba son corps et alla se coucher.

Carmen ne reprit ses sens qu'au lever du soleil. Plusieurs côtes cassées lui donnaient de la difficulté à respirer. Elle finit par se relever, de peine et de misère, les jambes engourdies. Son pied droit, fracturé, traînait et élançait terriblement. Se rendant soudainement compte de l'absence de *Sarracenia*, elle chercha partout dans la maison; peine perdue.

Elle tituba jusqu'au dehors et vit, derrière la maison du voisin, la cage écrasée de *Sarracenia*.

À genoux devant sa bien-aimée, elle pleura amèrement. Tout à coup, un bout de feuille tressauta, puis un autre. Bien qu'elle fût réduite en bouillie, *Sarracenia* vivait encore, comme par miracle, et ses feuilles se gonflaient, leurs veinules laissant pulser un sang neuf.

Carmen prit la plante entre ses doigts. Les quatre feuilles s'ouvrirent brusquement, se fusionnant en une seule feuille à la gueule béante, aux dents dix fois plus

longues, à la respiration mille fois plus puissante. Un éclat
de soleil embrasa Carmen qui fut soulevée de terre. La
gorge immense de *Sarracenia* était devenue un entonnoir
invitant.

Carmen s'y laissa glisser, tout doucement, comme on
s'enfonce avec plaisir, tête première, dans l'eau tiède de
l'océan. La lumière crue du soleil fit place à une autre, plus
tamisée, provenant du bout de ce tunnel attrayant, aux
parois lisses, à la voûte monumentale, aux effluves de rose
sauvage. Carmen cessa de souffrir et put respirer librement.
L'univers qui lui apparaissait était comme le cœur d'un
arbre millénaire, comme le ventre d'un volcan éteint qu'on
aurait visité en plongeant jusqu'au centre de la terre.

Il y eut un bouillonnement. Un grondement intense
retentit et un mur de lave vint tout à coup refermer l'entrée
de cette grotte. Carmen avait quitté le monde des mortels.

•

Sarracenia profita à merveille de cette nouvelle terre
d'accueil. Les premiers temps, elle se contenta de bouffer
les mouches, araignées, chenilles et limaces qui vinrent à
passer à la portée de ses crocs. Mais quand le voisin se
rendit compte des dons peu communs de la plante bizarre
qui poussait sur son terrain, il se mit à la nourrir avec le
plus bel enthousiasme. Il s'imaginait déjà devenu dompteur
d'une plante carnivore célèbre, dans un cirque qui ferait le
tour de la planète en montrant aux enfants avides de
connaître les choses insoupçonnables qui se passent ici-bas
et dont on ne se doute pas. Il se garda bien de divulguer à

sa tendre épouse le pourquoi de ses achats massifs de viande de bœuf et ce fut toujours avec beaucoup d'émotion qu'il gava *Sarracenia* chaque nuit, tout en lui enseignant les mille et une prouesses qui devraient faire d'eux de grandes vedettes.

Pendant ce temps, Jean-Paul souffrait beaucoup du départ de Carmen. Il devait préparer lui-même ses repas et, surtout, il ne trouvait plus moyen d'assouvir sa libido exubérante. Pourtant, jamais il ne se culpabilisa de la rossée qu'il lui avait administrée.

Un soir, alors que son « immense affection » le tourmentait particulièrement, il décida de chercher une compagne à qui il pourrait faire don de toute sa tendresse. Il parcourut donc la ville en automobile, préférant les quartiers plutôt gris, les ruelles étroites et les bistros enfumés, et finit par trouver Lolita, débordante d'une profusion de charmes. Devant les trois billets de cent dollars que lui présenta Jean-Paul, de plus en plus en mal d'amour, elle accepta presque avec véhémence de l'accompagner et de passer la nuit avec lui. Elle fut d'abord un peu surprise que cet homme lui propose son propre domicile, au lieu de l'habituel motel, mais il lui fit comprendre qu'il recherchait simplement une douce moitié pour lui prodiguer quelques gâteries.

Jean-Paul était follement excité à la pensée de partager sa couche avec cette affriolante Lolita. Énervé, il se gara si gauchement en arrivant chez lui qu'il érafla toute l'aile arrière de son automobile contre une borne-fontaine et arracha le pare-choc. « Bof, une baliverne de cinq cents dollars » se dit-il, l'âme en paix. « Qu'est-ce que l'argent quand on est en amour ! »

Ne prenant même pas le temps d'enlever son chapeau, il souleva Lolita dans ses bras — elle riait aux éclats en l'entendant bégayer des bribes de poèmes tout juste composés pour l'occasion — et la transporta jusqu'à sa chambre. La lune brillait devant la fenêtre grande ouverte.

Ce fut l'apothéose !

Ni souvenir, ni mal de vivre, ni angoisse absurde ne survécurent à la resplendissante envie d'amour de Jean-Paul. Après une dizaine de secondes de jouissance céleste, il se laissa retomber sur le dos, épuisé mais heureux, le sexe encore dressé comme un fanion fiché en terre après la bataille. Obnubilé par le repos du guerrier, il ne remarqua pas Lolita qui se levait pour aller faire un brin de toilette.

Il y eut comme un chuintement. Un bruit de feuille froissée. Une reptation le long du mur de la maison. Puis la silhouette géante d'une gueule ouverte qui se profilait devant la lune et pénétrait par la fenêtre. Une bave épaisse dégoulinait de chaque côté des larges mandibules munies de crocs luisants.

De la salle de bains, Lolita entendit un « clac » assourdissant suivi d'un hurlement. Accourant dans la chambre, elle entrevit la gigantesque plante qui avait saisi Jean-Paul par le tronc et le mâchonnait lentement. Des dents longues comme des poignards s'enfonçaient dans la chair et les os de Jean-Paul qui fut broyé avant de disparaître dans le fond d'une gorge violacée.

Et tombé sur le lit défait, il ne resta plus de lui que son sexe, tranché à la base, duquel giclait par secousses un sang brunâtre.

Histoire d'oignons
qui faisaient pleurer

Que j'aime donc me reposer! Comme je suis bien, couché sur le dos, en décubitus dorsal... les cubitus repliés sur la poitrine, les radius s'y jouxtant, dans une union tout ce qu'il y a de plus charnel, avec en bout de ligne les deux menottes jointes, dans un appel céleste à tout ce qui a existé et sera encore, pour l'éternité...

Je suis si confortable, à l'horizontale, les jambes allongées et les pieds relevés vers le haut, les orteils enfin libérés de ce fardeau quotidien qui aurait fini par les rendre complètement marteaux. Et surtout, contentement suprême! l'hallux valgus de mon pied droit est au repos. Ce maudit oignon détestable, qui n'a pas cessé de me faire souffrir durant toute ma chienne de vie verticale, dort enfin. Il m'en aura fait baver, ce tubercule de malheur, depuis le premier moment de sa conception, un jour de ma petite enfance lorsque j'avais botté de travers le coccyx du gros Tremblay qui me lançait des cailloux. Nous avions lâché simultanément le même cri de douleur, pour deux raisons anatomiques fort différentes, et j'étais revenu en boitant chez ma maman, tout penaud, le gros orteil démesurément gonflé.

Dans les années qui suivirent, mon oignon me fit pleurer à chaque chute de baromètre; dès que le moindre cumulo-nimbus se pointait au loin, un vague élancement naissait de ma phalange et se métamorphosait bien vite en spasmes épouvantables, me forçant à m'asseoir. Une chaleur infernale envahissait alors mon orteil qui virait du bleu au rouge et me laissait invalide pour plusieurs jours, m'enlevant toute envie de sauter à la corde ou de botter à nouveau le derrière des imbéciles.

Ma mère, évidemment inquiétée par de pareils soubresauts d'invalidité, consulta la médecine officielle à mon sujet. Malgré mon jeune âge, le vieux docteur du quartier songea immédiatement à une podagre: «La goutte du gros orteil!» tonna-t-il de sa voix éraillée par le tabac.

Intéressé au plus haut point par mon cas, il me palpa affectueusement, le gros orteil, pendant de longues minutes, assez pour se rendre compte qu'il s'agissait plutôt d'un simple oignon post-traumatique. Il me conseilla le repos et me suggéra d'éviter l'humidité. Lorsque l'illustrissime doc m'entendit demander à ma mère si nous déménagerions dans le désert du Nevada pour mettre mon tubercule au sec, il se mit à rire et affirma, la main sur mon épaule: «Il ira loin ce gamin-là... mais certainement pas en courant!»

Et il m'ordonna d'avaler une série de petites pilules bleues et blanches qui eurent le don de me tournebouler l'estomac sans me soulager pour autant de mon douloureux oignon.

Devant la défaite de la médecine traditionnelle et le décès de notre médecin de famille emporté par son rire trop gras et un cancer du larynx, ma mère décida de me jeter dans la gueule de la médecine parallèle. Elle me traîna chez un rebouteux qui s'exclama, en voyant mon orteil enflé et tout rouge : « Tu devrais le planter dans ton jardin c't'oignon-là ! C'est pas des pieds de céleri qui y pousseraient ! »

Mais malgré son humour assez grisâtre, il finit par me soulager en étirant adroitement mon membre tuméfié. C'est d'ailleurs grâce à ses conseils que je parvins par la suite à subir les inévitables orages d'été sans trop d'appréhension ; dès que la douleur apparaissait, je manipulais savamment mon orteil. Avis à ceux qui auraient des problèmes avec certains de leurs membres tuméfiés ! Ainsi en alla-t-il de cet oignon et de mon premier contact avec les maladresses de la Nature à mon égard.

C'est un peu grâce à ce souvenir que je profite pleinement de ce repos mérité, de cet arrêt dans la course de mon pauvre corps contre le temps. Quand je repense à toutes ces cicatrices accumulées au fil des années, je prolonge sans aucune gêne ce moment de dolce vita. Je détends avec compassion chacun de mes os, piliers de ce squelette qui me tint debout si longtemps et m'évita de ramper parmi les escargots, limaces et autres gastéropodes.

Je me souviens en particulier de mon tibia, parce qu'il rue encore souvent dans les brancards de mon passé. Un jour, après le plus extraordinaire dessalage de ma vie de canoteur, il s'était cassé net en heurtant un rocher.

Emporté par une exubérance toute printanière, je m'étais aventuré seul sur la rivière Métabetchouan et j'avais sauté le seuil d'un rapide classé «cataracte» dans le guide des rivières. Mon canot avait fait une cravate et s'était rempli d'eau. Propulsé à toute vitesse contre les rochers, j'avais pu sauter *in extremis*, pas assez vite cependant pour éviter que mon tibia gauche ne servît d'amortisseur au canot qui tamponnait une grosse pierre. L'os se cassa dans un craquement de biscuit soda, me donnant l'occasion d'expérimenter la douleur à son meilleur. Je perdis conscience, sous l'effet de l'atroce sensation qui montait vers l'aine et aussi de la noyade qui s'en venait à grandes goulées d'eau glacée.

Mais je ne mourus point! Emporté par de puissantes vagues, je dus voyager quelques centaines de mètres vers l'aval des rapides. Et dans un miracle typique des contes de fées et des histoires à dormir debout, je fus sauvé par des campeurs qui admiraient la beauté des détritus que charriait la rivière Métabetchouan en furie. À l'hôpital de brousse, un infirmier me demanda de mordre dans une guenille pendant qu'il déverrouillait ma jambe et l'ajustait dans une attelle. J'ai conservé une photo de cet infirmier dans une malle poussiérieuse du grenier, enveloppée dans la même guenille. On me fit un plâtre et on enterra les restes de mon canot dans le cimetière voisin. Quelques fleurs garnissent en permanence sa tombe. Il faut vous dire que dans l'arrière-pays de chez moi, on a du respect pour les canots victimes des rivières en crue et des chauffards qui les conduisent.

Les mois subséquents furent intolérables; au lieu de se souder, les fragments d'os se mirent à suinter et on dut me refaire un plâtre sec chaque semaine. Une subtance gluante, verte et odoriférante, jaillissait en permanence de mon membre inférieur, comme une source vive. On m'opéra, pour découvrir que je faisais une splendide ostéomyélite à salmonelle. On me taillada les chairs, on me grugea le tibia, on m'aspergea d'eau stérile, on me noya d'antibiotiques et on me ligota la jambe de fils résorbables. Quand j'appris que la bactérie en question (*salmonella typhimurium*) provenait sans l'ombre d'un doute des eaux souillées de la Métabetchouan, une fureur terrible s'empara de mon être, habituellement civilisé et bardé d'inhibitions, et je n'eus que l'envie de trucider tous les diarrhéiques campeurs du dimanche qui avaient pollué sans vergogne ma rivière. Ah! je rage encore contre ce monde excrémentiel qui fait pourrir tout ce qui coule et vit.

En ces temps mouvementés de mon existence, j'étais donc très souvent en colère, surtout lorsque je voyais pulser de mon tibia en éruption les laves de pus qui semblaient ne jamais vouloir se tarir. Pourtant, après de longs mois de traitements incessants, prodigués par les autres, et d'infinis apitoiements, psalmodiés par moi-même, je parvins à guérir. Je ne devais pas en rester trop infirme, bien que le séquestre de ma jambe, ce morceau de tibia frappé de nécrose, augmentait d'un cran les incapacités premières-nées de mon oignon podologique. Je sortis de cette guerre d'usure contre l'affreuse salmonelle maigre comme un clou et boiteux comme une béquille. Pourtant, je m'en libérai, et plus lucide justement: j'avais souffert, et la souffrance éclaire l'esprit humain. Sachez, chers esprits avides de philosophie existentialiste, que le martyre permet d'atteindre des extases d'une incommensurable dignité. Je dirais même, dans un mystique élan de sagesse orientale: à bas la santé qui avilit, vive la maladie qui sanctifie!

Mais je blague. Rien ne vaut la santé, surtout quand on a goûté aux affres sordides de la souffrance. Vous voyez que je suis devenu un sage, dans mon genre... J'ai peut-être boité durant toute mon existence, à cause de mon oignon droit et de mon séquestre gauche, mais la chance a voulu que ces deux accidents de parcours surviennent sur deux membres différents. Boitant également des deux jambes, mon apparence globale s'en est toujours trouvée améliorée et lorsqu'on me voyait marcher, on se demandait d'emblée si j'avais bu. Maigre consolation, me direz-vous? Morbleu, non! Il vaut mieux tituber et avoir l'air alcoolique, surtout si l'on est sobre, que de boiter pour un handicap qui ne prête à aucune confusion. La philosophie bouddhiste qui sous-tend ce raisonnement nous apprend ceci: l'homme sage est celui qui paraît fou tout en sachant très bien qu'il est sage. Quant à la philosophie taoïste, elle n'en dit pas grand-chose.

C'est pourquoi je me permets de sourire en repensant à tous ces cons qui ont ri de ma démarche. Ils riaient pour la mauvaise raison, et c'était là tout leur tort; il n'y avait que moi qui savais la vérité. Voilà tout le sens de ma démarche... intellectuelle!

Ma vie a été ainsi ballottée entre la paix de la santé et les tourments de la maladie. Je suis né et j'ai crû, malgré la destinée qui me harassait. J'ai su demeurer positif, comme un proton gravitant au cœur de sa molécule, et j'ai accueilli les maux qui m'assaillaient avec tout le courage dont j'étais capable. J'ai affronté les tempêtes la tête haute et la chemise ouverte, face à l'inconnu qui se faisait connaître; j'ai eu droit à ses gifles comme à ses coups de massue, mais toujours, j'ai su garder mon vaisseau à flot. J'ai bien souvent failli faire naufrage mais j'ai pu tenir la barre à deux mains, luttant frénétiquement contre l'adversité. Quand je songe à ce qu'a été ma vie, comme je me trouve admirable !

Je dois cependant admettre que j'ai aussi eu quelques faiblesses, quelques instants de profond découragement. Je n'ai pas toujours été le héros que je voulais être, courageux conquérant du temps qui passe et qui rend malade. Et pourtant, quand je me souviens de ma péritonite aiguë, je redeviens fier de moi.

Un jour, un caillou malotru décida de provoquer dans mon petit ventre la plus belle appendicite du monde. Je profitais plus que jamais de l'existence, courant, dansant et chantant, aimant, jouant et mangeant, quand une indicible douleur me fit plier l'échine. Avec un ami, je n'avais dégusté que trois ou quatre pizzas, accompagnées d'insignifiants amuse-gueule aux huîtres que nous avions arrosés de quelques litres de cuvée-maison. Peut-être était-ce le pepperoni, ou bien les anchois, mais quelque chose poussa ce calcul perdu, qui cherchait probablement sa mère dans une de mes boucles digestives, à se faufiler dans le secret

de mes boyaux et à obstruer mon appendice qui se gonfla
comme un ballon. Le temps d'avaler deux coupes de vin et
trois pointes de pizza... ça y était !

Comme j'étais jeune et peu préoccupé de mes destinées
physique et spirituelle, je n'écoutai pas ce premier signal
d'alarme et continuai à m'empiffrer toute la soirée. Stimulé
par la boustifaille italienne et les rasades de nectar
bachique, mon appendice s'enfla et s'enfla, se contentant
d'envoyer à mon cerveau grisé par les plaisirs de la chair
d'intermittents messages douloureux. Ce n'est que lorsque
mon intestin éclata que le signal de détresse devint assez
fort pour obnubiler mes papilles gustatives; je roulai sous
la table et mon compagnon de beuverie dut demander de
l'aide simplement pour me coucher sur un banc. Ratatiné
en chien de fusil, je râlais des vapeurs de sauce tomate tout
en implorant le Grand Boucher de m'extirper le mal qui me
rongeait les entrailles.

Ce fut une charmante chirurgienne, aux doigts de fée et
aux yeux de déesse, qui me raconta le lendemain l'histoire
de mon calcul. Elle me dit que l'opération s'était bien
déroulée mais que mes excès de table avaient failli me
coûter la vie. Avec un tuyau dans le bas-ventre, un autre
dans le nez et un dernier dans mon organe habituellement
érectile, je me contentai d'acquiescer à toutes ses
recommandations : je n'abuserais plus jamais de la pizza,
surtout aux anchois; je ne boirais plus de vin trop froid;
j'écouterais mon abdomen quand il me lancerait des cris
d'alarme. Il me fallut quinze jours pour me débarrasser du
dégât qui salissait mon intérieur abdominal. Mais comme
j'avais l'esprit ailleurs, je ne me laissais pas aller à la

dépression facile. Je combattais! Je luttais parce que j'étais positif. Je planifiais mon existence de plus en plus trépidante. J'organisais dans ses moindres détails le grand spectacle dont je devais être la vedette! Mon ventre, même amoché, était le dernier de mes soucis. Jamais l'idée de mourir ne m'effleura, pas même une seconde, car je possédais la jeunesse, cette suprême qualité qui permet de regarder résolument vers l'avenir, sans se préoccuper des incidents de parcours. J'étais jeune, donc j'étais beau; j'avais été malade comme un chien mais j'étais demeuré droit comme un chêne dans la tourmente. Hourra pour la juvénilité!

Maintenant couché sur le dos, je me délecte pleinement de ma situation de non-douleur. Mon ventre est souple, orné d'une magnifique cicatrice, et il ballonne vers le ciel. Ma jambe gauche, légèrement surélevée, se trouve sur un coussin de flanelle. Je peux même observer la petite bosse que fait mon séquestre, en plein centre de l'ancienne fracture à mon tibia. Et je ris de ces souffrances passées qui ne sont plus que des anecdotes parmi toutes les autres du grand livre de ma vie, enfouies dans les dédales de la Réminiscence.

L'atmosphère qui m'environne est toute chaude; je me sens comme un fœtus baignant au sein de l'amnios maternel, comme un chameau s'abreuvant à l'oasis saharienne, comme une crevette massée par le flux de la marée montante. Il règne, partout autour de moi, un calme olympien; pas un vent, pas un bruit ne vient troubler ma quiétude, mon confort, ma sécurité. Mon ego flotte dans un Éden de joie profonde; je suis un colibri gavé par le nectar de sa fleur. L'air que je respire n'est ni trop sec ni trop humide, embaumé de suaves effluves qui ondoient à l'unisson. Mes poils nasaux vibrent, au creux de mes cornets, dans un sensuel ballet olfactif. Je valse à la mesure de mes cils vibratiles, bercé d'odeurs mordorées de passé, emporté par l'univers odoriférant de mes souvenirs.

Ô réminiscences! Ô souvenances! Senteur des tisanes que me servait ma mère quand j'avais la grippe. Il suffisait d'un simple écoulement nasal, d'une petite toux ou d'un rhume insignifiant pour qu'elle me mette au lit et m'ordonne les plus agréables traitements. Enivré du bonheur de celui qui profite majestueusement de la maladie saisonnière, je me laissais soûler par ses frictions, ses remèdes à la camomille et ses couvertures chaudes. Les draps immaculés sentaient la lavande, la cuisine s'emplissait des parfums de thé au jasmin, de gâteau au chocolat et de parfait à la menthe. Toute la banalité du coryza disparaissait devant la grandeur des soins bienveillants qu'elle me prodiguait. Par la chaleur de sa main, ses sourires merveilleux, ses baisers sur mes joues en feu et la surabondance des délicatesses gustatives dont elle me gavait, je guérissais, sans qu'elle ait eu recours à aucune médication véritable. Je ne savais pas que j'expérimentais alors les vertus miraculeuses de l'amour et du placebo.

Je flotte dans un monde olfactif, entouré de mille exhalaisons qui s'insinuent au creux de mon naze et se fondent jusque dans les parties les plus intimes de mon cortex cérébral.

Et tout à coup je me rappelle une fraîche odeur de conifères répandue dans un sous-bois, un jour où je découvrais les vertus du printemps en compagnie de ma première flamme. Les troncs turgescents des épinettes blanches craquaient sous la poussée de la sève, laissant couler jusqu'à terre de longues traînées de gelée gommeuse. Elle était Diane, j'étais Apollon. Nous avions marché toute la journée, perdus dans une forêt enchantée, grisés d'un amour neuf. Je l'avais embrassée, elle avait répondu à mon baiser par un de ces attouchements merveilleux qu'une simple description ne ferait que ternir et que je ne décrirai donc pas, malgré votre secret désir. Nus comme des vers, isolés dans notre propre cosmos devenu cocon magique, nous nous étions aimés durant des heures, enlacés sur un tapis humide d'aiguilles de pins. Le soir était venu; nous nous caressions encore, éclairés par les reflets bleutés de la lune. Engloutis dans le bonheur, nous avions laissé la rosée se déposer en fines gouttelettes sur nos corps transis, juste assez pour qu'au petit matin, j'en attrape la plus fulgurante pneumonie qui soit jamais survenue dans toute l'histoire de la pneumologie mondiale. Quant à ma dulcinée, elle en fut quitte pour une larmoyante sinusite qui devait se chroniciser et l'incommoder pendant des lustres, longtemps après que mon mal eût achevé de nous séparer. Dans une lettre qu'elle m'envoyait, il y a quelques années, je l'entends encore m'écrire de sa voix nasillarde: «Monchour très cher abi, gomment ça va?»

Je passai six mois à tousser, cent quatre-vingt-trois jours à expectorer, deux cent soixante-trois mille cinq cent vingt minutes à râler. À cause d'une simple nuit d'amour vécue dans une frénésie toute élégiaque, de quelques grammes de jouissance éjectés à la face de la banale quotidienneté, je dus cracher des tonnes d'expectorations, évaporer des litres de sueur et chialer des centaines de dictionnaires d'invectives contre le mauvais sort qui s'acharnait sur moi et bafouait sans cesse ma santé.

La pneumonie: quelle maladie essoufflante entre toutes les autres, surtout lorsqu'elle se complique d'un pneumothorax suraigu qui affaisse complètement l'un des deux seuls poumons disponibles! Eh oui! Après de longs mois de fièvre et de sifflements, de faiblesse maximale et de maux de tête abrutissants, au moment où je me croyais enfin sorti de l'enfer dans lequel m'avait projeté la pneumonie, je fus éveillé un matin par une atroce douleur au côté droit. Persuadée que j'allais trépasser, ma famille éplorée m'amena d'urgence à l'hôpital où on constata la complication: «Intéressant! me dit un interne boutonneux à l'allure jekyllesque.»

«Un pneumothorax»! ajouta-t-il avec un cynisme repoussant. «Trop toussé»! enchaîna-t-il, antipathique. «Le poumon a tout simplement éclaté!»

Le misérable! L'infâme cancre médical! Qu'avait-il appris de la compassion pendant ses études? Rien! Il m'étudiait de son œil glauque, froid et calculateur, cherchant les détails qui lui permettraient peut-être, ô suprême contentement scientifique, de les publier dans une prestigieuse revue médicale. Qu'en savait-il, lui, de la toux et de l'impossibilité totale de la contrôler pendant une pneumonie? Rien de rien! Je mordais mes lèvres desséchées. Je me triturais les gencives. Je pourfendais la poussière qui voguait dans ma chambre avec d'effroyables clignements d'yeux.

Si j'avais alors eu la force de répondre à cet interne hideux, ne fut-ce que quelques secondes, je lui aurais fait connaître, à ma façon, les quatre vérités de l'essoufflé qui crève à bout d'oxygène ! Mais je ne le pouvais pas, ma situation étant tellement critique que je devais me contenter de me laisser tripoter, des amygdales jusqu'à l'oignon, sans réagir.

Finalement, on daigna me soigner : un chirurgien, d'allure pressée, mais plutôt adroit de ses mains, vint planter dans mon thorax une longue tubulure de plastique salvatrice. Je fus subitement libéré d'une portion de mes tourments, l'air vicié qui s'était aggluntiné au sommet de mon poumon se trouvant éjecté dans un grand souffle.

Ô joie ! Ô profond plaisir de renaître, après être passé si près de la mort charnelle ! Quel délire métaphysique de sentir le trépas nous frôler et puis nous abandonner sur son passage ! Quel plaisir suprême de faire un pied de nez à Madame la Faucheuse ! Maintenant délivré de cette pneumonie pénible mais formatrice, je me remémore avec un sourire en coin ma juvénile naïveté. Moi, faisant l'amour pour la première fois sur un lit d'aiguilles de pins, l'esprit ravagé par les effluves de résineux et de petite culotte, oubliant les plus élémentaires consignes d'hygiène que m'avait apprises ma maman. Demeurer tout nu dans la nuit, même en se réchauffant du corps d'une amante tourmentée elle aussi par le désir, ce n'est rien de très sain, me diront ceux qui soignent leur santé. Et ils auront raison. Que voulez-vous ! L'amour rend fou, aveugle, débile et exubérant. Il fait en sorte que des esprits aussi raisonnables que le mien succombent un jour et se laissent emporter par leurs désirs fondamentaux, abandonnant leurs organes et leurs poumons à tous les contaminants qui passent. J'ai eu une faiblesse, je l'avoue, mais j'en garde tout de même un souvenir ravi. La charmante, qui s'appelait Jacinthe, ou Pétunia peut-être, me permit d'accéder à certaines sensations hautement euphorisantes que je n'aurais probablement jamais connues autrement. Dieu ait son âme, maintenant qu'elle est morte depuis belle lurette... d'une syphilis tertiaire qu'elle ne couvait heureusement pas encore du temps de nos amours.

Je suis couché, émerveillé de ce souvenir aphrodisiaque qui ne cesse de provoquer en moi une foule de petits orgasmes intellectuels tout à fait divins. Ma vie a été frappée par la pneumonie, c'est vrai. J'ai connu les horreurs de la respiration laborieuse, larvaire et amibienne et j'ai pensé à la mort pour la première fois, c'est vrai. Mais je n'ai qu'à songer à ces instants apoplexiques pour que j'oublie tout, toux, tubulures et crachats. Ainsi l'esprit humain est-il fait: par un ingénieux système probablement développé aux heures grises de l'évolution préhistorique, le cerveau a l'extraordinaire pouvoir d'oublier en grande partie les souffrances et de ne conserver entièrement que les moments heureux.

Je ne ressens plus aucune douleur en ce moment. Je suis bien, extrêmement bien, et je me remémore avec délice les accidents de parcours de ma vie parce qu'ils mobilisent mon esprit et me permettent d'apprécier à quel point je peux jouir. Oui, je jouis, en ciboulette à part ça. Avec des roulements de tambour dans les tempes, des torsades de pointes dans les oreillettes et des convulsions dans la gangrène. Jouir, à en mourir. Connaître l'apothéose des sensations humaines; entendre des concertos de jouissance bercer le thalamus, toucher aux délices cutanées, goûter aux joies de la chair, renifler les aromates du désir et palper les troncs prêts à exploser de sève printanière. S'abandonner et se laisser croquer, tel un fruit mûr. Voilà l'essentiel, le modus vivendi existentiel. Sauf qu'il y a un hic! Tout va, mais seulement si chacun des instruments permettant la jouissance fonctionne. Il ne suffit que d'une simple incartade, d'un futile oubli, pour que des monstres vénériens contaminent le méat urinaire et viennent perturber la fragile harmonie du pénis en rut. Voilà! Le mot est lâché. L'esclandre peut avoir lieu!

Le jour de mes quarante ans, alors que la vie m'avait gâté — hormis quelques petites maladies déjà suffisamment décrites, j'avais tout eu: travail, honneurs, argent; épouse, enfants, vaisselle —, il me vint la malencontreuse idée de forniquer un peu trop et un peu vite... un peu trop vite, quoi. Il était écrit dans le ciel, quelque part autour de la ceinture d'Orion, peut-être un peu plus bas, que j'aurais un jour cet instant de faiblesse. Fidèle plus que jamais à la destinée qui guide mes pas, je l'eus donc. Un bar, un soir, une fille, inconnue, une chambre, jolie, un plaisir, accompli. Ce fut tout. Une semaine plus tard, l'organe en feu, je me perdais en injures contre les urétrites et les vicieux et les vicieuses qui les transportent et en redemandent. J'étais en partie responsable de mon malheur, mais cela ne le guérissait pas, bien au contraire. Maudite guigne qui s'acharnait irrémédiablement sur mon sort et provoquait les plus terribles écoulements. Uriner était devenu une torture, mais combien insignifiante comparée aux angoisses existentielles qui germaient dans mon esprit troublé : n'était-ce pas un cadeau empoisonné de la dame aux chlamydias qui me contaminait d'une bactérie résistante à tout traitement, vouée à s'installer définitivement dans mes canaux les plus intimes ? Je courus consulter. On m'écouta, me dosa, me guérit. Merci, médecine moderne, si bonne pour les membres de votre communauté, si douce à traiter les impotents de la terre.

Certains, qui n'auraient eu à subir que le quart de mes malheurs, pourraient demander un repos pareil à celui dans lequel je baigne en ce moment. Et ils l'obtiendraient ! C'est dire la profonde jouissance qui m'étourdit rien qu'à savoir que je mérite mon actuel apaisement. J'ai pu guérir de cette chaude blennoragie. Ma vie fut plus tranquille par la suite, c'est-à-dire que j'appris à planifier mes pulsions et à garder en permanence tout le matériel protecteur nécessaire qui s'imposait.

Cependant, je demeurais toujours un peu inquiet. Avais-je le mauvais œil ? Je n'osais pas réfléchir plus intensément et irriter mon imaginaire nyctomorphe, de peur de provoquer le destin, déjà passablement soupe au lait à mon égard. Je me tins donc coi pendant quelque temps, regardant les belles femmes du coin de l'œil, ne lançant que de rares œillades à la mienne, évitant les clins d'œil inopportuns qui auraient pu éveiller certaines jalousies mesquines. Je n'irais pas jusqu'à dire que j'avais mis des œillères, mais je demeurais sur mes gardes, me contentant de cultiver sagement mon jardin, mes œillets… et mes violettes !

Et la vie reprit son cours normal, comme un ruisseau de montagne après les débordements du printemps. Je m'habituai à mon handicap; on s'habitue à tout, il faut dire, puisque ma femme ne m'avait pas encore laissé. Je regoûtai pleinement à la vie et à ses charmes. J'avais vieilli... et plus le temps passait, plus j'essayais d'en capter tous les petits bonheurs. D'ailleurs, quand on se préoccupe de jouir de la vie, c'est presque toujours qu'on a plus de vie vécue que de vie à vivre.

Quel bonheur de pouvoir me reposer, la tête au même niveau que mes rotules, enfin libéré de ces envies de voyagement qui préoccupent l'esprit de tout humain normalement vagabond. Parce que moi aussi, comme beaucoup de mes semblables, j'ai aimé déplacer mon postérieur au large des servitudes de la chaise de cuisine et du banc de toilette habituel !

Un jour, je suggérai à ma femme de faire une promenade au sommet de la plus haute montagne du pays; histoire de voir jusqu'à quel point elle m'aimait encore. Elle accepta. Surpris, je faillis m'évanouir rien qu'à la pensée de cet alpinisme de trois mille mètres. D'autant plus que je faisais de l'angine de poitrine depuis deux ans et qu'on m'avait fortement recommandé de ne pas faire subir d'exercices trop violents à ma pompe. Mais il faisait beau et je n'avais pas eu de crise depuis des semaines. J'irais donc.

Le pays vivait un de ces splendides automnes, si rares il faut l'avouer, après qu'il eût plu quatre-vingt-six jours d'affilée pendant l'été. La nature éclatait de poésie : les arbres incarnats et jaunes pavoisaient dans l'azur immaculé, des armées de fauvettes frétillantes froufroutaient dans l'air frais, en partance pour des contrées plus clémentes, et un nordet enthousiaste soulevait les casquettes, ébouriffant les chevelures grisonnantes. Je marchais avec ma compagne, celle qui m'avait enduré toutes ces années, subissant dignement l'affront de mes incartades libidinales et se riant de mes urétrites. Nous avancions sur une route abrupte, cheminant parmi la rocaille et les herbes folles. Il faisait frisquet, j'avais chaud. Ma femme, hormonalement protégée contre les années qui apesantissaient nos destinées respectives, grimpait sereinement. Moi, touché par la masculinitude, je me sentais beaucoup moins en forme. Mon cœur se débattait, avide de sang, tel un vampire en manque d'hémoglobine, et tentait de propulser quelque énergie jusqu'à mes jambes flageolantes. Je dus m'arrêter à mi-chemin, complètement épuisé. Mon cœur battait la chamade, mes tempes battaient comme des cymbales et ma femme battait la mesure! Pour me stimuler, elle tapait dans ses mains en chantant «Hava Naghila». Quelle grande âme: vouloir fortifier son mari magané en lui chantant des chansons exotiques! J'aurais bien voulu lui giguer une petite polka pékinoise mais je n'avais pas le goût de plaisanter. Voyant ma mine abattue et mon faciès pâle et tiré, elle cessa ses élucubrations et devint plus attentive.

— Qu'est-ce qu'il y a, mon amour? me demanda-t-elle avec un accent yiddish. Tu as l'air un peu écœuré?

— Mais non, chérie, lui répondis-je pour la rassurer. Ce doit être le cipâte russe qui ne passe pas!

Cette conversation hautement intellectuelle me redonna quelques forces. J'avais voulu monter jusqu'au sommet de cette montagne, je monterais ! Mais après une centaine de mètres, un mal de cœur tout ce qu'il y a de plus malsain m'envahit. Je n'avais pas le cœur à rire, ma femme non plus cette fois-là. Quand je l'entendis fredonner le *Requiem* de Mozart, un frisson vint me secouer. Elle ne cessait de me dévisager.

— Tu as un drôle d'air ! me dit-elle. Tu dois être malade !

Oh ! Non ! Pas encore la maladie qui revient à la charge ! pensai-je. J'étais décidé à laisser ma mâle fierté de côté et à rebrousser chemin quand soudain, comme un coup de harpon dans la tête d'une baleine, comme un iceberg se fracassant dans la mer, comme une bombe à hydrogène qui aurait implosé, je ressentis un mal hallucinant qui me broyait le thorax et me déchirait le cœur. L'attaque, l'angine de poitrine, l'infarctus me terrassait ! En sueur, livide, la bouche écumante, je me noyais dans ma salive en cherchant des mots d'amour pour celle qui me soulevait sur ses épaules et me descendait, illico, vers la vallée, la voiture et l'inévitable hôpital... à condition seulement que le destin le veuille bien !

Et il voulut bien, le coquin. Mais je dus souffrir, pendant les quelques heures que dura ma douleur, autant que ce que j'avais enduré pendant toutes mes maladies réunies. Je perdis conscience une bonne dizaine de fois sur le chemin du retour, l'affreuse douleur me réveillant un nombre équivalent de fois. Profitant d'un épisode d'inconscience, je rêvai qu'un éléphant acrobate faisait le beau sur ma poitrine en se tenant sur une patte et tournoyait sur lui-même. Un peu plus tard, je m'imaginai être torturé par des sadiques qui me soudaient la cage thoracique à une voie ferrée et faisaient passer une locomotive dessus. C'est alors que je compris la raison des sudations profuses qui noient toujours les malheureuses victimes des infarctus du myocarde! Tout est dans la tête et dans l'imaginaire, n'est-ce pas?

Ma douce parvint à gagner notre automobile sans défaillir. Lorsque je l'entendis hurler *la Marseillaise*, je compris qu'elle avait réussi l'impossible! Je ne savais pas que j'avais épousé Édith Piaf. Ragaillardi par sa belle humeur, je pus ramper sur la banquette arrière en m'agrippant à l'air ambiant et je la remerciai avec une esquisse de sourire. Habile, elle démarra le moteur; forte, elle écrasa la pédale d'accélération; précise, elle me conduisit à l'hôpital.

L'infarctus, à cinquante ans, ça ne pardonne pas. J'eus droit à tous les honneurs de la guerre, avec en prime la croix de fer et la médaille du soldat inconnu. Une guerre, d'ailleurs, que je crus perdre quand on m'apprit, après huit jours de soins intensifs, qu'un énorme anévrysme s'était formé au cœur de mon ventricule gauche et qu'il ballottait, débile, empêchant le reste de l'organe vivant de se mouvoir convenablement et de faire son travail de pompe avec efficacité. Le médecin qui me soignait fut toutefois un brin plus courtois que l'interne acnéique qui diagnostiqua mon pneumothorax. Il me parla longuement de la vie et de la beauté de l'existence. Il me dit qu'il fallait un jour ou l'autre se résigner au décès. Il me rappela qu'il fallait laisser de la place aux autres, la terre étant surpeuplée à cause de Jean-Paul, son beau-frère gynécologue, qui ne voulait rien savoir des stérilets. Il ajouta quelques mots au sujet de la régulation des naissances qui s'amorçait difficilement en Inde et finit par me dire que de toute manière, j'avais réussi à me rendre à cinquante ans, ce qui n'était pas mal après tout, et que je n'aurais plus jamais à endurer de telles souffrances puisque ma vie s'achevait presque en beauté; qu'un anévrysme valait mieux qu'un sale cancer, et cætera, et cætera. Un long moment, il tint ma main dans la sienne, des larmes plein le nez, le mouchoir plein à souhait et le panier plein à ras bord. Il voulut m'embrasser dans un accès de compassion, ce que je refusai, gardant quand même un soupçon de dignité, et il m'avoua qu'il aurait donné sa vie pour la mienne s'il avait pu!!? Sa gentillesse me fit quand même du bien, car aussi bien préparé à la mort, je décidai de survivre. Ainsi fonctionne le paradoxal esprit humain.

J'avais un cousin anglophone, «Norman» de son prénom, journaliste et écrivain, qui avait souffert d'une terrible maladie lui aussi, et qu'on avait taxée d'incurable et d'inopérable. Pourtant, il s'était mis dans la tête qu'il guérirait... en riant! Et il s'était inventé toute une thérapie à base de vitamine C, de farces et de drôleries. Il s'était dilaté tant et si bien la rate, et les fesses, et le crâne et les épididymes, et la vésicule, et les oreilles, et la luette, qu'il avait fini par guérir, à la grande stupéfaction de tout le monde médical. Comme j'avais participé quelque peu à sa guérison en lui fournissant gratuitement, pendant six mois, les deux caisses de jus d'orange en poudre qu'il ingurgitait chaque jour, en lui faisant des grimaces et en lui montrant mes fesses, je décidai de suivre son exemple. Je me nourrirais de vitamine C et je me ferais rire. Trop faible pour me chatouiller moi-même et trop pudibond pour me montrer mes propres fesses, d'autant plus que le miroir de ma chambre était trop petit, je demandai à ma femme si elle n'aurait pas quelques plaisanteries dans son sac à souvenirs. Et elle me fit rire, comme un fou, tout en m'injectant de la vitamine C directement dans les jugulaires, en me racontant des anecdotes sucrées tirées de ses années de pensionnat. Elle me confia même ses propres incartades sexuelles, dont une nuit orgiaque avec le cousin Norman, qui l'avait séduite en lui racontant des blagues. Ces révélations tardives auraient dû me faire pleurer, mais elle me narrait ses infidélités avec tellement de cœur que je ne pouvais qu'en rire. Peut-être aussi se culpabilisait-elle de ses erreurs, voyant son brave mari si près de la mort, et voulait-elle se faire pardonner? Car, dans un ultime élan de miséricorde et de générosité, elle me montra ses fesses, qu'elle avait encore fort belles, et pas poilues pour cinq sous. Elle me dansa ensuite une rumba japonaise, me chanta une complainte arménienne et me caressa la nuque, ce qui avait toujours eu le don de me charmer.

Et je guéris. Comment? Par le miracle de l'amour et du rire, voyons donc! Quant à la vitamine C, on s'en fout! La science, toujours inquiète de la magie de l'art, s'aperçut avec effroi que mon anévrysme diminuait tout seul. Le corps médical constata que le mien reprenait des forces. Quelques mois plus tard, de retour à la maison, j'eus assez de vitalité pour imaginer la plus belle volée possible à mon infidèle de femme. Ma fierté de mari se devait d'être vengée. Mais quand mon épouse évoqua mes propres erreurs passées, j'arrêtai net d'imaginer que je la frappais avec mon égoïne. Forte du renouveau féministe, elle voulut

me donner un seul petit coup de marteau sur le crâne...
juste pour rire... et me faire réfléchir aux méfaits du
machisme universel. Mais elle aussi se retint, dans un
gracieux accès de bonté dont je lui sais toujours gré.

Ainsi va la vie. J'avais encore échappé à mon destin
mais la mort m'avait cette fois frôlé de très près; ce que je
n'ai pas osé dire, c'est qu'au deuxième jour de mon
infarctus, mes ventricules s'était mis à fibriller, en chœur,
comme ça, sans raison apparente. La belle de garde, une
douce jeune fille aux yeux ensoleillés, au teint de pêche et
au buste généreux, débordante de rondeurs rosées, avait dû
me choquer deux ou trois fois avec toute la puissance
d'une machine heureusement toute proche, électrisant mon
corps mort d'une décharge qui trépidait dans les quatre
cents joules. Je dois dire que la belle m'avait déjà électrisé
à plusieurs reprises lorsqu'elle faisait ma toilette matinale,
mais jamais aussi violemment.

Mon cœur avait cessé de battre. Immédiatement, ma
vue s'assombrit; apparut un voile rouge, rapidement suivi
d'un voile noir, le même qu'expérimente l'aviateur qui rate
un tonneau. J'entendis alors une musique, douce comme
celle de l'eau qui frémit dans la douche le matin, harmo-
nieuse comme le chant des walkyries. J'avais parfaitement
connaissance de ma mort mais, curieusement, je n'en
gardais aucune animosité. Au contraire, je vivais là le
premier vrai moment de non-angoisse de toute ma vie... si
je peux m'exprimer ainsi. Je flottais dans l'éther, béate-
ment, goûtant aux joies de l'anesthésie cosmogonique
transcendantale. Je naviguais, à mille fois la vitesse de la
lumière, vers le Big Bang originel. Cela me faisait sourire

parce que cette expression, «Big Bang», me rappelait ma première relation sexuelle. J'étais bien, extrêmement bien, communiquant dans une mythique béatitude avec toutes les forces universelles réunies.

Soudain, j'entendis une voix déchirant les ténèbres:

— Tu seras le bienvenu, mais un peu plus tard. Tu n'es pas encore prêt à faire le grand saut. Réintègre ton corps et souffre encore un peu!

— Merde! ai-je eu envie de m'écrier. Moi qui jouissais vraiment pour une fois. Je ne veux pas...

— Astine pas, le smat, ou je te fais goûter à mon gâteau d'absolu!

Obtempérant sagement à l'ordre céleste, je me revis alors, couché dans mon lit, les yeux fermés, tout mon corps crispé dans une formidable convulsion. La belle aux charmes provocants venait de m'appliquer l'ultime décharge électrique. Tout à fait réveillé, j'étais à nouveau confronté aux turpitudes de la vie terrestre, avant la mort.

Tout ceci a dû paraître assez anodin aux maniaques de science-fiction et de romans fantastiques. Tant pis pour eux! Mais je vous affirme que ma version, bien que tronquée, est la seule véridique et qu'elle possède l'insigne intérêt d'avoir été vraiment vécue. Les autres, provenant de tout le charabia de la littérature et de l'imaginaire dantesque que les auteurs en mal d'infini ont tenté d'inventer, ne sont que pures créations de l'esprit. J'ose croire que quelques bonnes âmes sauront apprécier l'exceptionnelle teneur du matériel didactique livré ici !

•

Ma femme était morte depuis six mois quand on m'amena de force au foyer du village. Comme je n'avais pas cessé d'être malade et que le rire était devenu la seule thaumaturgie qui pût me faire quelque bien, elle avait dû me montrer ses fesses en permanence. Elle en avait inévitablement attrapé son coup de mort une nuit d'automne où le thermomètre était descendu de quarante degrés d'une claque. Pauvre petite vieille, morte d'avoir trop aimé. Je l'avais enterrée dans le jardin, derrière la maison, je lui avais chanté tout bas une oraison funèbre et j'avais pleuré assez de larmes pour arroser le jardin au complet plus le champ d'à côté. Puis, je m'étais enfermé pour l'hiver, n'acceptant de recevoir personne. J'avais engagé le voisin pour qu'il m'apporte de la nourriture chaque semaine... et les mois avaient passé. Emmitouflé de solitude, je m'étais emprisonné dans ma maison, laissant la neige recouvrir le paysage et les jours heureux. Au printemps, lorsque je voulus rouvrir les fenêtres pour laisser entrer quelques frêles rayons de soleil, une meute de voisins enragés s'objectèrent et portèrent plainte à la municipalité.

« Ça pue ! » invoquèrent-ils. « Le vieux fou ne s'est pas lavé depuis la mort de sa vieille. Il faut brûler ce nique à rats ! »

Et la bonne dame du service social vint me chercher par la peau du cou, qui pendait passablement il faut dire,

pour me traîner jusqu'au centre d'accueil. Je ne lui offris
pas grand résistance parce que je pesais quarante kilos,
j'étais complètement aveugle — mes yeux ayant manqué
de vitamine A —, j'étais paralysé de la main droite et
boiteux.

Au foyer, on me décrotta, me frotta et me nourrit. Il
leur fallut trois mois pour me renipper; tout un ménage du
printemps! On m'administra des quantités astronomiques
de vitamines qui finirent par redonner vie à ma vision. Une
fois convenablement engraissé et revitalisé, je pus visiter le
plus épouvantable zoo humain qui ait jamais existé. Cent
locataires peuplaient cette terre d'asile pour moribonds et
autres légumineuses. Cent faces ternies par les trop
nombreux dégels, aux yeux vitreux de poupées, aux
cheveux rares et aux gencives indurées d'avoir manqué de
dents trop longtemps. Parmi ces pensionnaires, il n'y en
avait que deux à pouvoir exprimer autre chose que des
grognements ou des cris lancinants: Maryvonne et moi.

Je découvris Maryvonne plusieurs mois après mon
arrivée. Je la vis un beau matin, assise dans son fauteuil
roulant, tout au fond de la salle commune, appuyée contre
le rebord de la fenêtre. Qu'elle était belle, malgré ses
quatre-vingt-trois ans et ses deux jambes en moins. Elle
avait un sourire vaguement angélique qui me rappelait ma
femme. Les yeux brûlés par les larmes du bonheur, je
m'approchai délicatement. Elle me faisait tellement penser
à ma femme que ma première idée fut de lui demander de
me montrer ses fesses. Mais je me retins, ne voulant pas lui
faire subir un mortel refroidissement. Je touchai sa main,
toute raide, et j'y sentis une fraîche nervosité qui courait le

long de ses veines. Sursautant, elle leva les yeux vers moi, des quenœils encore pleins d'éclairs et de frétillements, et elle me dit: «Bonjour. Vous vendez du popcorn? Les vidangeurs doivent passer vers cinq heures.»

Je me retirai dans ma chambre, boitant encore plus péniblement que d'habitude, et je pleurai trois jours et trois nuits.

Peu de temps après, n'ayant pu trouver de corde pour me pendre, je décidai que je n'étais pas à ma place dans ce foyer. Une nuit, j'écrivis un petit mot aux gens du personnel pour les remercier de leurs bons soins, et ajoutai, en postscriptum, que je souhaitais ne pas leur avoir transmis trop de poux. J'espère qu'ils ont ri. Je mis quelques affaires dans un sac de plastique: ma brosse à dents, inutilisée depuis vingt ans, mon costume de bain, en souvenir des beaux jours, et un condom rouillé, pour ne jamais oublier mes antiques possibilités. Et je m'enfuis. Je marchai longtemps, jusqu'à la rivière qui borde le village, pour ensuite traverser le pont couvert et me réfugier dans une cabane à sucre isolée, que je savais depuis longtemps désaffectée. J'y trouvai une couverture de laine rouge et bleu, comme celle avec laquelle ma mère m'abriait quand j'étais petit, et je m'étendis sur un lit de planches dans un coin. Pour mourir. Pour en finir avec ce monde qui ne me faisait plus rire. J'étais plus démodé qu'un vieux tacot, plus ratatiné qu'une guenille de grand ménage, plus froissé qu'une feuille morte. Je laissai le froid venir me mordiller le bout des orteils, j'entendis le vent jouer du banjo dans la soupente, je vis courir pour la dernière fois un petit mulot, tout fier, qui vint me sentir le bout du nez. Et je mourus.

•

Je suis mort, depuis trois jours. Je suis mort, mort, mort! Des enfants qui jouaient à la cachette m'ont retrouvé, frette comme une boule de neige. On m'a transporté chez le croque-mort, on m'a placé dans une bière usagée et on m'a inhumé.

Et je ne suis plus bien du tout, étendu dans mon cercueil capitonné, couché sur ce dos qui me fait mal, avec les mains jointes dans une prière qui ne sert probablement à rien, cet appel désespéré à tous ceux et celles qui pourraient me sortir de ce merdier. Je ne suis plus bien, même si je l'ai été l'espace de quelques souvenirs, pourtant tous aussi souffrants les uns que les autres. J'ai peur, horriblement peur, et je souffre d'une angoisse lancinante, qu'aucun mot, qu'aucun cri ne pourraient exprimer. J'ai peur, et j'ai mal, dans le tréfonds de mes entrailles, dans ces viscères qui glougloutaient encore il y a quelques jours. Je crève de peur, devant cet infini et ce néant qui ne s'en vient pas.

Car je suis mort, irrémédiablement. Le sang stagne dans mes artères obstruées. Il n'y a plus d'air dans mes alvéoles. Mais je pense, donc je suis! Fadaises, toutes ces tergiversations de l'esprit qui pense. Rien ne compte plus, parce que je suis angoissé plus que jamais.

Pourtant, si je me fie à ma brève expérience de la mort, je ne devrais pas. J'ai pourtant bien vécu la vraie paix, celle qui annule l'angoisse. Qu'est-ce qui se passe? Rien ne va plus? Où est donc cette paix de l'âme? Pourquoi est-ce que je pense encore pendant que mon corps se décompose à toute vitesse, que déjà les vermisseaux s'affairent à leur travail écologique en vidant mes orbites et en bouffant mes intestins.

Je ne suis pas bien dans une tombe, prisonnier de l'inconnu. Je n'aurais jamais dû m'enfuir du centre d'accueil. J'aurais dû accepter de pourrir à petit feu, comme tous les autres, et me laisser ravager tranquillement par la vieillesse. J'aimais mieux mes maladies et mes souffrances, même les plus atroces. J'aimais mieux Maryvonne, avec ses veines nerveuses, même si elle alzheimait au cinquième degré. Elle avait au moins des yeux qui brillaient. Moi, je n'ai plus rien de tout cela. Je ne suis plus qu'un potentiel de peau trouée, d'os blanchis et de poussière grisâtre.

Je hurle mon angoisse, en silence, à la face de tous les vivants qui deviendront ce que je suis, très bientôt, inexorablement.

J'aimais mieux botter le derrière des imbéciles et me bâtir des oignons tangibles, exécrables peut-être mais qui ne me bouleversaient pas d'angoisse. J'aimais mieux la substance putride de mon tibia amoché, et les élancements nocturnes qui brouillaient mes pensées. J'aimais mieux les délices de la pizza aux anchois et la péritonite aiguë. J'aimais mieux les pneumonies d'amour et les crachats verts d'espérance en la guérison qui viendrait, inéluctablement, parce que le glas n'avait pas encore sonné. J'aimais mieux, j'aimais mieux. C'est tout ce que je trouve à penser en ce moment. Je suis devenu fou, anxieux jusqu'à la moelle, fiévreux face à l'au-delà qui semble inquiet de m'accepter et qui me laisse ainsi, tout seul, conscient de ma mort, entre l'infiniment grand de l'espace et l'infiniment minuscule de mon cercueil.

Je veux retourner à mes anciennes amours, à ce que j'ai connu, même si j'étais constamment malade. Je veux être malade, souffrir comme un dingue, et me thromboser le cœur tous les jours s'il le faut; parce que je veux me sentir vivre, et palpiter; je veux vibrer de l'air qui pénètre à petites bouffées dans mes poumons. Je veux revivre, même en cloporte, les ailes repliées mais prêt à bondir et à rire des premières fesses venues. Mon malheur vient de ce que je ne pourrai plus rire, parce que plus rien ne me rappellera ma propre déchéance. Quand ma femme me faisait rire, elle se transmuait en moi-même, avec mes défauts et mes lubies, et c'était cela que je trouvais drôle. Mais maintenant, plus rien n'est drôle. Tout est d'un macabre absurde, désespérant et abrutissant.

Se regarder pourrir, enseveli sous la terre humide, quoi de plus cynique !

Vivement que j'entende cette voix de musicien et que j'oublie tout, ma vie, mes jérémiades et mes angoisses. Vivement. Sinon... Sinon quoi? Je n'ai même plus la possibilité suprême de me suicider !

Vivement qu'elle m'appelle, cette voix à laquelle j'ai déjà cru, qui m'avait enlevé toute ma peur du cosmos géant qui doit s'emparer de moi.

Toi, là-bas, tout à côté de Bételgeuse, tends-moi donc la main ! Viens me libérer de ce que j'ai pu inventer de plus horrible, ma mort! Dis-moi que je n'ai fait qu'un mauvais rêve et que tout recommence, comme avant, avec les tisanes de maman, et les effluves de sapin, et les belles filles, et les montagnes fleuries. Ne me laisse pas tout seul. Raconte-moi que ma femme est tout près, qu'elle m'entend et s'en vient me rejoindre. Je ne veux pas subir le tourment de l'inconnu en solitaire, avec ce mal de dos qui m'éclate les vertèbres. Je ne veux pas être mort, entends-tu?

Je ne ris plus. Il n'y a plus rien pour me faire rire. Plus de calembours faciles, plus de fesses grossières, plus de situations abracadabrantes. J'ai de morbides flambées d'angoisse qui hantent ma tête et me broient les méninges... et je n'y peux rien. Je voudrais arracher le couvercle de ce cercueil inconvenant, je voudrais sentir la terre couler sur mon visage, comme un mort-vivant dans un cimetière, et faire peur à tous les rescapés de l'existence, pour qu'ils partagent avec moi cette angoisse qui me fait suffoquer.

Qu'ai-je fait de travers pour ne pas mourir simplement comme le commun des mortels? À moins que personne ne meure simplement?

Je dois me calmer. Attendre patiemment que ta voix m'appelle. Je ne veux pas être une simple poussière cosmique, née de rien et vouée au néant. Je veux être un oignon, une fracture, une pneumonie. Je veux ressentir à nouveau le vent, même la pluie, et me plaindre du temps qu'il fait.

Et je veux voyager en paix, vers Alpha du Centaure et les autres constellations, à travers l'espace et le temps, en me rappelant dans un grand rire qu'un jour, j'ai souffert, avec d'autres comme moi, tellement comme moi qu'il est impossible que je sois seul pour ce voyage qui semble vouloir durer l'éternité.

Le buck

Lorsque l'avion s'éloigna de la rive, je me sentis angoissé. Une fois au milieu du lac, le nez dans le vent, le monomoteur se cabra dans un vrombissement d'enfer, galopa sur l'eau et s'éleva. Un malaise inexplicable me comprimait la nuque.

Je n'en étais pourtant pas à ma première chasse à l'orignal: chaque automne depuis dix ans, je venais passer une semaine avec Michel au lac Brûlé, sur ce territoire giboyeux isolé de toute civilisation, sans aucun chemin d'accès.

Mais pour la première fois de ma vie, l'isolement causé par la forêt me troublait. Cet homme que Michel avait absolument tenu à emmener, un dénommé Leclair, un lointain cousin que je n'avais jamais rencontré auparavant, m'inquiétait. Le cri strident qu'il avait poussé en débarquant à terre, son attitude plutôt bizarre au décollage de l'avion — il avait lancé un caustique «Bon débarras»! —, enfin son comportement ne me disait rien qui vaille. Va sans dire que je n'ai jamais aimé partir à la chasse avec un inconnu. La forêt, sournoise, ne pardonne pas la moindre erreur et il est impératif de bien connaître ses compagnons.

Pourtant, j'avais fléchi devant l'insistance de Michel.

—Je lui dois bien ça; il m'avait prêté de l'argent quand nous étions au collège. J'avais oublié de le rembourser. Quand il m'a téléphoné l'autre soir, je me suis senti un peu obligé envers lui...

Nous rentrâmes le bagage dans la cabane et nous nous préparâmes à partir en canot tous les trois, en direction d'une presqu'île située au nord du lac, endroit propice pour *caller* l'orignal. Leclair monta dans l'embarcation, agrippant habilement les plats-bords. Cela me rassura un peu et je m'ordonnai de cesser de me faire des idées à son sujet. Il resta silencieux pendant tout le trajet, à contempler le paysage: des montagnes qui ondoyaient de chaque côté du lac en se mirant dans ses eaux sombres.

Aux commandes du moteur hors-bord qui nous faisait pénétrer au sein d'un pays exaltant, je me sentais mieux. Arrivé à la presqu'île, je débarquai avec Michel et me mis à *caller* l'orignal. Leclair, toujours assis sur son banc, immobile comme un chicot de plaine, restait obscur et impénétrable, les yeux rivés à la colline qui nous surplombait. L'après-midi se passa à attendre. Finalement, comme aucun orignal ne donnait signe de vie, nous décidâmes de rentrer au camp.

Le souper avec Michel fut très agréable. Il raconta toute une série d'histoires plus saugrenues les unes que les autres. Pourtant, Leclair ne rit pas une seule fois, ne goûtant même pas au ragoût de lièvre que j'avais cuisiné, se contentant de boire quelques rasades d'eau claire. Puis il sortit et alla s'asseoir sur un tronc d'arbre renversé près du lac.

Nous avions fait un feu et c'est avec plaisir que j'écoutais Michel me chanter ses nouvelles compositions en s'accompagnant à la guitare. À un moment, je l'interrompis pour lui demander si Leclair était toujours aussi taciturne.

—Je ne sais pas. Je ne l'ai pas vraiment beaucoup connu, me dit-il, insouciant.

—Drôle de bonhomme! ajoutai-je. Je ne sais pas comment il va réagir lorsque l'orginal va se présenter...

Michel ne répondit pas. Il fredonnait une ballade toute en trémolos passionnés.

Leclair refusa de coucher dans la cabane, préférant dormir à même le sol nu, sur la plage, enveloppé dans une simple couverture de laine.

Au lever, le lendemain matin, il avait neigé. Deux centimètres de poudrerie avaient recouvert les branches des sapins et la mousse du sous-bois. Assis sur le sable, face au lac, Leclair ne bougeait pas; il fixait l'horizon. Ce diable d'homme semblait invulnérable aux morsures du gel. Il ne voulut pas déjeuner.

— Il est en bois, ton cousin? lançai-je à Michel tout en cassant un œuf dans la poêle.

— Probablement! Mais on ne peut pas dire qu'il soit accaparant...

Il venta toute la matinée et nous dûmes attendre l'après-midi avant de retourner à la presqu'île. En embarquant le matériel dans le canot, j'entendis Leclair marmonner. Immobile, sa couverture encore sur les épaules, il prononçait des phrases que je ne comprenais pas, comme une incantation. Lorsque je m'approchai de lui, il se retourna vivement et se tut. Il me regarda et, pour la première fois, je crus remarquer une étrange lueur orangée qui émanait de ses iris. Il baissa soudainement la tête. Michel arriva au même instant, d'excellente humeur.

— Qu'est-ce qui se passe? Vous vous êtes chicanés? dit-il en nous voyant, l'un en face de l'autre.

— Non, ça va, répondis-je, embarrassé.

La bonne figure de Michel allégea l'atmosphère. Leclair nous aida à pousser le canot, prenant bien soin d'éviter mon regard.

Nous fûmes bientôt en vue de la presqu'île, à environ quatre ou cinq cents mètres. Michel n'avait pas cessé de fredonner, probablement excité par la chasse et le simple bonheur de se retrouver en pleine nature. Leclair, à genoux dans l'embarcation, gardait un silence imperturbable.

Soudain, sans raison apparente, il frappa Michel d'une retentissante taloche derrière la tête.

—Ferme-la! J'ai entendu un orignal marcher de l'autre côté de la pointe de sable!

Michel ne broncha pas et, chose incroyable, se mit à pleurer. Je n'avais pas eu le temps de réagir: au moment où j'allais engueuler Leclair, un énorme buck apparut sur la berge, surgissant justement de l'autre côté de la pointe de sable, comme un fantôme, déambulant nonchalamment juste en face de nous. Leclair saisit sa carabine et épaula. J'entendis une détonation suivie d'un cri. Une vague venait de faire balancer le canot et il avait manqué la bête qui s'enfuyait à grandes enjambées.

—Tu me l'as fait rater! me dit-il en grinçant des dents.

Il ne m'avait pas regardé. La carabine toujours orientée vers le rivage, il s'écria: *Hichquo!*

Il y eut un silence de mort. J'étais estomaqué! Comment avait-il fait pour entendre l'orignal, malgré la distance et le bruit du moteur?

Leclair souriait étrangement. Quant à Michel, il pleurait à chaudes larmes. Je ne l'avais jamais vu pleurer auparavant. Coupant le moteur, je voulus agripper Leclair par le bras, mais, plus prompt, il m'attrapa le poignet et serra à faire craquer les os.

—Pour qui te prends-tu?

Leclair me relâcha sans répondre, pointa du doigt la colline déboisée surplombant la presqu'île et lança d'un ton injurieux:

Hannasusque Hichquo Hannasusque Himso!

Par trois fois, il répéta ces paroles énigmatiques, jusqu'à ce qu'un long bramement sonore retentisse. Le buck, magnifique, le panache étalé au soleil, avait surgi au faîte de la colline. Hors d'atteinte, il demeura immobile un long moment avant de disparaître.

À ce moment, baissant les yeux vers mon poignet endolori, je vis les marques rouge vif qu'y avait laissées la main de Leclair, comme si ses doigts avaient été des tisons. J'aurais voulu hurler mais une intense fatigue s'empara de moi. J'avais envie de frapper cet intru maléfique mais une force extérieure me ratatinait sur mon banc.

Je parvins à toucher la corde du démarreur mais Leclair me regarda et j'en eus le vertige: ses pupilles paraissaient se dilater et se refermer à volonté, pulsant d'aveuglants rayons lumineux. Je faillis tomber à l'eau. Détournant son regard, Leclair fixa les eaux du lac. Un bouillon énorme jaillit devant le canot, faisant monter à la surface des dizaines de ouananiches le ventre en l'air. Leclair ramassa deux poissons et dit: «Faute d'orignal, on mangera de la ouananiche!»

Les éclairs se tarirent, le jaillissement s'apaisa et je fus libéré de l'envoûtement. À nouveau maître de tous mes mouvements, je redémarrai le moteur n'ayant plus qu'une seule idée en tête : retourner au camp. Je jetai un coup d'œil vers Michel qui demeurait prostré sur son banc.

Le canot accosté, Leclair prit les poissons et lança, guilleret : « Je vais vous faire un bon souper ! »

J'aidai Michel à débarquer. Le pauvre paraissait complètement anéanti. Je dus presque le rudoyer pour qu'il cesse de pleurer. Leclair étant déjà dans la cabane, je le questionnai à voix basse :

— Mais qui est ce fou-là que tu nous as emmené ? Un magicien ?

— Je le connais à peine...

— Je ne t'ai jamais vu dans un état pareil ! Qu'est-ce que tu as ?

— Sais pas... Je me sentais tellement bien. Puis, tout d'un coup, une épouvantable douleur m'a traversé la tête, comme si quelqu'un m'avait donné un coup de masse...

— Tu aurais dû réagir quand il t'a frappé !

— Je ne pouvais plus... J'étais paralysé.

— Moi aussi ! C'est avec ses yeux qu'il m'a... Je n'en ai jamais vu de pareils !

Je n'osais pas rentrer dans la cabane. Leclair y faisait un boucan terrible, cognant chaudrons et ustensiles. Je fis asseoir Michel. Lorsqu'il sembla un peu calmé, je le pressai de m'en dire plus sur son mystérieux cousin.

— Nous avons étudié au même collège... Je ne me souvenais même pas lui avoir emprunté cet argent. Il était du type solitaire... pas d'amis... toujours dans son coin... le genre de gars à qui on n'adresse pas la parole, qui vous met mal à l'aise à vingt mètres, qu'on cherche à éviter sans raison valable, qui vous bousille votre journée d'un seul trait du regard. Lorsqu'il m'a téléphoné, j'ai eu l'impression qu'il m'indiquait clairement dans quels recoins de ma mémoire je devais fouiller pour le replacer dans mon existence. Il a insisté pour nous accompagner à la chasse... Je me suis demandé un instant comment il avait su que je partais avec toi pour le lac Brûlé mais j'ai tout de suite dit oui, comme s'il avait forcé ma décision à distance...

Leclair sortit de la cabane avec trois assiettes garnies de filets de ouananiche. Michel, blême et affaissé, ne goûta à rien. Il ne but qu'un verre d'eau qu'il régurgita aussitôt. Malgré ma faim, je me résolus à ne grignoter que des biscuits secs qui traînaient dans mes bagages. Leclair mangea goulûment, s'empiffrant de toute la nourriture.

Michel alla se coucher dans le camp. Il s'endormit presque immédiatement, fiévreux, le corps en boule. Leclair fit la vaisselle en gueulant à tue-tête des chansons westerns. J'étais bien décidé à le questionner sur ses agissements. Comme je m'approchais, il se retourna subitement. Son œil droit devint brillant, la pupille complètement dilatée. J'étais prisonnier.

—Je n'ai pas de comptes à te rendre ! Je chasse, un point c'est tout ! Elle était bonne, ma ouananiche ! T'aurais dû en manger ! Et plus de questions, compris ?

Son œil se détacha de moi et je pus m'asseoir. Une violente migraine me martelait les tempes.

Leclair quitta les abords de la cabane et se dirigea vers le lac. Je me couchai auprès de Michel dont la respiration s'était faite plus laborieuse, plus sifflante aussi. Je priais pour que Leclair ne remît pas les pieds ici. Je sombrai bientôt dans un sommeil troublé.

Je fus éveillé en pleine nuit par des cris. Tremblant, je sortis de mon sac de couchage et regardai par la fenêtre. Leclair dansait autour d'un immense brasier de branches de sapin en récitant des litanies dans un jargon étranger. Soudain, j'entendis la phrase qu'il avait criée sur le lac :

Hannasusque Hichquo Hannasusque Himso !

Je fus secoué par un grand frisson. Leclair, en transe, psalmodiait sans arrêt et dansait autour de ce feu qui paraissait résolu à ne jamais s'éteindre. Rivé à la fenêtre, j'implorai le ciel qu'il ne me vît pas et que son œil ne me paralysât pas pour toujours.

Hystérique, la bouche écumante, les yeux exorbités, il se dandina jusqu'au petit matin.

Je parvins à réveiller Michel. D'une voix éteinte, il me dit qu'il n'avait pas même la force de se lever.

—J'ai peur, ajouta-t-il. Je vais mourir...

J'aurais voulu me sauver avec Michel et rentrer chez moi. Mais j'étais prisonnier de la forêt, sans radio ni aucun autre moyen pour rappeler l'avion. Et il nous restait encore quatre jours à attendre! J'essayai d'imaginer une façon de signaler notre détresse à tout aéronef qui survolerait le lac Brûlé. Terrorisé, je me décidai à sortir.

Leclair était assis sur une bûche. Il m'interpella:

—Salut, l'ami! Je t'attendais pour la chasse!

Je pris place dans le canot. Leclair s'assit à l'avant. Je n'osais pas bouger, cramponné au moteur.

Leclair me fit bifurquer vers une petite baie située à l'est du lac. J'aurais voulu faire renverser l'embarcation et le voir se noyer. Mais il existait une véritable rupture entre mes pensées et les actions qui en découlaient. J'obéissais, obtempérant aveuglément à ses ordres, sans y rien pouvoir.

Dès que le canot toucha la grève, Leclair sauta à terre: «Attends-moi là! Je vais renifler le gibier!»

Il prit le bois dans un vacarme de rameaux cassés et marcha plusieurs minutes en direction du fond de la baie. Soulagé de cette angoisse indéfinissable qui m'étreignait, j'essayai de faire redémarrer le moteur. Pourtant, des dizaines de tractions désespérées sur cette damnée corde de démarreur ne firent que m'épuiser. Furieux, j'enlevais les bougies d'allumage pour les vérifier quand un formidable cri jaillit de l'autre côté de la baie. Les bras au ciel, Leclair hurlait:

Hannasusque, Hannasusque!

Un bruit de pas dans l'eau me fit sursauter. Le buck, majestueux, se tenait debout dans le lac, à dix mètres de moi. Les naseaux écartés, de longs jarres bruns sur la poitrine, il me regardait en secouant son énorme tête de droite à gauche.

Un coup de feu retentit. L'orignal fit un bond sur le côté et décampa sous le couvert des arbres. Un écho de bramements fous emplit le lac et la forêt. Une longue traînée de sang rouge clair tachait l'eau et le rivage. Leclair exultait.

—Je l'ai eu! Je l'ai eu!

Lorsqu'il revint au canot, je m'apprêtais à lui dire quel piètre tireur il était mais il me devança:

— J'avais visé la patte avant gauche. Il va boiter toute la journée. Et il va souffrir... Énormément!

Leclair avait prononcé ces mots avec une sorte de ricanement. Comme ses yeux se posaient sur moi, je détournai prestement le regard vers le large. D'une voix forte, il m'ordonna de retourner au camp. Je replaçai les bougies et le moteur démarra du premier coup.

Toutes mes pensées étaient concentrées sur Michel. Je sentais que quelque chose lui était arrivé. La traversée du lac fut atrocement longue. Aussitôt accosté, je courus vers la cabane. Mon ami, toujours étendu sur son lit, grimaçait de douleur.

— Qu'est-ce qui s'est passé ?

— J'ai voulu chercher du bois sec dehors. J'ai trébuché contre une souche. Je suis tombé par terre, la jambe dans le dos...

En sueur, le pantalon déchiré, Michel geignait sans arrêt. Je lui fis une attelle, alignant tant bien que mal les deux parties de sa jambe cassée. Un bout d'os blanchâtre traversait une longue estafilade sanguinolente. Michel ne dîna pas. Moi non plus. Je demeurai assis devant la fenêtre, à surveiller les allées et venues de Leclair. Il édifiait un feu immense, ramenant d'un peu partout des brassées de bois mort. Je mourais de peur, incapable de mettre de l'ordre dans mes idées. M'enfuir avec Michel, le porter sur mes épaules, me terrer dans les bois, ou...

Le soleil était descendu derrière les montagnes, ne laissant dans le ciel que des placards de lumière rosâtre. Lorsque Leclair ouvrit la porte, mon cœur ne fit qu'un bond : je ne l'avais pas vu venir.

— Viens ! Le buck attend !

Je le suivis docilement. Une fois sur le lac, il se leva et montra la presqu'île du doigt : « Dirige-toi vers la pointe ! »

Nous étions à mi-chemin lorsque je vis le buck sortir du bois. Ce bougre d'animal agissait exactement comme s'il avait été commandé à distance! Il fit quelques pas sur la berge et s'arrêta tout près de l'eau. Il bougeait le mufle, reniflant l'air dans toutes les directions.

Leclair me fit signe de ralentir. Il prit sa carabine et se mit à genoux dans le canot. Le canon bien appuyé contre le plat-bord, il épaula. La tête en feu, je saisis mon arme et visai Leclair.

Quand le coup partit, je sentis mon épaule droite se soulever et je fus projeté dans le fond de l'embarcation. Un beuglement horrible et interminable s'éleva alors, suivi des cris de joie de Leclair. «Bravo mon gars! Tu l'as eu! Directement dans l'œil, comme je le voulais! Quel tireur! Avec l'œil arraché, il va encore souffrir... Énormément!»

Il avait parlé sur un ton moqueur. Quand il prit les commandes et m'envoya m'asseoir à l'avant, je ne réagis même pas. En me croisant, il posa sa main sur mon épaule. J'en ressentis une brûlure intense. Mon cri s'étrangla dans ma gorge. J'étouffais. Leclair me regarda droit dans les yeux et ajusta avec soin sa main sur mon autre épaule. Une douleur atroce me traversa le tronc. Je brûlais vivant. Vaincu par le mal, je perdis conscience.

Lorsque je me réveillai, une forte brise agitait le lac. J'étais affalé sur un banc et il faisait sombre. Une centaine de mètres séparaient encore le canot du rivage quand j'entendis Michel qui gueulait. Quelques secondes plus tard, je sautais à terre en maudissant Leclair. C'est alors qu'il me susurra:

« Prends ton temps, prends pas ta course ! C'est piquant, c'est déchirant ! »

Dans la cabane, Michel se tenait la tête à deux mains. Un sang noirâtre coulait sur son visage et il criait sans arrêt :

— Mon œil ! Mon œil !

Il se tordait de douleur. À travers ses lamentations, je parvins à comprendre qu'il s'était levé, avait trébuché contre un banc et que son œil avait donné sur la lame de la sciotte pendue au mur.

Je lui fis un bandage, couvrant l'œil noir dégonflé dans son orbite. Je pus le convaincre de se coucher. Il faisait pitié à regarder. Il me semblait avoir vieilli davantage en deux jours que durant les dix dernières années. J'étais consterné mais, surtout, je me sentais horriblement responsable de cet œil crevé.

La nuit fut épouvantable. Entre les lamentations de Michel et les incantations démoniaques de Leclair qui dansa des heures autour de son feu, je me sentais devenir fou. Mon compagnon finit par s'assoupir vers trois heures du matin.

À l'aurore, Leclair s'approcha du camp. Je fermai les yeux, implorant le ciel de m'arracher à cet insoutenable cauchemar.

Leclair siffla trois fois et cria : « Sors ! Le buck s'en vient ! »

De la fenêtre, je vis Leclair prendre sa carabine, la charger, avec des gestes lents, calculés. Puis j'aperçus un sillon dans le lac. L'orignal s'approchait à la nage. À quelques mètres du rivage, lorsqu'il posa la patte au fond de l'eau, il surgit dans un éclaboussement formidable. Il s'avança dans le sentier, son mufle exhalant de grandes traînées de buée blanche.

Leclair épaula.

Je sortis dehors en hurlant.

Je me trouvais à quelques pas de lui quand le coup partit. Le buck s'effondra, brisé net par une balle en plein cœur. Un sinistre râlement, en provenance du camp, acheva de bousculer ma raison. Je perdis conscience au moment où j'arrivais dans le dos de Leclair.

Il faisait nuit quand je m'éveillai. La tête encore bourdonnante, transi, je me levai de peine et de misère. Tout était calme. Depuis la porte grande ouverte, une flaque rougeâtre dégoulinait jusque sur le sol. Michel gisait dans son lit, l'œil droit toujours couvert de son pansement, la jambe tuméfiée, un immense trou dans la poitrine, plaie violacée et nauséabonde. Je l'enterrai à côté du camp, en silence.

Soudain, il y eut une clameur. Je vis une lumière qui flottait au-dessus de l'eau. On aurait dit une aurore boréale. Je distinguai une silhouette: Leclair! Je songeai au buck; aucune trace de sa carcasse!

Il se fit un roulement de tambour, puis un grondement sourd, et je perçus ces mots:

Hannasusque Hichquo Hannasusque Him...o !

Je courus. Vers le sud, vers la civilisation. J'en mourrais de fatigue ou d'inanition, mais je ne resterais pas dans cet endroit maudit une seconde de plus. Je fonçai droit devant moi, trébuchant contre les racines, déchirant mes vêtements. Je courus ainsi toute la nuit.

Au crépuscule, j'atteignis enfin le lac Noir, à quinze kilomètres du lac Brûlé. J'étais sale, à moitié nu. Mon corps avançait tout seul. Lancé en avant par la seule volonté de survivre, j'avais instinctivement trouvé mon chemin, sauté ruisseaux et torrents en passant plusieurs fois à deux doigts de la noyade.

Exténué, j'avais pratiquement rampé le dernier kilomètre, tombant à chaque bosse, devant chaque branche. Grimpant sur une souche, j'aperçus la cabane de Georges Daignault, un trappeur que j'avais connu l'été précédent. De la cheminée s'échappaient des nuages de fumée. Je jubilais.

Il ne me restait plus qu'à contourner le petit lac et j'étais sauvé! Je voulus crier mais seul un petit bêlement s'arracha de ma gorge desséchée. Je fonçai tête baissée dans les fardoches et les arrachis. J'arrivais à une clairière, toute proche de la cabane, lorsque soudain une affreuse douleur s'abattit sur mon dos et mes reins. Je tombai face contre terre et un mal lancinant me laboura les chairs, lacéra mes épaules.

Comme une brûlure...

Comme un fredonnement
de Glenn Gould

Cet automne-là, je me sentais bien seul dans ma maison sur la montagne, sans enfants ni compagne, tous partis en voyage pour trois mois. Chaque petite minute me semblait un gouffre d'éternité.

On m'avait laissé avec mon ordinateur, devenu un assemblage insignifiant de fils et de plastique clinquant parce que je n'avais plus le cœur à l'écriture. On m'avait abandonné ou plutôt, c'était moi qui avais fini par chasser la tribu, disperser les combattants, ceux-là même qui devaient constamment se battre pour survivre en ma présence...

J'avais réussi à créer un tel vide autour de moi que je ne pouvais même plus faire la seule chose qui comptât vraiment: écrire !

Mais il y a eu cette fille, ou femme, ou flamme, qu'en sais-je vraiment, même aujourd'hui. Elle est apparue dans ma fenêtre, un peu blême mais avec des yeux qui disaient bien plus que le ciel et la terre réunis dans les moments d'orage. Derrière sa silhouette, les feuilles cramoisies des érables tombaient une à une; j'ai eu le coup de foudre et l'ai rejointe dehors. Le froid vif m'a surpris. J'ai frissonné. Elle fredonnait.

— Vous connaissez Bach ?

— ...

— Vous fredonnez divinement. Vous savez Bach aussi bien que les plus grands musiciens.

— ...

— Ne me répondez pas. Continuez: cela m'est doux. Cela me fait penser au fredonnement de Glenn Gould lorsqu'il joue les *Variations Goldberg* au piano. Je vous fais sourire ?

— ...

— Eh bien, lorsque j'ai entendu Glenn Gould pour la première fois, cela m'a donné un choc: il semblait tellement captivé par la musique qu'il fredonnait, même en enregistrant ses disques ! On dit qu'il était excentrique... peut-être même fou... Belle folie, en vérité... Quand je serai fou, je voudrais l'être à sa manière, rivé à la musique, obnubilé par les sons. Vivre en transe, comme Glenn Gould, voilà mon idéal !

Ce jour-là, j'ai compris pourquoi les autres interprètes de Bach ne réussissaient qu'à me fatiguer: ils surchargent la musique de liaisons et exagèrent le phrasé dynamique, croyant ainsi obtenir un effet expressif. Glenn Gould, lui, donne une respiration rythmique à la phrase musicale, à un sujet ou à un thème. En d'autres termes, ce sont les extrémités des doigts qui agissent pour produire quelque chose qui ressemble aux sons merveilleusement haletants et sifflants des anciennes orgues.

—Il faut être un peu gaga pour fredonner comme Glenn Gould en plein concert devant mille personnes qui ont payé trente dollars le billet pour vous écouter jouer du piano... Vous ne croyez pas? Mais comme j'aimerais être aussi gaga que lui!

—...

—C'est ça. Ne me répondez pas. C'est beaucoup mieux ainsi. Continuez à me bercer de votre musique et j'aurai l'impression que les *Variations* coulent comme la source en forêt, sur des galets polis depuis des siècles. Je vous écoute et les sons ruissellent dans ma tête. Je suis inondé par la musique, par votre voix... Cette promenade me saoule, je vois des bulles pétiller au creux des rochers, des salamandres danser sur la mousse.

•

La fille s'est dématérialisée comme par enchantement, tout au bout du champ. Je n'ai pu la retrouver. Je me suis alors précipité dans la maison et j'ai écouté Glenn Gould. Je me suis laissé emporter par le génie de Bach, jusque dans le tréfonds des jouissances durables, celles-là qui persistent après l'orgasme, alors que les secondes s'étirent en éternités.

Le flot des notes m'envahit. Chaque variation monte et descend, librement, les deux mains du pianiste se multi-pliant. Il n'y a plus ni paumes ni phalanges, rien que des éclairs et des carillons voltigeant dans l'air. Et j'en oublie le piano, cet instrument d'égarement: il n'y a plus que la réalité pure de la musique.

Et je fredonne. Jamais aussi bien que cette fille. Jamais avec autant d'émotion que Glenn Gould. Et dire qu'on lui reprochait de faire des simagrées lorsqu'il chantait en jouant ou qu'il faisait des gestes de chef d'orchestre avec ses mains. C'est qu'on n'avait pas compris qu'il se concen-trait exclusivement sur la manière de mettre en œuvre la musique, sans prendre en considération les moyens physiques pour y parvenir.

Et je fredonne, comme un fou. Et dire que les *Variations Goldberg* ont été composées pour un insomniaque: quoi de mieux pour ne jamais arriver à trouver le sommeil !

•

La fille est enfin revenue. Je l'ai attendue trois jours et trois nuits pendant lesquels je n'ai pas pu fermer l'œil. Je n'ai rien mangé. Je n'ai bu que de l'eau claire...

Nous marchons ensemble dans un petit sentier ombragé. Le vent est frisquet. Elle marche pieds nus sur les feuilles mortes. Ses épaules sont nacrées, ses seins tout petits, bien ronds. Sa chevelure cache ses reins. J'entrevois les rondeurs de ses fesses. Elle ne paraît pas le moins du monde incommodée par le nordet qui souffle. Moi, je tremble, à cause de l'hiver qui s'en vient et de l'émotion qui m'étreint. Mais son fredonnement me recouvre, comme un édredon posé sur un corps bouillant de fièvre.

Cette fille fredonne et Glenn Gould m'apparaît, génial et racé, à la fois excentrique et merveilleusement équilibré. C'est lui qui disait qu'un interprète doit avoir une foi inébranlable en ce qu'il est en train de faire.

J'ai le goût de pleurer. La voix de cette femme est un don du ciel: je la suivrais n'importe où, dans le creux d'un ravin comme dans l'écume d'un torrent.

— Votre fredonnement me fait penser à celui de l'océan démonté qui se coucherait sur un rivage pour l'inonder. Si vous n'existiez pas, je me dessécherais, pareil à ces grands ormes morts au bord des chemins. Donnez-moi la main... S'il vous plaît... Ne vous éloignez pas... Restez près de moi, pour toujours, et faites revivre Bach. Votre fredonnement est tellement magnifique qu'il me semble irréel. Et j'ai peur de l'irréalité. Un seul mot de vous et j'en mourrai de joie.

— ...

•

La fille s'est envolée avec une brise de vent, emportée vers le faîte des grandes épinettes qui bordent le champ.

Son fredonnement s'est dissipé lorsqu'elle est disparue derrière un nuage.

Il s'est mis à neiger. J'étais alors très loin de la maison. De simples flocons, tout légers au début, puis une armée de papillons blancs me sont tombés dessus. Une rafale m'a fait chanceler, le blizzard s'est élevé et m'a jeté par terre à grands coups de tourbillons aveuglants. J'avais les yeux brûlés par des millions de dards. Péniblement, je me suis traîné sur le sol. Je ne voyais plus rien, rien qu'un désert de blancheur infinie et la poudrerie qui s'engouffrait dans ma gorge m'étouffait.

Mais il y avait la musique. Et ce fredonnement que je n'oublierais jamais. Je devais entendre la musique à nouveau, pour me sauver de l'hiver qui me glaçait sur place.

J'ai rampé pendant des heures dans la neige; il faisait nuit quand j'ai finalement atteint ma maison.

J'ai pu trouver la force de saisir la pochette des *Variations Goldberg* et régler le mécanisme de la table tournante qui ferait recommencer le disque automatiquement. Je me suis déshabillé puis je suis tombé sur le divan.

Je me suis gavé de Bach et de Glenn Gould, emmuré dans une bienheureuse torpeur. Le vent secouait mon logis mais je ne l'entendais plus hurler. L'art du plus universel des compositeurs jouait, interprété par le plus universel des pianistes. Et le fredonnement de Glenn Gould m'a pris aux tripes, tellement que j'ai pleuré toute la nuit, tout le jour qui a suivi, toute la semaine, probablement tout l'hiver aussi.

Un dernier cadeau pour Cornélia

Cornélia Pishum sifflotait tout en conduisant sa petite auto. Le soleil, radieux, créait de magnifiques chatoiements entre les branches effeuillées des hêtres tout en réchauffant son visage à travers le pare-brise.

En arrivant dans la rue des Parfums, en apercevant l'épicerie puis sa propre résidence, Cornélia Pishum sentit un coup de chaleur venir se loger juste entre ses seins. Elle dut déboutonner son chemisier.

Elle gara sa voiture, descendit dans l'allée bordée d'ifs sauvages et de noisetiers qu'Alfred et elle-même avaient plantés l'automne précédent et son cœur tremblota.

Toute vêtue de blanc, ses cheveux auburn ramenés en chignon le long de sa nuque, Cornélia Pishum était resplendissante. Un masque vermeil tachait cependant son beau visage ovale.

Elle jeta un regard furtif derrière elle tout en insérant la clé dans la serrure de la porte d'entrée. Personne. Elle ouvrit d'un solide coup de poignet et se précipita dans la maison.

« Ouf! Le pire est passé. T'aurais dû voir leurs bettes d'enterrement, mon bel Alfred! » dit-elle à haute voix tout en se débarrassant de son manteau.

Elle monta au deuxième étage et se fit couler un bain très chaud. Elle se déshabilla à la hâte et se laissa glisser dans l'eau bouillante. Elle prit grand plaisir à sentir courir le feu entre ses cuisses, sur ses fesses et le long de sa colonne vertébrale.

« Cher Alfred d'amour. Tu vas voir qu'on va être heureux comme jamais à partir de maintenant. »

S'étirant un bras derrière elle, Cornélia Pishum ouvrit une petite armoire de bois, suspendue au mur par un crochet de porcelaine. Elle en tira deux bouteilles en verre transparent. La première contenait un liquide ambré qu'elle versa tout entier dans l'eau du bain. La seconde était remplie d'une solution verte dans laquelle flottait quelques poils grisâtres pendus à deux narines toutes grandes ouvertes surmontées d'un gros furoncle.

Farfouillant avec deux doigts dans le contenant, Cornélia Pishum finit par en retirer le nez en parfait état de conservation grâce au formol. Le déposant sur la paume de sa main droite tendue à la hauteur de ses yeux, elle laissa échapper: « Si tu sens ce que je sens, tu dois être heureux, mon bel Alfred. »

Puis elle se laissa sombrer dans l'ivresse d'une jouissance sans bornes.

Au bout de longues minutes de halètement et de petits cris, elle déposa le nez sur le rebord de la baignoire et, avançant ses lèvres vers les narines quasi palpitantes, elle baisa le furoncle.

« Et dire que tout ça, c'est grâce à toi ! »

En effet, une semaine auparavant, un matin, Alfred Pishum s'était réveillé avec un petit bouton accolé à l'aile droite du nez. Au fil des heures, ce bouton avait grossi à un point tel qu'il avait valu à Alfred les sarcasmes de ses camarades de travail. Toute son attention accaparée par ce bubon disgracieux, Alfred s'était rendu aux toilettes à de multiples reprises dans l'espoir de le crever. Face au miroir, dans le privé de ce local servant aux exutoires les plus secrets et les plus morbides de la race humaine, Alfred avait donc compressé violemment entre le pouce et l'index son excroissance phlegmoneuse qui avait pourtant résolument tenu bon, se contentant d'enfler un peu plus à chaque compression au lieu d'exploser en pleine glace comme il aurait dû.

À la fin de l'après-midi, la taille du furoncle avait quintuplé, coiffant le nez d'Alfred d'une rougeur pulsative et presque éclairante. Même qu'une sauvage céphalée lui tamponnait la matière grise du côté droit du crâne, possible séquelle des trop nombreux quolibets qu'il avait dû souffrir.

Dès quatre heures, Alfred s'était empressé de se réfugier dans les bras de son épouse éternellement compréhensive. Comme de raison, Cornélia l'avait accueilli avec toute la dignité souhaitée, s'empressant de l'embrasser sur la joue gauche comme à son habitude, ajoutant cependant: « Mais qu'est-ce qui arrive à ton nez ? »

Le pauvre Alfred, dépité, avait alors raconté l'abracadabrante histoire de ce furoncle débridé, puis, les larmes aux yeux, il était monté à l'étage, sans prendre le temps d'enlever son paletot. Devant le miroir de cette même salle de bains, il s'était juré de faire éclater ce chancre de malheur. Ayant pris une formidable respiration, il avait écrabouillé de toutes ses forces et durant de longues secondes ledit bubon, jusqu'à ce que finalement se produisît une explosion de pus verdâtre. Enfin libéré de l'effroyable humiliation, Alfred avait cependant ressenti comme un coup de marteau qui lui fracassait le crâne, juste avant de perdre conscience sous l'effet du choc causé par le pus qui avait pris le chemin des veines de l'aile du nez, remonté dans les vaisseaux du cerveau et embolisé dans le sinus carverneux droit.

L'accident cérébro-vasculaire avait terrassé Alfred. Cornélia l'avait trouvé quelques minutes plus tard, les yeux rivés à son furoncle éclaté, la bouche tordue, le bras et la jambe gauche totalement paralysés, bouillant d'une fièvre cataclysmique. Le temps d'appeler à l'aide, de le traîner dans la chambre et de le hisser sur le lit, il était mort.

Le carillon de la porte d'entrée projeta Cornélia Pishum hors de son souvenir. Elle faillit glisser sur la céramique mouillée en sortant de la baignoire à toute vitesse. Elle enfila un peignoir et renvoya le nez dans sa bouteille, prenant grand soin de remettre le trésor à sa place, derrière une rangée de bouteilles de shampoing.

Tout en descendant l'escalier, elle fit de son mieux pour retrouver son calme. Rajustant les pans de son peignoir, elle entrouvrit la porte. « Cendrine ! Mais entre donc, vieille chipie ! »

Cornélia Pishum la fit asseoir au salon et lui servit une tasse de thé.

— Ta migraine est passée, j'espère ? minauda Cendrine Bastarache. J'avais tellement hâte de te parler, seule à seule. Si tu savais tout ce qui s'est raconté après ton départ du cimetière, ajouta-t-elle en avalant ses mots. Personne ne se préoccupait de toi. Il n'y avait que ce crime qui les intéressait. Mais moi, je pensais tout le temps à toi. Tu sais, une veuve comme moi, sans enfants, ça comprend bien des choses... Ça comprend tout, en fait. C'est drôle, à cause de ton sourire, tu donnais aujourd'hui l'impression d'une femme qui ne croit pas à la mort. Tu l'aimais beaucoup, Alfred, n'est-ce pas ? T'aurais pu faire des folies, tellement tu l'aimais, n'est-ce pas ? Comme moi, avec Rosario, quand il vivait. Tu te souviens de notre petit voyage d'amoureux à Saint-Félicien, dans ce motel sur les bords du lac Saint-Jean ? Je te l'ai déjà raconté je crois... Ah ! Tout ce qu'on a pu faire là ! Je n'ai jamais eu le courage de confesser ça au père-curé. Il m'aurait excommuniée, c'est certain... Mon Rosario ! Ton Alfred ! Deux hommes pareils... Extraordinaires ! Qu'on n'oubliera pas de sitôt !

Après ce long soliloque, Cendrine Bastarache se leva et déposa sa tasse sur la table du salon. Sur le pas de la porte, juste avant de sortir, elle chuchota: «Tu permets que nous venions toutes les trois te rendre visite? Demain soir? Nous voudrions t'offrir un cadeau.»

Cornélia Pishum, qui n'avait pu placer un seul mot depuis l'arrivée de son amie, voulut protester. Mais avant même qu'elle eût ouvert la bouche, Cendrine Bastarache l'avait embrassée sur les deux joues, remerciée de son invitation et lui avait juré qu'elle serait extasiée de leur surprise.

Le calme étant revenu dans la grande maison de la rue des Parfums, Cornélia Pishum ferma les portes à double tour. Se sentant un peu lasse, elle monta dans sa chambre avec une seule et obsédante idée: se coucher avec un morceau d'Alfred.

Nue, elle se laissa choir dans le grand lit aux draps de flanellette fleuris. Elle tira d'une commode une petite bouteille, la serra à deux mains, à la hauteur de ses yeux, admirant avec émotion l'oreille droite d'Alfred. Puis, de sa voix la plus douce, elle se mit à chantonner une berceuse. Flottant dans son formol, l'oreille paraissait danser au son de cette musique. Et chaque strophe de cette chanson improvisée se terminait par ce refrain:

Dors, dors, ma petite oreille,
Dors, dors, mon petit bébé

Terminant le dernier couplet, Cornélia Pishum étreignit la bouteille contre sa poitrine, en sortit l'oreille et la déposa avec précaution sur un oreiller tout à côté d'elle. Puis elle s'endormit aussitôt.

Tard dans la soirée, le carillon de la porte d'entrée retentit à nouveau. Il fallut plusieurs coups pour réveiller Cornélia Pishum qui dormait profondément, l'oreille d'Alfred accolée à une joue.

La veuve descendit au rez-de-chaussée seulement vêtue d'une robe de chambre. Deux hommes, casqués et vêtus d'imperméables gris, attendaient devant la porte.

— Inspecteurs Carpentier et Beaulieu, de la Sûreté du Québec, dit un policier en touchant le rebord de sa casquette. Nous pouvons entrer ?

— C'est qu'il est très tard... balbutia-t-elle en frissonnant.

— Nous serons brefs, madame. Mais ce que nous avons à vous dire est de la plus haute importance.

— Bon... bien... entrez.

Les deux hommes enlevèrent leurs imperméables qu'ils déposèrent sur le dossier d'une chaise. L'eau qui ruisselait du plastique des habits faisait une flaque géante que Cornélia Pishum se garda bien d'éponger, de peur d'indisposer ses visiteurs. Elle les fit asseoir et leur demanda la permission d'aller s'habiller.

Dans sa chambre, elle consulta son réveille-matin — vingt-trois heures et demie — et après avoir enfilé une robe, elle remit l'oreille d'Alfred, un tantinet desséchée, dans sa bouteille qu'elle cacha dans la commode.

Elle redescendit, inquiète. Les deux hommes s'étaient assis dans la cuisine au lieu de passer au salon comme elle les avait invités à le faire, et ils chuchotaient.

Dès qu'elle apparut, ils se turent et celui qui semblait le chef prit la parole.

— Vous nous excuserez de cette visite tardive, madame. Nous nous doutons que cette journée a sûrement été éprouvante. Mais nous devions vous faire part de ceci : nous avons maintenant la certitude que ce n'est pas « un » mais « plusieurs » criminels qui se sont introduits chez l'embaumeur le soir du crime.

— Ah…, fit Cornélia Pishum, un peu pâlotte.

— Voilà une bonne nouvelle pour vous.

— Ah oui ? Et pourquoi ? balbutia-t-elle.

— Parce que nous n'avons plus de raisons de vous soupçonner !

— Vous me soupçonniez ! Moi ?

— Évidemment ! fit le policier.

— C'est tant mieux alors… répondit Cornélia Pishum.

— Toute cette affaire paraît un coup monté…

— Non ! s'exclama Cornélia Pishum.

—Mais très certainement! Nous avons toutes les raisons de croire qu'un groupe de maniaques sexuels, acoquinés à la mafia de Montréal, ont perpétré ce crime abominable. C'est épouvantable de penser qu'on a si vicieusement amputé le cadavre de votre mari... même son pénis!

—C'est affreux! laissa échapper Cornélia Pishum.

—Vous l'avez dit, madame. L'escouade des mœurs s'occupe de l'affaire. Nous pensons qu'il s'agit d'un réseau qui aurait des ramifications à travers tout le pays... Même jusqu'aux États-Unis...

Comme Cornélia Pishum semblait décontenancée, le deuxième policier se leva et vint lui toucher la main.

—Nous ne vous dérangerons pas plus longtemps. Nous voulions seulement vous prévenir que l'enquête progresse normalement.

Les deux hommes s'excusèrent puis s'effacèrent, laissant la veuve toujours immobile sur sa chaise de cuisine.

Cornélia Pishum finit par sortir de sa torpeur et, se pinçant les joues, courut vers l'armoire au-dessus du réfrigérateur. Dans un gros bocal de verre flottait un œil, à l'iris d'un bleu éclatant. Le sortant du formol, Cornélia Pishum l'emporta dans le salon et le déposa sur le téléviseur. Puis, choisissant un disque de Johann Strauss, elle valsa au son de la musique viennoise, vagabondant follement à travers la pièce sous le regard d'Alfred dont la pupille se mit à se dilater et à se contracter, selon les allées et venues de Cornélia Pishum qui, emportée, caracolait entre les fauteuils et sur le long divan de cuir rose, s'enroulant du tapis persan, accrochant potiches et bibelots qui tombaient par terre en s'émiettant à qui mieux mieux.

Cornélia Pishum, enivrée par un bonheur frénétique, vit soudain les portes d'un petit vaisselier s'ouvrir d'elles-mêmes et le couvercle d'une grosse fiole se dévisser afin de laisser sortir deux mains, coupées aux poignets, aux doigts graciles et aux ongles parfaitement limés. Patinant à toute allure sur le plancher, elles sautèrent sur son visage et se mirent à la caresser. Puis, les dix doigts descendirent en pianotant sur sa peau satinée. Cornélia Pishum fut déshabillée en deux temps trois mouvements; ballottée entre l'extase et l'épouvante, elle s'abandonna aux ongles, aux phalanges et aux paumes humides qui remontèrent par petits coups le long de chaque cuisse, plongeant sur le pubis et de chaque côté du nombril avant de se glisser sous chaque aisselle, puis autour de chaque sein avant de venir se nouer autour de son cou.

À ce moment, Cornélia Pishum sombra dans l'inconscience.

Au petit matin, elle s'éveilla, étendue sur le tapis du salon, son corps nu zébré de marques violacées, la gorge encore comprimée par une tenaille invisible. L'œil d'Alfred n'était plus sur le téléviseur; les mains n'étaient plus sur son corps. Chancelante, elle alla vers l'armoire au-dessus du réfrigérateur. L'œil dans le bocal tourna soudainement sur lui-même, la pupille se fermant et s'agrandissant à plusieurs reprises. Apeurée, elle claqua le panneau. Pourtant, cinq minutes plus tard, elle ne put s'empêcher de vérifier le contenu de la fiole du vaisselier. Les deux mains, qui baignaient dans le formol, se joignirent et les dix doigts, enlacés, se convulsèrent les uns contre les autres, de manière à faire craquer les jointures.

Cornélia Pishum s'enfuit dans sa chambre et plongea sous les couvertures. Il lui fallut des heures avant de retrouver un certain calme. Finalement, elle se résolut à s'habiller et à redescendre, lentement, marche après marche, à l'écoute attentive de tout bruit suspect. Les portes du vaisselier encore ouvertes, elle jeta un regard furtif vers le récipient de verre. Cette fois, ô soupir, les mains ne bronchèrent pas.

Elle repoussa les idées folles qui l'assaillaient, se forçant à prendre de grandes respirations. Puis elle attendit la visite de ses amies, résistant à l'envie de les appeler pour annuler le rendez-vous. Elle avait finalement grand besoin de leur compagnie.

Bien sûr, Cornélia Pishum avait été ravie de découvrir l'oreille droite d'Alfred dans la maison, quelques jours après sa mort. Bien sûr qu'elle aimait cet œil, ces mains, ce nez, même surmonté de ce furoncle ! Aussi n'avait-elle pas ressenti le moindre dégoût, la moindre peur... jusqu'à ce que ces organes se mettent à bouger, danser, virevolter, s'épivarder...

Vers sept heures, Cornélia Pishum entendit du bruit. Elle n'avait pas bougé de son fauteuil de tout l'après-midi et lorsqu'elle se leva pour aller à la fenêtre, ses jambes engourdies faillirent ne pas la soutenir. Dehors, on riait.

Elle ouvrit la porte et aperçut les trois veuves, toutes habillées de blanc. Savamment coiffées et fardées, elles étaient élégantes comme jamais dans leurs longues robes de taffetas. Augustina Malouin, qui précédait les deux autres, tenait précieusement un petit sac de plastique.

— Si tu savais ce que nous t'apportons comme cadeau, ma chère, dit Amandine Aubut en embrassant Cornélia Pishum sur les deux joues.

— Quand trois veuves veulent le bonheur de leur plus grande amie… dit Cendrine Bastarache en s'assurant que la porte était bien verrouillée.

— J'ai tellement hâte… renchérit Amandine Aubut en fermant soigneusement les persiennes de toutes les fenêtres.

Cornélia Pishum, hébétée, se laissa conduire jusqu'au milieu du salon et tomba presque à la renverse dans un fauteuil qu'avait tiré vers elle Augustina Malouin.

— Attends de voir ça! dit-elle en présentant son petit sac tel un trophée.

Rayonnante, elle en sortit un paquet de forme oblongue, enveloppé d'un papier brillant couleur fuchsia qu'elle tendit à Cornélia Pishum d'un geste solennel.

— Mais… je voudrais vous raconter…

— Ouvre ! On en parlera après !

Cornélia Pishum, tremblante, déballa le cadeau. Dans une boîte se trouvait une longue bouteille de verre où flottait une langue rosâtre qu'elle reconnut tout de suite.

— N'est-ce pas ragoûtant ? s'écria Cendrine Bastarache en se serrant contre l'épaule de son amie.

Le cœur dans la gorge, Cornélia Pishum fondit en larmes et faillit échapper son cadeau par terre. Cendrine Bastarache la délivra de ce présent qui semblait peser des tonnes et le tint à bout de bras, comme s'il s'agissait d'une relique précieuse.

Certaine que Cornélia Pishum sanglotait de joie, Amandine Aubut fouilla dans sa sacoche avec enthousiasme et en retira une petite flûte à bec noire.

Augustina Malouin applaudit. Retentirent alors les premières notes d'une mélodie rythmée. Après quelques mesures, la langue se mit à se dandiner dans la bouteille dont le bouchon se dévissa de lui-même. À grands renforts de contractions spasmodiques, la langue se hissa hors du contenant pour choir sur le sol où elle entreprit une sarabande endiablée.

Cornélia Pishum tomba durement sur le plancher du salon, tout à côté de la langue.

La musique cessa, la langue se recroquevilla. Cendrine Bastarache et Amandine Aubut portèrent Cornélia Pishum sur le divan pendant qu'Augustina Malouin replaçait l'organe d'Alfred dans son contenant.

Les trois veuves s'affairaient à réanimer leur amie quand Augustina Malouin s'écria:

—Mon Dieu! Mais qu'est-ce qu'on va faire avec le dernier cadeau pour Cornélia?

TABLE DES MATIÈRES

Repères bibliographiques

Les textes suivants ont déjà été publiés dans des revues ou collectifs, sous des formes parfois légèrement différentes :

« Une heure dans la vie de quelqu'un » dans *l'Écrit primal*, n° 6, printemps 1988 ;

« La fleur que tu m'avais jetée » dans *l'Horreur est humaine*, collectif publié chez le Palindrome éditeur, avril 1989 ;

« Histoire d'oignons qui faisaient pleurer » dans *Meilleur avant 31/12/99*, collectif publié chez le Palindrome éditeur, sous le titre « Risibles angoisses ou histoire d'oignons qui faisaient pleurer », novembre 1987 ;

« Le Buck » dans *XYZ*, n° 16, hiver 1988, de même que dans le collectif *l'Horreur est humaine*, avril 1989.

Cet ouvrage composé en Times corps 12
a été achevé d'imprimer en novembre 1989

Achevé   Imprimerie
d'imprimer Gagné Ltée
au Canada Louiseville

More Praise For "Love Without Limit"!

"*Love Without Limit* presents a view of life rooted in pragmatism; not the practice of self-interest, but a pragmatism which binds self-interest to the good of all. This is brought out in every one of Pastor Williams' examples, from 'keeping the Sabbath' to 'loving one's enemies.' His interpretations transform the message of the Scriptures from the dictates of a tyrannical, arbitrary deity to the benevolent advice of a loving God demonstrating 'invincible good will'—infinitely flexible, expanding to include all life and further all creation."

—**Winslow Pels**, Artist/Author

"This is a book which should speak to the condition of lay people and clergy alike. Pastor Williams' well written and well researched picture of the "saved" and of the power of love is life enriching. It transforms the image of God from a demanding deity, to that of a loving Lord who is always concerned about and working for our welfare. It changes obedience to God, from the drudgery of duty to the discovery of the wisest and most beautiful way to live.

—**Diane Crawford**, Author

"*Love Without Limit* is an enlightening study of the Bible's description of God's love for us and his gifts to us. It should soothe the troubled spirit and cleanse the guilty conscience. The author provides new insight on many passages and helps us see God's laws and Christ's Sermon on the Mount as treasured gifts of love rather than threats or impossible requirements. I believe this book will provide a new perspective for all of your future Bible Study.

—**Joyce Egginton**, *NY Times* bestselling author,
From Cradle To Grave, Circle of Fire, Day of Fury

"Absolutely groundbreaking! Offers a fresh, positive and loving view of God. Anyone who reads this book will become convinced of it's true Christian message. Written by a Minister, the book presents the revelation that God's will is synonymous with the greatest wisdom for living, which makes *Love Without Limit* valuable for secular as well as religious readers."

— **Father James Sheehan**, author, *The Father Who Didn't Know My Name*

"*Love Without Limit* helps the reader feel loved and accepted by God, which fosters self-acceptance. It then explains how this leads to the love and acceptance of others. It also contains the best advice I have seen on how to understand and overcome anger, whether my own anger or that of others."

—**Mathias B. Freese**, author, *i*

"Books of ethics explore what is right. Self-Help books usually deal with the methods people can use to achieve a better life. *Love Without Limit* combines ethical guidance with ways of really living that good life. I was impressed by the advice on how to become untroubled by insults and at the same time how to benefit from criticism. The helpful insights in *Love Without Limit* reveal religion as meant to enrich rather than restrict our lives. It also shows how that more beautiful life can be ours. "

—**Gary Anderson**, Syndicated Columnist

"Explaining how the love of God is different than the 'romantic love' we usually think of, makes clear why God's love is unconditional and will never fail us. The certainty of salvation that results from God's limitless love, allows us to focus on living this life wisely and well. The book devotes most of its space to learning how to live the best life on this earth."

— **Dr. Glenda Gnade**, *Return to Paradise in New Heights of Glory*

"This is explosive stuff! In *Love Without Limit* startling scholarly ideas about salvation are revealed finally to the general public. These insights show God is more loving than generally portrayed. Examination of the Sermon on the Mount reveals that the spirit of God's law shows people the wisest way to live."

—**Richard Staley**, author, *Last Kiss*

"The fresh interpretations of familiar scripture passages are very enlightening and valuable. They free the reader from worry about salvation and give good guidance for living this life. Lessons from psychology reveal the problems of human nature and ways to overcome them."

—**Eldon Thomas**, author, *Table For Three*

"A minister's discovery that God's love is great enough to save *everyone*—along with the convincing evidence he found in scripture. His testimony can help people feel loved by God and also help them love God, themselves and others. The book goes a long way to free people from religious manipulation which is perpetrated by fear of hell or other punishment."

— **Billie Marie Zal**, author, *The Fabric of our Lives*

"Anyone concerned about salvation will find assurance in this book. Anyone seeking a better life can benefit from the good guidance the author finds in the Sermon on the Mount. The psychological insights in the book help the reader to overcome problems like anger or insults."

— **Rev. Basil Sharp**, author, *The Adventure of Being Human*

Love Without Limit: A Personal Journey to the Heart of God
Copyright © 2004 by Walter E. Williams
Probe Publishing Company

For further information, contact the author through Probe Publishing Company

Published by:
Probe Publishing Company
Post Office Box 395
McAlisterville, PA 17049 ⊕ Email: probepubco@yahoo.com
(717) 463-3878

Book designed by:
The Floating Gallery
331 West 57th Street, #465, New York, NY 10019
(212) 399-1961 www.thefloatinggallery.com

Cover Design by Winslow Pels

Love Without Limit: A Personal Journey to the Heart of God
By Walter E. Williams

1. Author 2. Title 3. Inspiration 4. Religion
Library of Congress Control Number 2003107034
ISBN 0-9742463-0-1 (Paperback)

Printed in Canada

LOVE WITHOUT LIMIT:

A PERSONAL JOURNEY TO THE
HEART OF GOD

by Walter E. Williams

Probe Publishing Company
McAlisterville, Pennsylvania

This book is dedicated to the many people who loved and accepted me, despite my faults. They enabled me to love myself and others more completely. They also inspired and confirmed for me the vision of God's unconditional and unlimited love, which I present in this book.

This book presents God's unlimited and unconditional love as the absolute assurance of our salvation. In the last judgment good people are not separated from evil people. We are all a mixture of good and evil. In the end God frees us from the evil within us, which torments us and others on this earth, so we may enjoy heaven purified and free from trouble.

Even on this earth, God tries to free us from the faults that mar our existence. So the second section of the book focuses on this life, where God's loving guidance shows us the path to the best and most beautiful life. Finding and following God's will enriches life, rather than restricting it, thus it is the wisest way to live.

Christ's Sermon on the Mount goes beyond the letter of the law to reveal its spirit, which deepens our understanding of God's will.

The seemingly paradoxical beatitudes are actually profound statements which can produce the promised blessings now as well as in the future.

The Sermon on the Mount also contains passages which, combined with psychological insights, can enable us to understand and overcome anger, insults and condemnation.

The sermon's advice to "Love your enemies," far from being an unworkable ideal, is the wisest way to live on this earth. The God-like love referred to here, means active concern. We should be concerned about the welfare of our enemies because unhappy people can be cruel and desperate people do desperate things.

In this book the image of God is transformed from a demanding deity, to that of a loving Lord who is always concerned about and working for our welfare.

Table of Contents

PREFACE

HIS BOOK IS ABOUT GOD'S love, and the gifts He gives us because He loves us so much. I believe that God is much more loving than we have been led to believe. Many people say that God loves us; but in the next breath they tell us that He will condemn us to hell if we do not measure up to the standards *they* lay down in His name. Over the years, I learned to love people more, as they showed me their love. Finally, I could not believe that God would exclude anyone from His salvation.

At first, when I wanted to believe that everyone was saved, I was sure that I must be wrong. After all, I had never met anyone else who believed that; and I knew all too well what the Bible said.

One day, I discerned a new possible interpretation for a portion of scripture that could imply universal salvation. I began to look at the Bible with new eyes, and I found more verses which could mean that God would ultimately save everyone. I began to deliberately take on the verses that had been interpreted as meaning that some people would be damned eternally. I found that there were other ways of interpreting those scriptures, so they did not mean some would be condemned. I felt then I could believe that everyone could be saved, now with the backing of the Bible.

Gradually, I began to preach about this more loving God; and people did not stone me. Still, it was not often that I brought this new belief up outside my congregation. Then I began to discover other ministers who agreed with me, but they were just as silent about their belief.

Now I have discovered scholars and theologians through the ages who have written about their belief in universal salvation. I wondered then, how many people there might be who believe, or would like to believe, that God loves everyone so much that He will ultimately save them all.

It seemed sad to me that God is preached as a threatening, judgemental God openly and boldly over the airwaves and through many other media, while those who believe in a more loving God are so shy and cautious about spreading the good news.

I remembered part of the Preface of the 1855 edition of *Leaves of Grass* by Walt Whitman where he wrote:

"Re-examine all you have been told

At school or church or in any book,

Dismiss whatever insults your own soul"

The threatening God who is going to send us to hell if we do not follow His commandments and believe what He wants insults my soul; and I think it insults God. I have followed Walt Whitman's advice and reexamined all that I have been told or read. I have found a God of greater love than I had known before.

It was then that I decided to write this book, to give courage to those who believe in this unlimited love and salvation, but think they may be the only ones. I am amazed now at how many years it was before I even had the courage to share my belief with another; and to my amazement, find agreement. What a shame if this great message of love is hidden, while a far harsher God is preached widely without any compunction.

I do not write this book to convert anyone to my belief who does not want to believe, or doesn't already believe, in the loving

God whom I have come to know through life first, and then the scriptures. I write this book to confirm in like-minded people their belief, and to strengthen them in their convictions, by letting them know they are not heretics, and they are not alone.

I am also writing this book to share the love that I have found from God and other people, which fills my heart and overflows. I want the reader to feel the love of God as I have felt it, an unconditional love and complete acceptance which brings joy to my heart. It inspires me to love as I have been loved by God.

Now I have found that many people I talk to would like to believe that everyone is saved, but there are so many scriptures that seem to say it cannot be true. It would take a book longer than I would care to write, or you might care to read, to deal with each and every scripture that I have found troubling people on this point.

I will reexamine many scriptures in this book. The new insight I have found into their meaning results in interpretations that do not insult my soul. I hope you will join me in this reexamination and find that the Bible and religion need not insult anyone's soul.

In the first section of the book, I lay down a theological argument for the loving God who will save everyone, and I present my belief that the law of God is also a gift of His love. In the second section of the book, I examine the Sermon on the Mount and reveal some beautiful and practical insights into the meaning and benefits of Christ's loving advice in that famous sermon.

I hope you will find this book full of love. I hope it will help you feel the love that God has been trying to convey to His children throughout the long history recorded in the Bible and particularly through His son, Jesus Christ. I hope this book will convey to you my love, and show you more about loving each other. I want you to feel that God is love and that loving is the best way to live on this earth. This book is my gift of love to you. I hope you will accept it, and feel loved.

SECTION I: THEORETICAL JUSTIFICATION

Chapter 1: What is Love?

*L*OVE IS THE MOST BEAUTIFUL and important thing in life. I think it is probably the greatest dream of people in their youth. I fear it is often the greatest disappointment later in life. Maybe that disappointment comes because love is so misunderstood. When I mentioned the title of my book to people, they almost invariably thought of romantic love. Romantic love can be very beautiful and fulfilling. In this book, I wish to discuss a love even better than the best of romantic love. That love is the love of God. I will first explain the differences between these two types of love.

In Greek, there are several words, each of which we translate "love" in English. What I call romantic love is referred to in Greek by the word *eros*. Romantic love, or eros, is love for something or someone who is desirable, whom we like. To love someone romantically, we must like that individual and find that person desirable or attractive in some way. Nothing else makes sense.

The problem with romantic love is that people sometimes do things we do not like. Then we get angry at them. At that point, we no longer feel any romantic love for them. If they do enough things we do not like, we may stop loving them forever. This is where the agony of romantic love comes in. Even when the love seems strong and secure, there is still the worry about how long it will last. When we love each other in this romantic sense, we are always falling in and out of love, and fighting to get what we desire from the other person. In our romantic desire, we want to possess the other person, and we want the other person to fulfill our wants and desires. The fighting and heartbreak that ensues makes us wonder if love is worth it.

There is also the worry about how deep it goes. We try to put our best foot forward to impress the other person, and to win his/her love. Then we wonder if they would love us if they knew all about us, for we all have some less desirable traits. Romantic love is a great joy, but it is also a great worry.

Romantic love is really love for oneself, more than for the other. It is like someone saying, "I love that car." What he really means is, "I love myself, and I want that car to make me happy." If he gets the car, he is happy and continues to love the car as long as it does his bidding and makes him happy. If the car starts to give him too much trouble, or if a more attractive car comes along, he stops loving that car or starts loving another. At this point, if he is able, he trades his old car in on a new model. Such is romantic love.

Romantic love and all the other loves we give and receive from each other on this earth are limited and conditional. People love us if we are desirable for one reason or another. They love us if we are not too much trouble. There always seems to be some limit to how much, or how long, they will love us. Because of that, we might assume that God's love has similar limits. God is often presented as one who loves us, but who will reject us if we do not conform to certain conditions.

God loves us and He is trying to save us from eternal damnation. However, if we do not listen, believe, and shape up, He will give up on us, turn His back on us, and we are lost forever. God's love is perhaps more patient and more forgiving than those we have known on this earth, but it is basically the same. Therefore it also has a limit.

I reject the idea that God's love is limited like the loves we receive from the people on this earth. I believe, and the Bible says, that the love of God for us is not just greater than any earthly affection we have experienced, but it is also different.

The first hint I had that God's love was a quite different love was the words of Paul in I Corinthians 13:4 which say, "love is not jealous..."

Now one of the main characteristics of romantic love is jealousy. A Scottish proverb underlines that when it says, "Love is never without jealousy." Yet Paul is telling us about a love that is not jealous. That is certainly not romantic love or eros. In fact, the word eros is not even used in the New Testament either to refer to the love God has for us or the love we should have for each other.

In the New Testament, the word *agape* is used to refer to love. Agape is what this book is about. In the remainder of this book, whenever the word "love" is used, it is agape which is meant unless the words "romantic love" are used, in which case eros is meant.

Agape is love even for that which is not desirable. It is love that has nothing to do with the characteristics of the person who is loved. It is love that is totally dependent on the nature of the one who feels and gives the love. God loves people, not because of what they do, or feel, or believe, or are, but because of what God Himself is and thus feels.

In I John 4:8 we read, "God is love." This agape is the very nature of God, and it causes Him to love us with a different, unlimited, unconditional love.

Victor Hugo once said, "The greatest happiness of life is the conviction that we are loved—loved for ourselves, or rather, in spite of ourselves." This is the very kind of love that God feels for us. It does not matter how we respond, or if we respond at all.

In I John 4:10 we read, "In this is love, not that we loved God but that he loved us and sent his Son to be the expiation for our sins."

So it is the love of God on which our assurance stands and, as the verse also says, our salvation. God loves us by His very nature, and by the very nature of that love He sends His Son to assure us of our salvation. When we really understand what God's love is like, this agape, there is no need to fear that He will never punish us, reject us or stop loving us.

The writer of I John understands this, for he writes in I John 4:18, "There is no fear in love, but perfect love casts out fear. For fear has to do with punishment, and he who fears is not perfected in love."

Thus, if we really understand God's love, we have no fear of punishment or hell.

Paul gives further assurances in Romans 8:31-33 when he writes, "What then shall we say to this? If God is for us, who is against us? He who did not spare his own Son but gave him up for us all, will he not also give us all things with him? Who shall bring any charge against God's elect? It is God who justifies; who is to condemn?" What greater sign could He give of His love than the giving of His Son? If that does not convince us that He loves us, what will?

And once we are convinced, Paul goes on to assure us that nothing can separate us from that love, saying in verses 38-39, "For I am sure that neither death, nor life, nor angels, nor principalities, nor things present, nor things to come, nor powers, nor height, nor depth, nor anything else in all creation, will be able to separate us from the love of God in Christ Jesus our Lord." Truly, God's love is without limit. His love extends to all of us freely, fully and forever.

Chapter 2: Is Salvation for All?

*O*BVIOUSLY, IT IS GOD ALONE WHO decides who will be saved and how. In Romans 8:30 we read, "And those whom he predestined he also called; and those whom he called he also justified; and those whom he justified he also glorified."

In other words, God predetermined or predestined who would be saved. Our salvation is entirely God's choice and His doing. We may object to the fact that we can do nothing to change our fate. For me, it is a wonderful relief that my ultimate salvation is completely in God's hands. If my salvation depended on me in any way, I am sure I would mess it up.

We should all be happy if God has sealed our salvation. But what if He has chosen to condemn us? Then it is surely unfair that there is no way we can redeem ourselves. This problem does not arise if God chooses to save everyone, which I believe to be true.

I Timothy 2:3-6 says, "This is good, and it is acceptable in the sight of God our Savior, who desires all men to be saved and to come to the knowledge of the truth. For there is one God, and there is one mediator between God and men, the man Christ Jesus; who gave himself a ransom for all,"[1] It is God who decides and He wishes all of us to be saved. God will surely have His way and we will all be saved. Karl Barth, the most prominent theologian of the twentieth century, agrees that God will save us all.[2]

Is there no act so bad that salvation would be lost? What deed could be worse than the crucifixion of Christ? Can God forgive those who killed his own Son? Can Jesus forgive even those who are crucifying him? We read in Luke 23:34 that Christ in the midst of his suffering on the cross said, "Father, forgive them; for they know not what they do." He asks God to forgive them not because they believe in God, repent of their wrongs, love God or Him, understand or any other positive requirement, but because "they know not what they do."

If anyone fails to fulfill this, it is those who are Christians, and particularly ministers, for they have studied and claim to "know" just like the Pharisees. Yet I believe that Christians, even ministers, like the scribes and Pharisees, "know not what they do."

Everyone, then, is included in Christ's plea for forgiveness, and that request is certainly granted by his Father. Thus, the worst sin of all time becomes the greatest sign of God's limitless love and forgiveness. There is nothing people can do to prevent God from forgiving them, and there is nothing they can or must do to earn that forgiveness.

I have known people who are consistently mean, and I know that they are just as consistently unhappy. They want to be happier, but they have no idea how to find that happiness. In their ignorance, they lash out at others. Hopefully we, like Christ, can say, "Father forgive them for they know not what they do."

Although I can not imagine any deed more deadly than the crucifixion of Christ, there is in scripture the so-called "unforgivable sin." We read in Luke 12:10, "And every one who speaks a word against the Son of man will be forgiven; but he who blasphemes against the Holy Spirit will not be forgiven."

Jesus is indicating that to oppose the Holy Spirit is worse than to oppose Him and is unforgivable. The work of the Holy Spirit is to make us believe in the love and forgiveness of God. Now forgiveness, to be effective, must not only be given but also believed and accepted. No matter how surely God forgives us, we do not feel that forgiveness unless we believe in it. If we do not believe in God's love and forgiveness, we have rejected the work of the Holy Spirit. We do this in ignorance because we know not what we do. God forgives us anyway, but we feel nothing as long as we do not believe in it.

When we die, we will see clearly and finally feel God's limitless love and forgiveness for us and for everyone. Then our salvation will be sure and secure, just as God in His love has always intended. It is sad, however, if we do not feel the joy of our salvation now on this earth. It is sadder still when we teach people about an angry judgemental God who will condemn some, maybe them, to hell. If we do that, we surely blaspheme against the Holy Spirit by undermining His attempt to convince every one of the love and sure salvation which is theirs through the free gift of God's grace.

Therefore, I have written this book to assure people that God's love is without limit. That means God's forgiveness is without limit and their eternal salvation is beyond doubt. When they believe this, they may feel here and now the beauty and joy of God's love and the certainty of their salvation.

What about Evil and Justice?

FOR GOD TO save everyone does not seem fair to many people. What then of evil and judgement? Justice cries out, and one cannot ignore its seeming necessity of punishment. Evil must be dealt with and eliminated. I will therefore take a closer look at the justice and judgement of God. But first, I deal with the ultimate disposition of evil.

My first hint of universal salvation in the scriptures came when studying John 16:8-11 for a Sunday School lesson. A peculiarity of the wording intrigued me. Talking about the coming of the Holy Spirit, Christ says, "And when he comes, he will convince the world of sin and of righteousness and of judgement: of sin, because they do not believe in me; of righteousness, because I go to the Father, and you will see me no more; of judgement, because the ruler of this world is judged."

I have always thought of the writer of this gospel as a very careful theologian. This wording is not a careless mistake or a meaningless phrase. The writer meant to say that it is not us who are judged and perhaps condemned, but the "ruler of this world." This might mean the devil personified, if such a wayward spirit exists, or it could mean the force of evil in each of us. It seems that evil is judged, but evil is part of each of us and not all of any of us.

What the writer of John is saying becomes even clearer in John 12:31-2, "Now is the judgement of this world, now shall the ruler of this world be cast out; and I, when I am lifted up from the earth, will draw all men to myself."

Evil, whether personified in Satan or as an ingredient of each of us, will be cast out, overthrown; but all of us will be gathered to Christ for salvation. This is good news; for the evil within us, or which rules over us, is what makes for hell in our lives. Its overthrow will make for heaven.

The idea that only evil, and not people, is overthrown is implied in several other scriptures. God intends to cleanse everyone, not cast them out. That could be the meaning of the judgemental words of John the Baptist in Matthew 3:12. John speaks of Christ's coming thus, "His winnowing fork is in his hand, and he will clear his threshing floor and gather his wheat into the granary, but the chaff he will burn with unquenchable fire."

At first glance, this would appear to go against the concept of universal salvation. Instead, I will present a novel interpretation that occurred to me. Each grain of wheat consists of both kernel and chaff, even as each person contains both good and evil. To take away the chaff is not to take away the whole person, but only that part of them which is evil and worthless. The valuable part of each person will be gathered into the granary. In other words, everyone will be saved and freed from the evil power that binds and oppresses them. As the chaff imprisons the kernel, so evil imprisons people. On the threshing floor, everyone will be freed, finally and forever.

The concept which I have presented above is even more clearly expressed in Malachi 3:2-3 as he describes the coming Day of the Lord. "But who can endure the day of his coming, and who can stand when he appears? For he is like a refiner's fire and like fullers' soap; he will sit as a refiner and purifier of silver, and he will purify the sons of Levi and refine them like gold and silver, till they present right offerings to the Lord."

This concept, that man is purified rather than destroyed in the end, is also put forth by the Roman Catholic theologian Hans Küng.[3]

As we face God, I believe we will see everything clearly for the first time. When we realize the truth, we will reject evil finally and forever. It says in John 8:32, "the truth will make you free." Free at last from all evil, we will be amazed and overjoyed by the complete love and acceptance of God; despite our past misdeeds.

Rather than being condemned and destroyed, we will be welcomed home like the Prodigal Son. Malachi 3:6 tells why we will not be destroyed. "For I the Lord do not change; therefore you, O sons of Jacob, are not consumed." God remains faithful even when we are faithless. Therefore, His love still saves us, no matter what we do.

Now let us consider the justice of God. Justice seems to say, "It is not right that all people be saved." or, "It is not just and God is just."

I do not deny the justice of God. Instead, I say that God defines justice, rather than our concept of justice defining God. For example, the concept "eternal" is defined by God; because only

God is eternal. So eternal life, as used in the gospel of John, can be seen as a Godlike quality of life; rather than merely an endless quantity of life. I say that God is just, and, in fact, God is the only standard by which we can define true justice.

Often we take our idea of justice and insist that God must fulfill our concept. Instead we should try to understand God and His way of being "just," for that is truly justice. The justice of God, which we see in Jesus Christ, is love and forgiveness. Therefore, true justice is love and forgiveness; not punishment, revenge, or retribution. This is a strange idea, because the world has long conditioned us to think in its way, rather than God's. Thus, universal salvation is true justice, and does not contradict it. Universal redemption conforms to God's deepest feelings about how to deal with the apostasy of His people.

For those of us who cannot buy the concept of justice I have outlined, we can always use the sacrifice of Christ as the expiation, propitiation, ransom, price, payment or whatever else for the sins of all people. That should satisfy even a vengeful God. However, I consider that approach barbaric, and a crack through which people can rationalize all types of punishment and vengeance toward others. There must be a correspondence between the way God tells us to feel and act toward others, and the way He feels and acts Himself. Many times we are instructed to forgive as we have been forgiven. If God only forgives some, and then only after requiring a sacrifice; what does that say about our requirement to forgive others? If repentance, belief and other requirements are added; we can demand the same of others before we forgive them. What kind of Christianity would we have then? We might as well go back to legalism.

I do not believe that God, in His love, requires some payment or retribution before He forgives. I particularly do not believe that He would require His Son to die as payment for sin. But if Christ's death was not payment for our sins, why did He come and die on the cross? I believe that He came because He loved us, and He wanted to tell humanity that God loves us and will surely save us. I think Christ also wanted to give us some loving advice from our Father in heaven as to how to live the best and most beautiful life. He came to teach about love, and to demonstrate that love in His own life. He knew that if He came with this good news, He would be persecuted like God's messengers before Him; and that, in His case, He would be killed. Yet He loved us so much that He came anyway.

Christ was willing to suffer and die so we might know of God's love for us, and about our sure salvation because of that love. This is the same belief that William Barclay, my favorite Bible commentator, holds concerning Christ's sacrifice. [4]

If we could be assured of our salvation, we could stop worrying about hell and get on to the task of living this life, which is why God put us here. As it turns out, Christ's death on the cross only made God's love that much more believable. Also our salvation is proved even more, because what greater proof of God's love could we have than the sacrifice of Christ? That was a willing act of incredible love. What greater act of forgiveness could we have than the forgiveness of the worst sin in all history, which was the crucifixion of God's only Son?

From the cross, Jesus said, "Father, forgive them; for they know not what they do." (Luke 23:34)

If God could forgive even that, is there anything beyond His love and forgiveness? The death of Christ was not wished or required by God; still it served as the ultimate sign of God's love and forgiveness. What greater sign of our sure salvation can we ever imagine?

Sometimes I wonder if it does not make God and Christ very sad that, after doing so much to assure us of our salvation through God's love and forgiveness, which was supremely and at such high cost demonstrated by Christ's death, some still do not believe in their salvation, or try to limit it to a few so-called "good" or "faithful" people. Instead, we should spread this good news of sure salvation to everyone. We should be making God's love and salvation free and full, as He intended, rather than restricting access to some "sweet selected few."

We no longer sing the old hymn, "We are the sweet selected few. The rest of you are damned. There's plenty of room in hell for you. We can't have heaven crammed."

If we are repelled by the harsh words in that old hymn, we should be equally repelled by the same ideas dressed up in today's theologies that condemn people to hell. In the hymn, the thought is so absurd that one almost laughs at it. Yet it is hard to laugh at those who impose this thinking on people today as serious theology.

Accepting Salvation for all

SALVATION FOR EVERYONE has always seemed to me to be a possibility that would be cause for rejoicing. Instead, it is met more often by horror, cries of heresy, and militant rejection. People try to talk others out of such a terrible belief. Apparently the prospect of everyone being saved threatens them in some way. Otherwise, it would not evoke such an emotional response. Therefore, I will examine some possible reasons for this strenuous objection to an overly generous God.

One reason may be that it implies that everyone is equal in the sight of God. For those who strive really hard to be good, it seems quite unfair to equate them with the lazy and evil people. All their good works seem to be for nothing, and thus much effort has been wasted on their part. Certainly a just God would not be so unfair.

I believe, however, that by following God's loving will I have had a far more beautiful and fulfilling life than those who ignored God's will. They need heaven more than I do, and I would want them to have it. I have found that the will of God has not restricted my life. Following God's will has enriched my life. By following the wisdom I have discovered in the will of God, I have missed out only on the suffering and grief that result from foolishly disobeying his guidance. I feel sorry for those who ran away from God and sought happiness in other ways. I also feel sorry for those who found doing God's will a great burden, so they are envious of those who did not do it. I would wish both of these groups to have God's salvation. I would not begrudge His salvation to anyone.

Perhaps there are people who find some others so detestable that they could not bear to be in heaven if those evil ones were there. People who feel that some are so horrible they can't be in heaven, are blind to their own shadow sides; which they have repressed below their level of consciousness. The very things they detest in others reside in that dark part of themselves hidden in their own subconscious minds.

Walt Whitman writes of this in his poem "Song of Myself," saying, "In all people I see myself, none more and not one barley-corn less, and the good and bad I say of myself I say of them."

It is understandable that we have repressed and denied our dark sides, because we want to feel acceptable. To accomplish this there are various methods. One is to rationalize everything we do, to justify it as right, no matter how horrible it may be. For this to work we must brainwash ourselves into believing our own rationalizations. We must lie to ourselves and fool ourselves, and therefore the effort has to be unconscious on our part. Probably Hitler and his followers even rationalized the Holocaust. We usually rationalize smaller things, like cheating an insurance company. We tell ourselves that insurance companies are always ripping people off with excessive rates, so padding our auto repair bill is our chance to get even. We might also think that a big rich corporation like an insurance company will never miss the small sum we are milking them for. In fact, the outrageous rates that we complain about are partly caused by people cheating the company.

When we rationalize things, we distort the truth. It is hard enough to make wise decisions in this life when we are thinking straight and have all the facts right. If we lie to ourselves, deceiving ourselves, we may make disastrous decisions without ever realizing it until it is too late. It is a dangerous game to play.

An even more subconscious technique is to repress the unacceptable parts of ourselves so far below the conscious level that they are invisible to us, although perfectly visible to others. Then there is the tendency to project these characteristics onto others and to be really horrified by those traits in them. We vehemently oppose some things because we are trying to keep them repressed in ourselves. This strategy of repression may seem necessary, because we could never accept ourselves if we knew all that is part of us.

In a sincere effort to be good, we fool ourselves into believing we are better than we are and judge others for the very things we have repressed in ourselves.

Paul cautions us about this in Romans 2:1 where he writes, "Therefore you have no excuse, O man, whoever you are, when you judge another; for in passing judgement upon him you condemn yourself, because you, the judge, are doing the very same things."

How can we stop this? We need to look deeply and honestly into ourselves and see all that is there, both good and bad, light and dark.

But if we saw everything which is inside us, how could we ever face ourselves or God? That is one reason why we have to understand the limitless love and acceptance of God. It is only through feeling God's complete acceptance that we will ever be able to accept ourselves as we really are, more or less, love ourselves, despite all our faults. Whenever we reject another, we reject part of ourselves, and whenever we condemn another, we condemn part of ourselves.

We will never feel completely accepted and loved until we learn to accept everything human, for, as psychiatrist Carl Jung has pointed out, nothing human is alien to us.

Jung also asks, "What if I should discover that the least amongst them all, the poorest of all the beggars, the most impudent of all the offenders, the very enemy himself—that these are within me, and that I myself stand in need of the alms of my own kindness—that I myself am the enemy who must be loved—what then?"[5]

Walt Whitman echoes Jung's question in his poem, "You Felons on Trial in Courts":

"You felons on trial in courts,
You convicts in prison-cells, you sentenced assassins
    chain'd and handcuff'd with iron,
Who am I too that I am not on trial or in prison?
Me ruthless and devilish as any, that my wrists are not
    chain'd with iron, or my ankles with iron?
You prostitutes flaunting over the trottoirs or obscene in your
    rooms,
Who am I that I should call you more obscene than myself?
O culpable! I acknowledge—I exposé!
(O admirers, praise not me—compliment not me—you make
    me wince,
I see what you do not—I know what you do not.)
Inside these breast-bones I lie smutch'd and choked,
Beneath this face that appears so impassive hell's tides
    continually run,
Lusts and wickedness are acceptable to me,
I walk with delinquents with passionate love,
I feel I am of them—I belong to those convicts and prostitutes
    myself,
And henceforth I will not deny them—for how can I deny
    myself?"

Perhaps the realization that God loves, accepts, and ultimately will save everyone can help us in our goal of total self-acceptance. If we no longer have to hide from God, perhaps we will not hide from ourselves, either. The increased honesty and self-awareness that results can help us to lead a wiser and thus better life.

I feel God means to get our minds off the question of our future salvation, and onto the living of today. In His love, God alone secures our salvation; and proclaims it as a sign of His amazing love and grace. Through Christ, God seeks to assure us of that certain salvation in as dramatic and convincing a way as possible, so we will stop worrying about it. Having received this message, the good news of the gospel that the church should convey to everyone, those who believe never need to think again about their future salvation.

Chapter 3: What is God's Law About?

*W*HEN YOU TELL PEOPLE THAT God is going to save everyone, they often see no reason to follow God's commandments. After all, if what they think or do will not affect their salvation, they might as well think and do whatever they want. The same problem can arise if you tell people they are saved by faith, as a free gift of God.

Protestant theology says that people cannot be saved by good deeds, but only by God as a free gift. Paul had to argue that this did not make the law irrelevant, and his letters always had long discourses on Christian ethics.

I find that most people cannot quite believe that good or bad works do not somehow determine whether they will be saved or not. I think the usual position is that salvation is made possible by Christ's redeeming sacrifice on the cross, is made accessible to the individual by his faith in Christ, and is secured by good works. So most people still believe in works-righteousness, and dedication is born of fear for one's salvation. With all the talk of love, fear still haunts the common Christian, and the God who speaks softly still carries a big stick of eternal damnation.

I believe, however, that God, in His sovereign power and will, has chosen, out of love, to save us all, no matter what. Faith is really another work and thus only a more subtle form of the good deeds that people think will save them. Not even faith is needed for our salvation, which is fortunate, because our faith can be as unsteady as our conduct. We are all saved no matter what we believe or do.

I Timothy 4:10 says, "We have our hope set on the living God, who is the Savior of all men, especially of those who believe." This means all people are saved and this includes even those who do not believe.

So there is no need to fear, or to obey God's will out of fear. Still, I cannot believe we are to ignore God's law. Paul ends each of his letters with ethical instructions. Christ gives a long discourse on ethics in the Sermon on the Mount (Matthew 5-7).

Jesus ends his sermon with this story in Matthew 7:24-27. "Every one then who hears these words of mine and does them will be like a wise man who built his house upon the rock; and the rain fell, and the floods came, and the winds blew and beat upon that house, but it did not fall, because it had been founded on the rock. And every one who hears these words of mine and does not do them will be like a foolish man who built his house upon the sand; and the rain fell, and the floods came, and the winds blew and beat against that house, and it fell; and great was the fall of it."

So we should follow God's will because it is wise and will lead to a better life. I find that following God's law does not restrict our lives; rather it enriches our days. God's will leads us into the most beautiful and fulfilling paths in life. God's law also tries to help us avoid life's pitfalls. To ignore God's guidance is foolish, and we, along with others, will suffer for it.

I read the Bible as the story of God's reaching out in love to His children, His creation. God tries to show them His love by giving them His loving guidance as any parent would. As His first gift of love, God gives everyone, through Jesus Christ, the assurance of their salvation. As His second gift of love, God tries to help people along the path of this life, through the wisdom that is found in His commandments and Christ's teaching.

The Law as a Gift of Love

GOD, IN HIS love, not only assures us of our future salvation, but He also gives us His loving guidance for the living of this life.

In I Timothy 2:3-4 Paul says, "This is good, and it is acceptable in the sight of God our Savior, who desires all men to be saved and to come to the knowledge of the truth."

Previously, I had noted God's desire that all men be saved. Now I point out His other desire that everyone "come to the knowledge of the truth." It is this truth that He always tries to teach us, so we might make the wisest decisions in living our lives.

Christ spoke to this truth when He said to the Jews who had believed in Him, "If you continue in my word, you are truly my disciples, and you will know the truth, and the truth will make you free." (John 8:31-32)

This is a novel idea, that following Christ's word will make us free. Most people think that obeying Christ restricts life. People think of religion as a restriction because of all the laws and commandments they feel they must follow. But that view gets things backwards. It is sin, disobeying God, that restricts life. Following God liberates life.

Sin enslaves; as Christ points out in John 8:34 saying, "Truly, truly, I say to you, every one who commits sin is a slave to sin."

God wants people to know the truth, so they see the grip sin has on them and thus have the will and the wisdom to break that grip. Those who do not know the truth fall prey to lies. God, in His love, tries to show us the truth and the way to truly live through His revelation contained in the Bible.

When we realize that the scriptures are God's gift to us, as a guidebook through our very complex and often perplexing existence, we will eagerly seek to follow the instructions we find, because we know they are in our best interest.

This concept, that God's commandments are not tests of obedience or restrictions imposed to fulfill the whims of a judgemental tyrant, but God's loving revelation which will show us how to live a freer, fuller, more beautiful and abundant life, can be accepted without believing in universal salvation. But the idea never occurred to me until I had asked the question, "If everyone is saved, then what of the law?"

People can believe that the law is God's loving gift of guidance without believing in universal salvation. But I think that as long as salvation is dubious, people will always be seeking the basis for God's judgement and the criteria for separating the sheep from the goats. Casting around for a basis for judgement, they almost inevitably seize upon the law, and works-righteousness creeps into their belief.

Subtly, but surely, the law becomes demand, rather than gift, in their eyes. The love of God is undermined in their minds, and they begin to see God as their adversary. They begin to hide from God and themselves, pretending to be more righteous than they are, and doing God's will out of fear and/or hope for a heavenly reward. Only belief in universal salvation makes salvation irrelevant, removes the last trace of fear, and allows people to really believe and feel that the law is God's gift of guidance for more abundant living.

This concept, that the law of God is for our sake, not His, explains nicely Christ's words recorded in John 10:10. "I came that they may have life, and have it abundantly."

As we try to guide our children into the best paths in life, so our heavenly Father tries to guide us, His children, wisely and well. Of course, our ideas of what is best for our children are sometimes wrong. God's ideas are never wrong.

There are many other complications, of course, such as whether we interpret God's advice correctly. Much of the guidance in the Old Testament is to a particular people in their specific historical circumstances. To make that advice apply literally to all people everywhere is a mistake. So it is not a simple matter to understand how God's guidance in the scriptures applies to us today. But it is of the utmost importance that we try to understand, because it is the quality of our lives that is at stake, not a matter of pleasing God.

In an effort to get His children to do what is best for them, God will use whatever means are most effective, and this means that He might use fear sometimes. Human parents sometimes threaten and even punish their children to help them to learn and follow the best path. Even so, our heavenly Father sometimes coaxes and coerces us because of our stubbornness. Human parents do this in their children's best interest, and do not ultimately cast them out forever. Likewise, their heavenly Father, even when He seems stern, will not ultimately cast them into eternal damnation.

The realization that people have nothing to fear from God concerning this life or the next, brings about a real change in the way I speak and act. I was attracted to Christianity because of the love I found there. I pursued the ministry because it was a chance to serve people by giving them love and acceptance, while also conveying the good news of the gospel. It is these positive, warm and generous aspects of Christianity that I love about my faith.

But in the past I was always torn by the belief that ultimately God may not accept some people. Then I felt that I had to condemn these people for the sake of their own salvation. In a sense I had to burn their bodies at the stake to save their souls, as church officials claimed during the inquisition.

I remember hospitals having problems with zealous conservative Christians going into patients' rooms where they heard that people were dying, and getting them all upset about whether they were going to heaven. It seemed to me that it was a cruel thing to do to people who already were suffering enough; yet I understood that it could be an act of great love and concern on the part of those Christians. In their eyes, the anguish they might cause these patients in their final time on this earth would be nothing in comparison to the fact that they were trying to save their souls for all eternity. When one believes that some will truly be damned, such cruel measures as this seem more than justified.

I am glad that my belief in universal salvation keeps me from having to treat people cruelly on this earth for the supposed sake of their eternal salvation. In my heart, I cannot bring myself to thus condemn people. I feel that my words would bring only destructive guilt and would not help them at all.

Carl Jung confirms my feelings when he says in *Modern Man in Search of a Soul*, "We cannot change anything unless we accept it. Condemnation does not liberate, it oppresses. I am the oppressor of the person I condemn, not his friend and fellow-sufferer."[1]

Now I can talk of wisdom, not sin. I can point out the wisdom of God's law, and recommend it to people as helpful, rather than laying a destructive burden of guilt on them. I can speak of following God's loving guidance as wise, rather than using the morally charged word "right." I can speak of going against the wisdom of God's will as foolish, rather than labeling it "wrong" or "evil" with all the guilt that is implied by those words.

I can now approach people and say, "I am here to serve you, not to judge you."

People hide from God; they hide from ministers; they even hide from themselves; because of guilt. If they understood the intent of God's law to be loving guidance rather than a tool for judgement and condemnation, they might seek God's will eagerly, rather than running from it fearfully.

My belief in universal salvation solves many ethical questions for me. For example: "If we are supposed to love everyone, even our enemies, how can God reject some of His enemies, condemning them to hell?"

If God in the end does not forgive some people, that leaves a big loophole for us to use to rationalize our hatreds. On the other hand, if we understood that everyone is completely forgiven by God and will be in heaven with us, perhaps it would encourage us to learn to love them now. We really have no grounds for rejecting people if they are all accepted by God now and forever.

So universalism answers a question and closes a loophole. I, like God, am to love and accept everyone. It also makes it a lot nicer answering the questions of people whose loved ones have died, and whom they fear will not get into heaven. I can assure them they have nothing to fear, without feeling I am bending the truth just to make them feel better. I am happy to give them the good news, with the confidence that it is true.

Universalism also changes the motivation for following God's will. It elevates that motivation, from fear, or hope of reward, to accepting God's will as best for us. It should make it easier to love God.

This was a problem that plagued Martin Luther. He found himself unable to love the God who seemed to demand that love of him.

Love is never fostered by demanding it. The fact is that God does not demand that we love Him. Instead, God loves us, forgives us, accepts us, and always seeks our good.

In I John 4:10 we read, "In this is love, not that we loved God but that he loved us and sent his Son to be the expiation for our sins."

Thus God wins my love, imperfect as it may be, by loving me. It is a wonderful thing to love one who loves you. It is hard to love one who demands love from you. It is love that we receive from God, and not demands. The law is an expression of that love, not demands or a test of obedience that we must pass to be saved. This understanding fills the Christian life with joy, rather then work or fear.

Suppose I serve God for fifty years and another never even lifts his finger, but we both enter heaven. I do not feel it is unfair that he got in, nor am I angry about it. Instead, I feel sorry for him, because he missed the beauty and warmth of knowing and walking with a loving God all those years of life.

It is a funny, yet tragic thought, to think of the Good News Club that used our church building. They met to share good news with grade school children. They told them that Jesus loves them, and they must love and obey Him, so they can go to heaven. And they also warned them that if they did not accept, love and obey Christ, they would go to hell and be punished forever. If that is good news, I don't understand the meaning of the concept.

I like to preach about a God who loves us so much that He has, at great sacrifice, come in Jesus Christ to bring the good news of our certain salvation in the future, and who also helps us each step of the way to that future with His loving guidance.

Now that is good news! And that is the good news that I am trying to share. If I am mistaken, I would rather err on the side of love and acceptance than on the side of judgement and condemnation.

I would like Christianity to be a joy, not a burden. I would like to make the circle of love and acceptance larger, not smaller. So I tell people of God's love for them. If they can believe, and really feel loved by God, they might be able to love others and even themselves more.

Seeing no limits on God's love, I try to make my love limitless also. The love I feel for people and demonstrate to them may make the love of God more believable.

Love fulfills the law; is the motivation for the law; and the motivation for our desire to follow it.

Paul says in Galatians 5:14, "For the whole law is fulfilled in one word, 'You shall love your neighbor as yourself.'"

Belief in universal salvation frees us from all fear and concern about future salvation, so we can concentrate fully on living a life of love now. That is why God put us on this earth. God's law is His gift of love to guide us in that very important life on this earth, so our life may be freer and more abundant.

Section II: Ethical Implications

Chapter 4: Can We Follow the Sermon on the Mount?

In Section One, I discussed universalism and its implications for ethics abstractly. In this section, I will apply my viewpoint, that the law is for our benefit, not God's, to specific ethical teachings.

I have chosen to analyze the Sermon on the Mount, because it was always the most difficult ethical teaching of Christ for me to handle. Finally I began to understand it. Now I feel the Sermon on the Mount is the most valuable ethical instruction I have seen anywhere.

When I was a teenager, I had not had my rebirth experience. So I thought in terms of works-righteousness as the way you got to heaven. I was very troubled by the Sermon on the Mount, and I interpreted it quite literally.

One particularly distressing passage was Matthew 5:29, which says, "If your right eye causes you to sin, pluck it out and throw it away; it is better that you lose one of your members than that your whole body be thrown into hell."

This was a terrifying passage of scripture, since as a young teenager I was finding many sexual desires springing up inside of me and making me want to do things that I felt sure were wrong.

I seriously considered plucking out my eye, even both eyes, and might have, except I thought it out enough to realize that in my mind's eye the fantasies would continue. Therefore, plucking out my physical eyes was no solution.

This left me with an even greater dilemma, because I did not know how to get rid of the sinful thoughts and desires that tormented me and endangered my salvation. In 1984, I read in the newspaper of a teenager who actually mutilated himself physically because of this very passage. I could well understand his thoughts, and I was very sad. The fear generated about hell, and the propensity to interpret the scripture literally led to this tragic deed.

As an aside, I might discuss the attitudes toward sex which caused me such torment and that other teenager such tragedy. In a book on child rearing and religion, I read that the tendency to portray sexual feelings as somehow evil comes home to roost in the teenager. Suddenly he finds these feelings springing up within him. He becomes convinced he is evil since he cannot get rid of these desires. This makes him ripe for the preaching that portrays him as evil and in need of repentance and God's grace. He is ready for the conviction of sin and the rebirth experience put upon people at revivals. So he walks the sawdust trail or has a dramatic conversion experience and feels saved.

What then of his sexual desires? He usually represses them, denying that they any longer exist, or he funnels them into marriage and denies any desires for people other than his spouse. I have used masculine pronouns, but all this applies equally to women. This results in the projection of these feelings onto others and many other difficulties dealing with sexual issues.

For example, one of the reasons it is felt that sex education is not very effective in increasing the use of birth control among teenagers is because they are deceiving themselves to avoid guilt.

If they prepare wisely to use birth control, they feel that the premarital intercourse, condemned as fornication by the Bible, was premeditated. Then they will feel guilty of breaking God's law intentionally. So they pretend to themselves that they were just carried away by their feelings on the spur of the moment. Thus they feel they are not morally responsible for their actions.

Unfortunately, nature does not care what psychological tricks they play on themselves to avoid guilt. Girls get pregnant all the same. Thus the fear of guilt leads to foolish and dangerous self-deceit. In fact, the warnings against premarital intercourse are because it is a risky business, and God does not want them to get hurt.

Sex is a part of God's creation and is therefore perfectly natural. Moreover, sex is good, because God declared all of His creation good. But sex is a powerful natural drive, and it should be handled wisely. Sex is a very special gift of God and it warrants special treatment by society and religion. Thus marriage is part of every society, to manage the sexual relationship and care for the children that may result. Far from being evil, sex is sacred, so there is no reason to be ashamed of this gift of God. If sex is cherished and dealt with carefully, much torment and tragedy can be avoided. Then sex can be appreciated as one of God's most beautiful gifts.

In my first year of college, while reading a letter by Martin Luther, I suddenly understood his teaching about justification by faith alone, and I had the traditional rebirth experience. I now recognize that dramatic rebirth experience as really a flash of intellectual understanding. I was overjoyed and overwhelmed. I never again worried about my salvation. I concentrated instead on spreading this good news and, out of gratitude, serving God to the best of my ability. I became very evangelical. I wanted to save souls. But I was bothered by the fear that some, perhaps many, were unsaved and thus lost forever. Now the Sermon on the Mount contained no fear for me, because I was saved by the grace of God, not by works.

Still, I was troubled by these great ethical teachings because I could not understand why Christ preached a sermon full of impossible commandments. I really wanted to please Him, but I could not deal with difficult, surely impractical, ethical advice, such as "Turn the other cheek" or "Love your enemies."

When I studied Paul's letter to the Galatians in seminary, I learned of his belief that the law was impossible to fulfill. Indeed, the law was to force us to accept the conclusion that we can be saved only by the grace of God. The idea that the law was made impossible so we would see the failure of works-righteousness seemed to make sense of the Sermon on the Mount, and especially Christ's statement, "You, therefore, must be perfect, as your heavenly Father is perfect."(Matthew 5:48)

But the idea that the Sermon on the Mount was impossible to fulfill made it even more impractical and irrelevant. The Sermon on the Mount became something to be practically ignored. I felt these ethical teachings had to have more meaning than just to back you into an impossible moral dilemma, in order to destroy any illusion of salvation by good works.

It was not until I began to examine this sermon again, this time as being given to guide us into a better and more beautiful life, that I began to look at what Christ said more deeply and seriously. I began to probe beneath the literal surface interpretation, as if digging for buried treasure. When I did this, following the spirit of what was said and examining in my heart and mind what would be the results, I began to find great treasures. Now I see that no other way of living makes sense. The Sermon on the Mount is now the richest and most precious of all Christ's teaching to me.

In the rest of my book, I hope to share these insights. I will unpack and explore the deep treasures I found when I sought what good and loving advice our Father in Heaven is trying to convey to us, his beloved children, for the living of a more abundant life.

Taking the Law Seriously

SOME PEOPLE THINK that belief in universal salvation will lead to disregard for the law of God. That may be one of the reasons many people oppose the view. It was certainly one of the criticisms of Paul's preaching of justification by the free gift of God's grace, accessible through faith alone.

Jesus was criticized not only for being lax on the law, but even for breaking it. One of the things that surely led to the death of Jesus was the fact that He often broke the law in the eyes of the scribes and Pharisees. With His constant consorting with sinners and accepting all kinds of people, Jesus was undermining the morals of the people and the religion so dear to those religious authorities.

Many times, seeing His acceptance of "sinners," I also felt that Jesus was lax on the law. Of course, I wanted to see Him that way. Then I would not have to judge myself or others harshly, so I could love and accept them.

Still, the Sermon on the Mount troubled me. I could not write off the law, or the Sermon on the Mount, because Christ Himself in that sermon said that He did not write off the law.

In Matthew 5:17-18 Jesus said, "Think not that I have come to abolish the law and the prophets; I have come not to abolish them but to fulfill them. For truly, I say to you, till heaven and earth pass away, not an iota, not a dot, will pass from the law until all is accomplished."

Surely a sarcastic smile must have formed on the lips of the religious authorities, and perhaps more than one knowing wink was exchanged when they heard those words. They must have thought, "This Jesus sounds like one of the strictest of all the scribes and Pharisees, this lax lawbreaker. What an imposter!"

Even some Christian scholars have speculated that Christ could never have said the words in Matthew 5:17-18. They seem so unlike Him who accepted everyone so easily. But most scholars cannot imagine such an uncharacteristic statement being invented and inserted into the gospel. Jesus must have said it, or it would not be reported. So we are faced with a puzzle as to what it means.

As I have studied scripture, I have found that taking seriously and struggling with the most difficult verses of scripture have led to the greatest leaps in insight for me. Those seemingly impossible scriptures force me to leap over my usual ways of thinking, to some radical new truth, which opens up vast new avenues of understanding. So it was with these words of Christ, which I refused to ignore. I have found that this emphasis on the law contains, in some ways, the key to the whole sermon; which is a collection of seemingly legalistic demands by Christ that are clearly impossible to fulfill. I hope it will also help you to unlock the mysteries of this most difficult of ethical discourses.

It is obvious to me now that Christ came to reveal to us the spirit of the law of God, which, if followed, fulfills that law even better than following the letter of the law.

Sometimes the spirit of the law seems to contradict the letter. That is why the Pharisees thought Christ broke the law. This seems a simple insight to be given such a big buildup. It is not as simple as it seems. It is very difficult to probe deep enough into the spirit of the many cryptic passages of the Sermon on the Mount to find the treasure.

Even on simple passages, one can be misled by misunderstanding the spirit intended by God. I will illustrate this by starting with a seemingly simple law that is not in the Sermon on the Mount. I have chosen for this purpose the law of the Sabbath.

The Sabbath law is the commandment Christ was most frequently accused of breaking. It is also a law that is widely misunderstood today, causing much dissension and guilt.

We find it first in Exodus 20:8-9 where it begins, "Remember the sabbath day, to keep it holy. Six days you shall labor, and do all your work; but the seventh day is a sabbath to the Lord your God; in it you shall not do any work . . ."

Now the scribes understood that you were supposed to follow the spirit of the law in all its implications. So the religious authorities of Christ's day tried to interpret the spirit of the law. They worked hard to refine and interpret its meaning, so it would be clear how to fulfill it exactly. For example, they tried to define what work was. One form of work would be to carry a burden. Then burden must be defined. According to scribal law, a burden is any food equal to a dried fig in weight. A swallow of milk is a burden. Enough ink to inscribe two characters of the alphabet would be a burden. These were only a few of the burdens that were precisely defined.[1]

There were many matters still open to question, and these were endlessly debated. The matter of whether artificial teeth or limbs constituted a burden was discussed. Was picking up your child a burden? They pondered whether a wig or jewelry was too much to carry. In my mind, this excruciating examination of what was permitted on the Sabbath was too much to bear. [2]

Volumes were written interpreting the smallest details of the law, in order to precisely define and obey God's will. It was not that they did not try to follow the spirit of the law from the start. They seemed to feel, as I suspect many people do today, that the purpose of the law was to restrict their freedom and activities in order to somehow show respect or obeisance to God. They then tried to define exactly how their activities must be restricted to please God in His whims. After all, the gods of Old Testament times were all whimsical and unpredictable. Of course, many of the restrictions seemed ridiculous, but they could not see any reason for the law of the Sabbath to begin with.

Christ, on the other hand, understood and said that, "The sabbath was made for man, not man for the sabbath."(Mark 2:27)

The Sabbath law, like all of God's other laws, is for our benefit, not God's. It was to spare us the folly of working seven days a week, thus never taking any time off to enjoy life or to rest for our health's sake. There may have been many times in history when we would have been required to work seven days a week, if it were not for the law of the Sabbath. It is a blessing, and not a curse, to have a day off. On that day, it is good to worship God, so we remember the source of our blessings and take time to seek His wisdom for the living of the days ahead. But it is also good to enjoy that day in whatever way we find best, whether pursuing a hobby, playing a game, going to a movie, or other recreation.

Recreation comes from the word re-creation. Play re-creates us and renews us for a new week of work. The Sabbath is a day of greater freedom because we do not have to work, not a day of restricted freedom. Who wants to work seven days a week anyway? If we do enjoy work so much that we would call it play, be warned that we need a break to maintain our physical and mental health. Wanting to work seven days a week may mean that we are workaholics, which can be a dangerous disorder. To argue whether Saturday or Sunday is really the Sabbath is ridiculous, since the idea is to have regular days off for the sake of our well being. The Sabbath law is for our benefit, not a random restriction to glorify God's vanity.

So it is with all of God's laws. They are not to restrict our lives, but to show us the way to a better and more beautiful life. The spirit of these laws is love. They grow out of God's love for us, and they point out to us that love is the only way to live. "Love your enemies" is not an unreasonable requirement, but the way to a more beautiful life than we think possible. Some may think I do not call on us to do anything, because I always talk of love. But I am really laying out the most difficult of all guidelines to follow, yet the only one that is truly worthwhile, and surely the most beautiful. I seek to teach people to do more than follow the letter of the law, indeed, to follow its very spirit.

Likewise, I believe Christ, by loving us and advising us to love, was laying out a more difficult task than that which the scribes and Pharisees laid out. The scribes and Pharisees followed the letter of the law, not understanding its true spirit, and they were called righteous by the people of their day.

Christ, who is always loving and accepting people, says, "For I tell you, unless your righteousness exceeds that of the scribes and Pharisees, you will never enter the kingdom of heaven."(Matthew 5:20)

Is this a threat worse than that of the legalists? No, it is better guidance than that of the legalists who follow the letter of the law, to gain salvation in the end. Following the letter of the law out of fear or to get into heaven after we die is folly. To love is to enjoy a piece of heaven right now. Love is what heaven is all about, and only those who love enjoy its fruits. Finding these fruits, they love more freely and fully, as they overflow with beauty. It is almost like there is no law, because love points the way.

Long ago Saint Augustine said that the Christian life could be summed up in one phrase: "Love God, and do what you like."

Paul wrote in Galatians 5:14, "For the whole law is fulfilled in one word, 'You shall love your neighbor as yourself. '"

Learn then that love is what life is all about. Learn to love as God intends, and you will be free to enjoy the kingdom of heaven, for you will already be basking in its beauty.

So far, I have tried to point out that the commandments of God were given for our benefit, as a loving gift to us. I have also tried to show that the spirit of the law is love. These assertions may be true, but they are general and abstract truths. Understanding what God is trying to say specifically in each of His commandments, and how that will benefit us, can be more difficult to determine. Of course, we could just trust that His advice is best, and try to follow it on that presumption. However, we would have difficulty in really understanding what that guidance meant in all the complex situations and decisions we face, unless we understood the specific spirit of each lesson He tries to teach us. To illustrate how the specific may add to the general, I will look again at the words of Christ from His

Sermon on the Mount, which gave me so much difficulty when I took them literally as a teenager.

Jesus says in Matthew 5:29, "If your right eye causes you to sin, pluck it out and throw it away; it is better that you lose one of your members than that your whole body be thrown into hell."

As I said at the beginning of Section II, I was afraid of this terrible threat and even considered plucking out my eye, but I knew all too well that plucking out my physical eyes would not spare me the temptations that tormented me. My mind's eye would still be there, and the fantasies created would still cause me to sin, at least in my thoughts. This knowledge just made my situation more hopeless, because I could not find any way of overcoming my sinful desires. I was surely lost. Only later, when I realized that we are saved by the grace of God, could I be at peace with these words of Christ. Then I assumed I would never be able to fulfill this commandment, so I ignored it. It was no longer a problem to me, but neither was it any benefit.

Now I look at these same words as containing some treasure if I can only understand them. When I look for that benefit, I find it. We all are sometimes unhappy because we cannot have something we desire. More than making us unhappy, these desires can make life hell for us.

Christ is trying to tell us how to avoid that hell. The torment will continue as long as we let that desire rage within us. The way out of that hell is to root out the desire that is tormenting us. This is not done by some physical mutilation, but by cutting out the desire. He even hints at some reasoning that may help us. We may feel that we cannot live without having our desire fulfilled, that to live without what we want would be like living without an eye or a hand.

He says, "It is better that you lose one of your members than that your whole body go into hell."(Matthew 5:30)

He is pointing out that this desire is putting you into hell through the torment it is causing you. Surely, to do without that one thing is better than this constant torment, which is making your whole life hell. When we realize that, we may find it easier to finally lay this desire aside, thus freeing our life from its domination. This is a very beneficial lesson in how to deal with our desires when they get out of hand.

People have destroyed their lives and the lives around them by either brooding constantly about what they cannot have, or going after what they should not have and losing what was most precious to them. It is probably not accidental that Christ's advice is in the paragraph about adultery. If people want to commit adultery, but cannot, they torment themselves with what cannot be. If they commit adultery, they also destroy much, for marriages are damaged or destroyed by such acts.

When a desire dominates you and threatens to destroy you, remember this advice of Christ. It is better to give up that special thing, even if it seems as dear to you as an eye or a hand, than to destroy your whole life, making it a living hell.

Now I feel good about this passage from the Sermon on the Mount. It is a treasure, rather than a threat or an impossible demand to be ignored. It is in this way I will examine other passages from the Sermon on the Mount. My belief in everyone being saved has led to a new perspective, That has unlocked the mysteries of many difficult passages of scripture. This makes me more confident that I am on the right track.

Chapter 5: How Can the Beatitudes be True?

*I*T SHOULD BE IMMEDIATELY APPARENT that The Sermon on the Mount is going to be difficult to understand, since it starts right off with a list of seeming contradictions called the beatitudes. Sayings such as, "Blessed are the meek, for they shall inherit the earth." (Matthew 5:5), are so obviously opposite to the realities of life on this earth that they are usually written off as only possible of fulfillment in some future paradise. Indeed, the term "shall," and in this case "inherit," tend to point to some fulfillment in the future, probably after we die or at the end of this world. It is temptingly easy to write them off as irrelevant for this life, other than in terms of trying to obtain some distant reward.

Since I have proposed that everyone will be saved ultimately, this concept of a reward in the end only for those who comply with the conditions of the beatitudes doesn't make sense. On the other hand, if everyone is to get those ultimate rewards, then any reason for following the advice in the beatitudes seems to have vanished.

If the beatitudes are to have much value, it must be in the present, in this life. I will try to show that the benefit is in this life. I think this will make us take them more seriously, because we will usually be more concerned about today, *i. e.* , this life, than some promise about the hereafter.

My whole approach makes this life more significant, rather than directing the attention so much to the next life.

It was William Barclay who opened my eyes to the realization that the beatitudes reveal a blessedness that can be ours here and now. Barclay believes the beatitudes are exaltations proclaiming that blessedness.[1]

How appropriate the form of the beatitudes is. They are not stated like commandments or demands. Instead, they are guidelines to blessings. They seem to thus confirm my feeling that God gives His commandments as loving advice to lead us to the most beautiful or blessed life.

Starting with the word "Blessed" is really the most appropriate, since all of God's commandments are meant to be blessings. Throughout my examination of the beatitudes and the other teachings of the Sermon on the Mount I will show how the law is a gift of God's love.

As I have been saying, God's first act of love is to assure us of our eternal salvation, so we do not worry about the next life. His second act of love is to show us the way to the most beautiful and abundant life on this earth. I begin by exploring the blessings that the beatitudes contain for those who understand and live them.

The word "Happy" has, in recent times, been substituted for the word "Blessed," but that word cannot do justice to what Christ is talking about.

William Barclay points out that the root of the word "happiness" is "hap." "Hap" means chance. So happiness is a matter of chance. Circumstances might bring us happiness, but chance can as easily destroy that happiness. The blessedness that the beatitudes speak of is a joy that no turn of fate can take away. It is a joy which sustains us through suffering, as well as good fortune.[2]

This joy, which has its secret within itself, serene, untouchable and self-contained is what we will find and feel if we can understand and live the life proclaimed "blessed" in the beatitudes. This joy is one of God's gifts of love, intended for us. Surely such a prize is worth seeking.

The Poor in Spirit

THE FIRST BEATITUDE in Matthew 5:3 says, "Blessed are the poor in spirit, for theirs is the kingdom of heaven."

For this first beatitude we must understand what Christ is talking about when he speaks of being "poor in spirit."

"Poor in spirit" certainly would not refer to being demanding or proud. It would seem more to refer to being humble, and to the willingness to accept what is. When we think then of these two contrasting attitudes, we might imagine people who want everything their own way, and demand that it be so. We can imagine such people not even being happy in heaven, because they will not get to run the show there. Such people surely have difficulty being happy here on earth, because things often do not go as they would wish. They demand everything, but life does not deliver everything. Therefore, although they may have far more than others and bully others into pampering their whims, they are generally not happy.

The person who has learned to humbly accept the vicissitudes of life might be happier than the demanding person, despite more meager circumstances. Happiness is really a matter of what they will accept in comparison to what they have. Some with a lot are unhappy. Some with a little are happy. Happiness springs from a humble and accepting heart, not from a proud, demanding spirit. To illustrate this, I will look at how life and attitudes may change as we grow older.

Many say that youth is wasted on the young, because they have so much and seem to appreciate it so little. They usually have their health and a future full of opportunities ahead of them. They are not weighted down by the mistakes of the past, or crippled by failing health, yet they are not generally happier than older people. Older people may end up happier, although their circumstances are clearly worse.

As I look back on life, I find I appreciated what I had more, after I had lost it. Many of those treasures of our youth cannot be reclaimed. The clock cannot be turned back. Still, I find I can be as happy now as before. Time and circumstances have taught me humility and acceptance of what is. I look back now at that brash young man that I was, and I am glad that I have learned some humility and acceptance. I feel wiser and more contented. I have not the frothy exuberance of youth, but a more durable and seasoned joy. I hope I am now better prepared to withstand the storms of life.

I have also learned that I am not in control of my life. In my youth, I thought I was captain of my own ship. I thought I did not need God or good fortune to forge ahead in whatever direction I wanted. I had many abilities, and I could do whatever I turned my mind to. Circumstances have taught me that I am not in control, and life can take nasty turns, wrecking all my plans. It was an uphill battle learning to accept that lack of control, and learning to accept circumstances as they are. Understanding how little control we have can be very disturbing. Yet, once realized, it cannot be denied. The only way to peace of mind is to trust God, who is in control of that which is beyond our control. To realize that the most important things in life are beyond our control and to learn to really trust God is a characteristic of the "poor in spirit."

In Aramaic, the language Christ spoke, the word for "poor" describes a person who, because he has no earthly resources whatever, puts his trust in God. Such a person will realize that true happiness and security cannot be found in the things of this world that are transient, but only in the will and purposes of God.

58

Of course not every person with little or no money puts their trust in God. Some who are financially poor are devastated by that poverty spiritually, mentally and physically. Still, the poor are more likely to trust God, because, unlike the rich, they have nothing else to trust. Therefore, it was the poor who mostly flocked to Christ. It was the poor who constituted most of the early Christian church. Even today, the most promising group of people for evangelism is the lower class. They are usually the ones converted at revivals. They are the most zealous and the most concerned about their eternal salvation. If you think about it, for many of them, this life and this world do not offer much, so they place their faith in the next life and in their Savior, Jesus Christ. This desperation makes them prey to manipulation and exploitation in the name of religion. But those who realize that God loves them and will surely save them, will put their trust in God alone, not in some preacher who tells them that only if they support and follow him will they secure the precious prize of personal salvation.

The rich are usually less zealous than the poor about God and religion. There are many good things in this life for them. It is those good things that they trust and enjoy. The rich may trust their money or their abilities, but if they are really wise, they will realize that tragedy can render their material wealth worthless. Some people who have material wealth may put their trust in God, understanding it is the only way to achieve real peace of mind. Still, if they have money, there is a tendency to place their trust in that, even if they think they are trusting only God.

I had a friend in seminary who had a wife and several children to support. He had saved up some money and decided to quit his job so he could enter seminary and study to be a minister. He told me he trusted God to provide for his needs and the needs of his family while he sought to serve God in this new way. He felt secure in his trust of the Lord until he got down to the last thousand dollars in his bank account. Then he realized, as his sense of security slipped away, that he had really trusted his bank account more than God.

We often say we are trusting God, when we really trust money, or our ability to manage, or some answer that has always made us feel secure.

Life has a way of shattering these things. The generation who went through the stock market crash of 1929 and the great Depression will never feel quite secure about money or other possessions. Our understanding of life can also be shattered. We think we understand life and God, and in that understanding we feel secure. Then tragedy befalls us and we ask, "Why? "

Suddenly our understanding and our faith are inadequate. At times like that we may realize that we really trusted our supposed knowledge, more than God.

I have found that life can destroy all of our answers and undermine our understanding. Therefore, I have always liked Philippians 4:6-7, which says, "Have no anxiety about anything, but in everything by prayer and supplication with thanksgiving let your requests be made known to God. And the peace of God, which passes all understanding, will keep your hearts and your minds in Christ Jesus."

By always thanking God, we will concentrate on what is good rather than on what is bad. Thereby we can be more joyful, despite the dismal circumstances we may confront. By basing our peace on trusting God without requiring understanding, we will find a security that cannot be destroyed by circumstances that shatter our answers and defy our understanding. If we trust God even when we do not understand, our peace of mind is secure. We do not need to understand in order to obey God's good and loving guidance. To obey God and His eternal purpose should be our goal. Then we should find our security in God alone. We will know that God alone can bring us help, and hope, and strength. Therefore, our trust and allegiance will be in God.

Now the kingdom of heaven, or as some gospels say, the "Kingdom of God," is surely a place where God rules. To be in God's kingdom is to recognize God as king. So those who are poor in spirit, in the sense that they give their whole allegiance to God, are, by definition, in His kingdom. The beatitude, "Blessed are the poor in spirit, for theirs is the kingdom of heaven." is literally true.

The poor in spirit have learned to trust God, and in this, they have found peace of mind. They have learned to accept life as it confronts them, and thus they can be happy in less than ideal circumstances. Their blessedness is more than that happiness life can give or just as quickly take away. It is more like that serene and untouchable joy that comes from walking in the company and in the presence of Jesus Christ.

Of course, our trust in God is never perfect on this earth, or our allegiance to Him complete. Therefore, we do not totally possess joy or peace, because we do not live completely in His kingdom now. The complete fulfillment of the beatitude may be in the future, but in so far as we can understand and follow its direction now, we will enjoy the benefits of its promises in the present.

Those Who Mourn

THE MOST DIFFICULT of the beatitudes to deal with to my satisfaction is Matthew 5:4, where Christ says, "Blessed are those who mourn, for they shall be comforted."

Its difficulty lies in the subject, which appears to be suffering. Anyone who has really suffered knows that, particularly in the midst of that suffering, there is no satisfactory answer to the question of suffering. It is even more difficult for me to think of giving some trite formula to others who suffer. In the face of suffering, words often fall powerless to the ground. The word that is used in Greek here for mourning is the strongest one possible. It is the word used for mourning the death of one who is loved passionately. There is no way that I will ever feel I have found words or answers for such suffering.

Still, there are things that can be said about this beatitude which have value. There are three ways that this beatitude can be taken and I think each reveals some valuable insights.

The first interpretation is the usual one and the most difficult, because it deals with one's own personal suffering. What can be said about suffering? Many things can be said about suffering. Each has some truth, and thus some value.

I remember seeing a poster at church camp which said, "Suffering builds character." I thought to myself immediately, "Well if it's all the same to you, Lord, I think I will do with the character I have." Even though I have learned much from suffering, I thought, "Only the young could put up such a poster."

The beatitude tells us it is those who mourn who will be comforted. In seminary, we were instructed about grieving for a lost loved one. We were taught in pastoral psychology that people need to really grieve, rather than running away from the pain. If they tried to evade the suffering of mourning their loss, they would never really recover from that loss.

Psychology teaches us that one cause of neurosis is the attempt to avoid suffering necessary pain. Psychology thus confirms the need to mourn if one is to ever find real comfort. Indeed, emotional honesty is always best in the long run, even if it means experiencing pain now.

I would not wish suffering on anyone, but it comes anyway. Then we have two choices. We can be defeated by it, or we can face it bravely and try to rise above it. I confront my pain and disability every morning when I wake up. I mourn the loss of my health for a few minutes, but then I decide to make the best of that day. The worse the suffering, the greater the triumph when it is overcome. The wisdom and strength gained is a help in meeting all the challenges of life.

I can say that I have learned much from suffering. I am a wiser, better person for it. But, if I had my choice, I would rather not have suffered. Some lessons may be worth the pain, but some are, at most, a compensation that is salvaged from the wreckage.

The Arabs have a saying, "All sunshine makes a desert."I can agree with that. But mourning, such as Christ speaks of, I could not wish on anyone, no matter what they learn from it, or how much they grow because of it.

The only thing I presently know that will really deal with the worst suffering or mourning is for it to be relieved or taken away. The suffering that I find the hardest to face is that which I feel will go on forever. A very sharp pain can be endured if it is brief, while a smaller pain will drive one to despair if no end can be hoped for.

The beatitude promises what is needed. It says, in essence, that none of us will suffer forever. Its assurance is that those who mourn will surely "be comforted." Relief or release from suffering is the best solution imaginable.

As youth, we stumbled over pebbles. I remember one day seeing a little girl, about two, crying because she couldn't get her lollypop. I remember thinking, "Boy, if all I had to worry about was losing a lollypop, how happy I would be."

As we grow older, we find life becomes more difficult. One day I told a Sunday School class that my newest proverb was, "You might as well be happy with the way things are now, because in the long run they will surely get worse."

Well, the young people in the class were horrified by such a philosophy, but the people over fifty backed me up. Life becomes more difficult, so we need to get wiser and stronger. To our eventual amazement, we find ourselves climbing over walls that we would never have dreamed we could even face, much less surmount.

We may find ourselves happier than when we were younger although we have far less. The difficulties of life have tempered our expectations and our demands. So we have learned to be happy with what we have, rather than always wanting more, as is often the tendency of youth.

I do not criticize youth for their desires and drive. That is the way they are meant to be. If they knew as much as older people, they might not have the courage to marry, or have children, or to forge a life for themselves.

As we grow older, we learn to do with what we have. We need to surmount higher walls than those of youth, the walls of suffering and the walls of mourning, as we lose so much that is precious to us. Finally, when the wall that faces us is too high, God rescues us from this pilgrim path. When our cup of suffering is full and we can not drink any more, He takes us home. There we get the ultimate and eternal comfort.

The promise, "for they shall be comforted" is fulfilled. Of that time we read, "and God himself will be with them; he will wipe away every tear from their eyes, and death shall be no more, neither shall there be mourning nor crying nor pain any more, for the former things have passed away."(Revelation 21:3-4)

That hope may help us endure personal suffering on this earth. It is this simple assurance of comfort for those who mourn that is the most common interpretation of the beatitude, and it seems to be comforting just to hear the words without any explanation.

A second interpretation is that the mourning is not for one's own suffering, but the suffering of others or the world in general. Even if we ourselves are fortunate, there is always more than enough suffering in the world to cause much mourning. This mourning grows not out of personal suffering, but out of our concern for others who suffer. At its most intense level, it comes from the suffering of someone whom we love very much. It comes out of love, and it can cause us much grief.

Since there is always much suffering in the world, how can we find any comfort? Here, as in many other cases, the answer is only found when we really follow this beatitude to experience the result. We must love someone and mourn for their suffering. Only in this way may we eventually find the comfort.

I will draw from personal experience, and what I felt. I remember one case in particular. I heard that one of the teenagers in my youth fellowship whom I had grown to love, was facing a very dark future. It upset me to the point of depression. For at least a year I mourned her fate. I felt great pain, and I wondered sometimes if caring so intensely was worth it. I knew that I could stop the pain by simply stopping the love. Yet I preferred the pain to the emptiness I would feel if I stopped caring.

To not love is to have an empty heart, and I prefer a heart full of people and feelings about those people, even if they are painful feelings. After about a year, a feeling came over me that comforted me. I felt that my love would, in some way, make everything all right. It doesn't make any logical sense, but I felt that because I loved this girl, although she suffered terribly, she would survive. Somehow my love would keep her from being destroyed by the degradation that she would experience. My love surrounded her and would protect her from being lost. My love for her would keep her from being completely alone in the face of her trials.

Later, I looked at my feeling logically, and understood that it was really the love of God, which would never abandon her and would ultimately protect her. That is a nice logical statement which now makes some sense. Still it is my love that makes me sure that she will be safe.

I am sure that we will all suffer in life, some more, some less. Now I also have in my heart the assurance that we will all survive and be comforted, and this comforts me. When I see people suffer, my love for them grows, until it seems to envelope them and holds them securely, in some sense, safe from the slings and arrows of outrageous fortune. I am sure then that God will do as much and more for them. That is the real source of comfort.

I can look at it from the other side also. When I am suffering, it is a great comfort to me to feel that I have people who love me. Again, it is more logical to look to the love of God for my ultimate protection. After all, human beings do not always have the power to spare me any suffering, much less to assure my ultimate survival. Yet it is the love of people that convinces me of God's love, and thus gives me faith that God will help me in my suffering. So logic has little power, compared to the heart.

If we wish to really understand the loving advice in the Sermon on the Mount, we must, in love, follow that advice, until our heart feels the result. Our own heart then becomes the source of our assurance of God's loving intentions.

I spoke once at a funeral of the joy of husband and wife reunited in heaven. Later, the daughter said she wished that she could feel that it was so. For me, the love in my heart assured me of their certain reunion. I could feel it in my bones, and it needed no scripture or further proof.

God is love, and the good news of the gospel is about love. The truth and implications of the gospel are not felt or understood by logic, but by loving. The comfort I found when I mourned for others came out of love, even in the face of suffering that I was powerless to prevent or alleviate. Of course, if it is in our power to prevent or alleviate the suffering of another, the path to comfort for both is obvious. I chose to deal with the more difficult case of unavoidable suffering. I found, even there, that those who mourn for the suffering of others will be comforted. They will also be blessed by a greater feeling and understanding of love. Their heart will be full of feelings that, even in sadness, will have a certain beauty, because they spring from love.

Finally, there is a third, surprising interpretation of this beatitude. It may be the main meaning. It is that one mourns for his own sins. This may fit into the idea of sin that I am putting forth in this book.

I feel that sin is more foolish than evil. We suffer and cause others to suffer when we foolishly ignore or go against the wise and loving advice of God. This suffering does not occur because God punishes us. Indeed, God gives us His loving advice to steer us toward happiness and to spare us needless suffering.

Sin is not always the cause of suffering. That was a mistaken belief of the Old Testament Jews. Yet sometimes you do cause your own suffering through disobeying God's good advice. When you sit in the midst of the mess you have caused by your own foolishness, you will mourn your folly and have no one to blame but yourself. That may make you more depressed. But out of that realization and sorrow may come true repentance and the wisdom to begin living according to God's will. So, in the long run, you may be blessed by realizing the desirability of following God.

If things always seem to work out well when you are following your own foolish way, you may never wake up to how far you have gone astray and what beauty and fulfillment you are missing. You may trample on other people and bully your way into a position of wealth or power or prominence and feel quite successful, never realizing that you have missed out on the loving relationships that are really the heart of life.

The poem "Tamerlane" portrayed a world conqueror looking back over his life and wishing he had stayed in his rural home with the girl he loved. For him, it was too late to recover what he had left behind and lost.

I have always hoped that when I take a wrong turn in life I will quickly fall into a pit. Hopefully I will find out how foolish I am before I have done too much damage, or gone so far astray that I cannot find my way back. When things fall apart at my feet, I mourn the trouble and suffering I have caused. But I will more likely repent and start over on a far better path and have a happier life as the consequence. Once more, the beatitude is true, and, in a way, seldom thought of. The comfort comes in the present when I repent, that is, wise up, and change now.

Whatever interpretation is correct, it is clear that Christ gave this beatitude for our benefit or blessing. This beatitude is a gift of God's love.

The Meek

ONE OF THE beatitudes that seems most contradicted by the reality of this earth is, "Blessed are the meek, for they shall inherit the earth."(Matthew 5:5)

It is obvious to anyone that the strong and often the ruthless are in the positions of power on this earth. It looks clearly as if the fulfillment of this beatitude must be in the future. It is even implied by the use of the words "shall" and "inherit."

Still, I am claiming that the beatitudes were given to help us now. Of course, the message of this beatitude brings comfort to people now, even if its fulfillment is in the future. Seeing how the power and privileges of this world often go to those who grab what they can get, stepping on the heads of others along the way, the meek can look for a future day when justice will be done. Then the meek will get the chance to receive their fair share; or even the whole earth.

I was discussing the beatitudes with someone recently, and they said that they had often heard the beatitudes read; but never preached on. Perhaps this is because the message is seen as a comfort; but, since the fulfillment is in the future, they see no particular relevance for this life.

I have challenged myself to find the fulfillment in the present for the beatitudes. So I will look for how the meek inherit the earth in this present life.

One thing most scholars agree on is that the word translated "meek" does not mean "weak." As I thought of the word "meek," "humble" came to mind: or thoughts like "quiet" and "accepting." I began to see similarities to the words "poor in spirit. "In fact, some early manuscripts put this beatitude right after the one about "poor in spirit." Apparently they also saw a similarity.

Who, then, are the meek? The meek are not aggressive. They concentrate on their duties rather than their rights. They quietly seek and follow the will of God. They have a silent strength that might be misinterpreted as weakness. They are content with their lives and see no need to contend with others. If others push them, they step aside to preserve the peace, because they are not needy like the pushers of the world.

Still, the meek are clearly not the kind of people that are in control of this world, nor will they fight to wrest control from others. So how can this beatitude be fulfilled in the present?

Let us look at two types of people again, from another perspective. The aggressive people fuss and fume. They shove and grab to get what they want on this earth. The meek simply accept and enjoy what they have been given.

James 3:13 says, "Who is wise and understanding among you? By his good life let him show his works in the meekness of wisdom."

The meek, in their wisdom, are already enjoying God's blessings, instead of fighting to get more. The fighters have no peace, never get all they want and are not satisfied. They may have power and have legal ownership on paper of many of the physical things on this earth; yet they do not feel that they have inherited the earth.

The meek, on the other hand, may realize that you cannot really possess or own anything on this earth. So they find fulfillment like a little child in the wild flowers or the sunshine; that is, without requiring any exclusive claim to the flowers or the sunshine.

In a sense, every child inherits the earth. There is a time, before they know about private ownership, in which they assume that everything belongs to them. Watch how a child explores everything within its reach without ever asking permission. Notice how a child can become absorbed in the simplest of things and experience great bliss, although at that age he really owns nothing and is completely at the mercy of the people around him.

Such contentment is not found in the positions of power in this world. Everyone has inherited the earth, but some try to claim parts of it exclusively for themselves. This goes against nature and God's intent. Perhaps the Indians were right in claiming they could not sell their land, for it was given to them by God. They would share it, but they would not sell it. The meek enjoy what is within their grasp, and do not covet or fight for what has not been granted to them.

What has been granted is a gift or an inheritance from God, and is to be used not for one's exclusive right or pleasure, but is to be shared with others to serve God's purposes.

The illustration of public lands occurs to me, or all of the public facilities in America. People are always clamoring for lower taxes so they can buy more things for their exclusive possession, at the expense of the parks and libraries and subways and even water, plumbing, police or fire protection.

Perhaps the folly of this is most evident in the area of clean air. People want to do away with clean air regulations, so they can have more money for themselves. But they have all inherited the same air, and they have to share it, whether they like it or not. There is not yet any private ownership of the air. If they pollute someone else's air, they pollute their own. The air jumps over boundaries and private property lines. So if they do not take care of the common good, they all suffer together. If the rich and powerful think that they will be able to own their own private air, their folly is evident. All their grasping for more money and power so they can gain exclusive ownership of the world is madness.

The Indians lived here at least ten thousand years before the white man came. At the coming of the white man, this country was as pure and bountiful as the first day the Indians came here. The Indians could have lived here forever, using, sharing and always nurturing the resources of this land. The white man has lived here less than five hundred years and he has already depleted and polluted the land, so his days here may be very limited.

The land has been raped and pillaged for personal gain. The greedy and aggressive have taken what they wanted and they will not inherit a good and bountiful earth, but ecological disaster and devastation. For money, they have destroyed the inheritance.

The Indian prophesy may come to pass, which says that if you take more than you need, you will someday find the earth barren, so even your needs will not be met. Those who try to grasp the earth for themselves will not inherit the earth. They will destroy the earth in their greed. Yet even when they have the most, they will never feel they have enough. What they grasp will slip through their fingers like the dust of the earth they have despoiled and depleted.

Happiness and the real sense of having inherited the earth belong to the meek. Meekness is a sign of happiness and contentment. The meek do not need to push others off the earth to enjoy it. One of the reasons they do not need to push is that, far from being weak, they are the strong. Meekness is a sign of strength, as well as happiness and contentment. The meek, who are really strong, have no need to push or shove or fight or kill. Violence is the tool of the insecure. Who was really stronger than Jesus, yet Jesus was meek. .

When Jesus would not speak in his own defense, Pilate said to Him, "'Do you not know that I have power to release you, and power to crucify you?' Jesus answered him, 'You would have no power over me unless it had been given you from above.'"(John 19:10-11)

The earth is the Lord's and always will be. He has no need to fight for ownership. He shares it with everyone, and when He came to this earth, His power was shown in meekness. It is the insecure and unhappy people who must fight, trying to get more than their share of the inheritance.

Even on this earth, people fight over the inheritance from their earthly parents. There is no joy or gain in such fighting.

I was told that my ancestors were quite wealthy back in the 1800s. When those wealthy parents died, the children fought so much over their inheritances that the lawyers ended up with all the money.

In this nuclear age, people may fight over the earth until there is nothing left.

God knows we must learn to share the earth that we have inherited from Him. It is for our own good that Jesus says, "Blessed are the meek, for they shall inherit the earth."

Because God loves us, He has given us this beautiful and bountiful earth. He is also trying to give us the guidance we need to keep the earth beautiful and bountiful, and to live together, sharing its benefits in peace. Here in the present he wants us to enjoy His gift of love, which is this earth. When we realize all this, we have no need to be anything other than meek.

Those Who Hunger and Thirst For Righteousness

THIS BEATITUDE SEEMS simpler than the last one. It says, "Blessed are those who hunger and thirst for righteousness, for they shall be satisfied."(Matthew 5:6)

It raises another question, however. Whenever we hear a word like righteousness we might think "religious requirements" or "demands of God." I have been contending that God's advice, *i. e.*, commandments, is for our sake, not His. It will be my challenge to show that to be true as I look at this hungering and thirsting for righteousness.

The idea that righteousness is something we hunger and thirst for, rather than something that is demanded of us, may hint at how important this righteousness is to us, more so even than to God. When we realize that this righteousness is really the best thing for us, we will hunger and thirst for it, and we will be happier or more blessed for it.

It is interesting that everyone seeks the "good" life. If only they realized that it is found by being "good." So let's look at being "good."

We would all like to be good, and we put some effort into it. But we want a lot of other things also. We may find ourselves tempted to twist the truth or hurt someone by pushing to get something we want. Sometimes we choose the good, and sometimes we go for something that seems more important. We operate from mixed motives and, if we are honest, we know and admit that.

If we are honest, we also know the guilt we feel when we know that we have chosen our own desires over what we feel is really right. The sense that we did not do what we should have, detracts from the pleasure of getting what we wanted. Even if our waywardness seems to succeed, we are a little uncomfortable. If we betray our principles and we do not succeed in getting the goal we pursued, our remorse is without relief. If our betrayal blows up in our face, we are defenseless.

On the other hand, the person who really does what he feels is right can look failure straight in the face, because he knows he did his best. His defense is his integrity, and his stable platform is the principle he based his actions on. Even if he is proven wrong, he knows he acted with the best intentions and only went astray in ignorance. Herein lies much of the happiness or blessedness of the person who hungers and thirsts after righteousness. He can look himself in the face in the mirror in the morning, and he can face others, knowing that he tried his best.

Many successes and failures will come to each of us in life. But we cannot enjoy our successes fully unless we acted with integrity, and we cannot face our failures if we betrayed our principles. No matter what we do or say, some will praise us and some will criticize us for it. But we will not be able to accept the praise and feel good about it if, in our heart, we feel our actions were base and deceptive. If, on the other hand, we feel that we acted on noble motives, even the harshest criticism will bounce off without a mark.

But who has such pure motives, such singular intentions? As I said, we are all a bundle of mixed motives and conflicting desires. Certainly, we would be happier if we could achieve such singular strength of purpose that we would no longer be tormented and torn apart by conflicting feelings and temptations.

Paul speaks of this very problem in Romans 7:21-24, saying, "So I find it to be a law that when I want to do right, evil lies close at hand. For I delight in the law of God, in my inmost self, but I see in my members another law at war with the law of my mind and making me captive to the law of sin which dwells in my members. Wretched man that I am! Who will deliver me from this body of death? "

Surely if we could be free of these tensions because we so intensely want to be righteous, we would be blessed. Perhaps Christ gave this beatitude to show us the reason for such pure purpose.

When Christ speaks of those who hunger and thirst after righteousness, He uses words which may be stronger than we can comprehend. In this affluent land we do not understand the hunger of the poor people of Palestine to whom Jesus spoke, where on the best of days they had barely enough to eat. Many times they might go for days without having anything to eat. Hunger was an everyday feeling, not an occasional pang. Thirst, working under the hot Mideast sun, could also be unbearable. A man might be on a journey and, in the midst of it, the hot wind would bring a sandstorm. There was nothing for him to do but wrap in his cape and turn his back to the wind and wait. Meanwhile, the swirling sand filled his nostrils and his throat until he was ready to suffocate for breath, and until he was parched with an unbelievable thirst.

There were no mixed motives in such a moment. Water dominated the thirsty mind, and one would pay any price for it. Such single-mindedness is practically unknown in our comfortable lives. Yet such a single-minded desire for righteousness is what Christ speaks of here. Nor is the hunger and thirst He speaks of an occasional feeling. It is a constant daily drive.

Suffering can bring great singleness of mind and purpose. It can dominate and obsess the mind. I have found such a hunger and thirst for righteousness growing in me more each year, as I realize how I have suffered, and how I have caused others to suffer by my foolish straying from God's will. I am far from perfect and will never be perfect on this earth. Yet how I wish that I had been perfect, that I could be perfect. Then so much suffering and grief would be avoided.

As I get older, I see ever more the suffering that could be avoided if we would only love and care for each other as God intends. Then the ache in my heart grows; an ache that wishes for God's loving will to prevail in my life and the lives of others.

In my youth, it seemed that God demanded so much of me, but now I see the truth. It is not God who demands this precious righteousness. It is my very heart and soul that desires, indeed, demands it of me. How the suffering that my folly has caused grieves me. How much my probable future foolishness frightens me. The suffering I have caused is multiplied by the suffering caused by all the people on this earth, and it is more than my heart can bear.

Oh how much I agree with Paul in Ephesians 5:15-16, where he says, "Look carefully then how you walk, not as unwise men but as wise, making the most of the time, because the days are evil. Therefore do not be foolish, but understand what the will of the Lord is."

The beatitude is true. As I feel that single-minded desire for righteousness, a sense of satisfaction, a good feeling flows in. Maybe I have had mixed motives in the past, but now I will seek only the right path. I feel strong, as if I can resist any temptation. I know that as long as I really desire only that goodness, I will be able to ward off all temptation. There is almost a feeling of invincibility, as if I can, with integrity, stand up to anything life throws at me. The feeling is wonderful, full of love and beauty.

It is truly a blessing. We can look into our own hearts. In our hearts we know, if we really look, that we are not satisfied with less than the best. God also knows this. After all, He made us. He knows the key to our fulfillment, the answer to the malaise that so often overcomes us. He knows the answer is to strive with singleness of mind and with every fiber of our being to be the best person we can be. He also knows how easy it will be to become selfish in our desire to find happiness, and how that selfishness will tempt us to leave integrity behind in the pursuit of other things that we think will bring fulfillment.

God knows that He has put one true hunger within us, and that is for righteousness. Nothing else will truly satisfy us. We are blessed when we finally realize this and pursue it with our whole being. That is why God tells us that it is in single-mindedly hungering and thirsting after righteousness that we will be truly satisfied. If we really understand and believe in the extreme importance of pursuing righteousness, it is important that we find a way of achieving that goal as far as possible right now, in this life.

In thinking about the goal of finding and following the good or Godly life, I have some ideas. It is not unusual for us to ask ourselves in the morning what we will do with that day. That is a good time to renew a daily pledge to do what seems right or righteous. During the day, we face many decisions and temptations. As we review our options, we should look for the right decision, which is the righteous one. We need, in other words, to focus our mind increasingly each day on righteousness as the goal of every decision. It will not come in a day or a week or even in a year, but it will gradually become habit to make morality the dominant motive in our life. From this will grow peace of mind and strength of character, and a satisfaction that is more secure and fulfilling then any other goal we might have pursued, even if we achieved it.

Of course, we will always fall short of the mark, but a goal, once achieved, loses its glamour and its meaning, anyway. We need a goal that will never really be reached, so it will always draw us onward, but one that also brings satisfaction each step of the way. Knowing that we will always fail to perfectly fulfill God's will, should make us more understanding and accepting of everyone else, since we all fail in even our best efforts.

Christ says nothing about achieving perfect righteousness in this beatitude, only about earnestly and honestly desiring it. If we really desire it, we will try our very best. Then we will find satisfaction, even though we miss the mark somewhat. This is because the heart and soul, as well as the goal, of righteousness is love. Love, although never perfectly found on this earth, is beautiful, even in imperfection. Love is not a narrow, puritanical, icy righteousness, but bountiful, soft and beautiful. Love causes life to blossom with warmth and beauty. Love is not a harsh and demanding requirement, but an alluring and fulfilling feeling, which woos us and wins us. It is the outgrowth and outpouring of our deepest heart and soul. It is a hunger and thirst that is in each of us. It is only when our efforts to satisfy that most basic need for love are frustrated that we turn to other things to try to fill the emptiness.

So when we question ourselves, "What is the right thing to do?" perhaps it would be better phrased, "What is the loving thing to do?" or even, "What is the loveliest thing to do?"

Righteousness, in the narrow negative sense that many see, tries to avoid doing anything wrong. Righteousness, in the true sense of love, is always looking for ways to extend itself and its love to help others, even those people some would call unworthy. If righteousness does not add beauty and satisfaction to life, even though imperfectly achieved, perhaps it is because it is that negative, narrow misunderstanding of righteousness. We need to pursue the positive, real righteousness which flows from the pure love of the heart, and satisfies the deepest needs of the soul. Truly that is something to hunger and thirst for, and it will surely bring satisfaction and an abundant life.

The Merciful

"BLESSED ARE THE merciful, for they shall obtain mercy."(Matthew 5:7)

This beatitude poses problems for me as I try to say that everyone will be saved, since that means everyone will obtain mercy.

Some might say that this beatitude implies that only the merciful will obtain mercy. If that is true, some will not obtain mercy, and thus they will not be saved. Of course, I can say that to state the positive does not make the negative true. This verse does not say that anyone will not obtain mercy, thus that negative is not proven. However, if I say that everyone obtains mercy, is this beatitude useless? Why should anyone try to understand or follow this beatitude if everyone is going to obtain mercy anyway? Here, especially, we have to show that the beatitudes are speaking definitely about present fulfillment. The merciful will obtain mercy in the present. My statement that everyone will be saved means that in the future, in the end, everyone will obtain mercy. As I have stated before, God's first act of love is to assure us of our ultimate salvation, which is for everyone.

He also, as a second act of love, tries to show us the best way to live our life in the present, so we might have the most fulfilling life now. This beatitude is trying to show us the way to obtain God's mercy now, so we can enjoy it in this life, being then spared much worry and unhappiness on this earth.

Am I saying that God only gives His mercy to some people now? Why would He be so selective now and so free with His mercy and salvation later? Such a God sounds a little cruel. So you see, this beatitude poses many questions.

Mercy has several meanings, and the first I will examine is "forgiveness." There are some scriptures hinting that if we do not forgive, we will not be forgiven.

Jesus, later in the Sermon on the Mount, says, "For if you forgive men their trespasses, your heavenly Father also will forgive you; but if you do not forgive men their trespasses, neither will your Father forgive your trespasses."(Matthew 6:14-15)

This sounds very threatening, and I have been trying to show a God who is kind and loving, not angry and demanding. I don't believe that God will withhold forgiveness from anyone, either in the present or the future. But how can this be true? The scriptures clearly state that those who do not forgive will not be forgiven.

God is really trying to tell us about reality. The reality is that forgiveness may be given, but to be received it must be believed. God may be merciful to everyone. But only if we believe in His mercy now, will we feel, and in that sense obtain, His mercy now. I am not splitting hairs, but speaking of psychological realities. If we believe that some people or some actions will not be forgiven, are not forgivable, then we cannot believe deep inside that we are forgiven. This is true no matter how much we think we are better or different from others. If forgiveness is in doubt for anyone, it is in doubt for us. We may suppress those doubts. We may rationalize our faults or say they are forgiven, while condemning the faults of others as unforgiven. Still, deep inside, this places our own forgiveness and salvation in doubt. Our sense of God's mercy is determined by our own sense of mercy. If we cannot accept others, we cannot accept ourselves. Deep inside, we realize the truth that we are not any better than others.

Walt Whitman realized this and expressed it in his poem "Song of Myself," as he wrote, "In all people I see myself, none more and not one barley-corn less."

Thus, until we learn to love and forgive others, we will not really love and forgive ourselves, nor will we be able to feel or believe in God's forgiveness for us.

Many evangelical Christians claim that they know they are saved. They go about proclaiming their salvation and trying to save others who, they are equally sure, are lost. They are always proclaiming their salvation and presenting their path as the only way to salvation. With all their talk and concern for salvation, I think they protest too much. They are really unsure of their salvation and their supposed truth. Consequently, they must convince others they are right, in order to continually convince themselves. If you disagree with them, you are a threat to their certainty, which is not very certain at all. It is no wonder they are so zealous; their own repressed doubts are dogging them.

This beatitude is trying to tell us the way to really obtain that certainty of God's mercy. The key to receiving that assurance of God's mercy is to have mercy on everyone else. If we find it in our heart to forgive others, then God's forgiveness becomes believable, thus receivable. Only if we learn to understand and forgive every fault will we feel that every fault in us is likewise forgiven by God. God never withholds His love, forgiveness, acceptance or mercy from anyone. When we truly understand, and find ourselves willing to love, forgive and accept others, we will be able to truly believe, feel and thus obtain God's mercy. Then finally we can forgive ourselves.

The idea of forgiveness is certainly contained in this beatitude, but William Barclay looks even deeper into its meaning. The New Testament was written in Greek, but Jesus spoke Aramaic, which is similar to Hebrew. So we need to go back to the Aramaic word Jesus probably used to express the concept of mercy. Although this word is untranslatable, Barclay sees it as far deeper than mere sympathy. It is more like identifying with a person so completely that we feel that person's feelings as if they were our own. It also means to see things like that person and even think like them [3]

To be merciful in this sense is to feel in perfect harmony with the other person. Sometimes it is sad, if the other person is sad, and sometimes it is happy, if he is happy. When we really feel what it is like to be that person, forgiveness is easier. How can we help but be merciful, when we understand so completely?

The French have a proverb that says, "To know all is to forgive all." This understanding is also necessary when we look at parts of ourselves, if we are to believe ourselves worthy of mercy. Such understanding breeds compassion for parts of ourselves and others that we would otherwise condemn.

So if you have difficulty forgiving others, the route to that forgiveness is understanding, in the very deep sense of identification. Such full understanding takes great time and effort, but it is worth it. If you do manage that union of yourself with others, you will find their hearts filling up yours. You will find your heart growing not only fuller, but also richer. You will find yourself drawn to them with compassion. Your heart will bleed with their sadness, and rejoice with their joy. Whether it is joy or sadness that is evoked, it is a beautiful thing to care about another, even if he does not know it and cannot respond. You will find yourself finally able to accept and love yourself completely only when you have accepted and loved others equally. As you learn to love others and thus yourself, even so you will obtain the assurance that God also loves all others and yourself even more than you have learned to do.

Far from being only true in the future, this beatitude is really strictly true only in the present. After death, we will all face God and find His mercy. Then we will finally believe and feel that we are forgiven and saved. But God, in His love, wants us to feel and enjoy the assurance of His mercy now also. Therefore, Christ came to earth to help us believe and thus receive that feeling of forgiveness now, on earth. However, to feel his mercy now, we must feel mercy in our own hearts for others. Only in that way will we know that such mercy is a possibility, and, in fact, a reality. When we take the time to really understand others, as the Indians said, "to walk a mile in their moccasins," we will forgive.

Christ walked in our shoes, and he understands us completely and forgives us completely. Blessed are we when, through being merciful to others, we have found this mercy. In this beatitude, Christ tries to show us and steer us into this beautiful path full of mercy. Jesus' advice here, as always, is for our sake, not His. It is a good gift, not a demand or a requirement for salvation.

The Pure in Heart

"BLESSED ARE THE pure in heart, for they shall see God."(Matthew 5:8)

I have often said, "Only the pure in heart want to see God."

When God has revealed himself to someone, it has often been to give him an assignment he did not want. Consider Jeremiah. He was not eager to be a prophet. When God first called him to be His prophet, Jeremiah said, "Ah, Lord God! Behold, I do not know how to speak, for I am only a youth."(Jeremiah 1:6) There were many other times when he wished he had never seen God, or heard His call.

Think of Moses hearing the call of God from the burning bush to go to Egypt and bring out the people of Israel. Moses saw God and God had a mission for him. Moses was not glad to see God. Instead, Moses said, "Oh, my Lord, send, I pray, some other person."(Exodus 4:13)

The fact is that having God too close makes us a little nervous. I know that we try to serve Him sometimes, but we also have times when we want to do our own will. We might wonder if we would have any life of our own if God were too close. We try to please God, but mostly we want to please ourselves. To have God hanging over our shoulder could make us more than a little nervous. Deep in our heart, we know that we hide a lot from Him, from other people, and from ourselves. We would be more than embarrassed if that was all exposed, particularly to God.

When Christ came to this earth, people did see God, and they crucified Him.

John 3:19 says, "And this is the judgement, that the light has come into the world, and men loved darkness rather than light, because their deeds were evil."

Why did they crucify Him? That is explained in the very next verse, "For every one who does evil hates the light, and does not come to the light, lest his deeds should be exposed."(John 3:20)

Those who are not honest with God or themselves, fear being exposed. It is only the pure in heart, that is, those who are not hiding the truth or trying to deceive, who can come to God without fear. They have already admitted the truth and there is nothing further to be exposed by the light.

Somehow, when we are not thinking about God, which is most of the time, we forget that He sees us and knows us through and through. Deep in our heart, we know there is no hiding from God, but then we don't look very deep into our hearts. Such deep thinking is too revealing, too disturbing. Often we play the radio or try to be constantly busy, so unwanted thoughts don't pop into our heads.

In this and many other ways, we avoid God and ourselves. Thus we miss out on life, life as God intended it to be. We run from life, even as we run from God and ourselves. When we do not listen to God, when we avoid Him and ourselves, there is always a sense of missing the mark. We sense that life is not what it was meant to be. Still, we are afraid to ask what God wants us to do, for fear it will be too difficult or dangerous. So we entertain ourselves with small pleasures, and try to appease God with occasional service. We do not realize that we are cheating ourselves out of the beautiful and bountiful life that God intended for us.

We need to stop deceiving ourselves and look into our hearts honestly, so we may become pure. We need to face God openly, so we can see Him clearly and understand Him more completely. You see, all our hiding is wasted because He sees right through us. But worse than wasted, it is depriving us of seeing God as He really is. In the midst of all our hiding, there is deep in our hearts the desire that we could expose ourselves totally and find ourselves completely accepted and loved just as we are.

What a beautiful wave of warmth and relief would wash over us, and what peace and freedom we would feel. No more need to run and hide, or to be afraid of being found out. It is a real blessing to be able to finally face ourselves and accept ourselves. What freedom and joy it will be to tear down the walls and dance in the open unashamed. But that is exactly what God wishes to give to us. He comes to us with that limitless love and complete acceptance, but because we cannot believe it, we run and hide.

When we have faced up to ourselves and God, we become pure in heart, and we see God as He really is. We feel His love and acceptance and have no more need to hide. Then we are truly blessed.

But that is only the beginning. When we have discovered that God is love, we know that He has much more in store for us. We know that His will is what is best for us, because we trust His love for us. Now we seriously seek out His will for our lives. We stop keeping busy, or playing the radio to avoid the thoughts that come into our heads. Instead, we spend our time seeking out the deepest thoughts and feelings. Those thoughts and feelings will guide us to the deepest treasures and the richest life.

We are tempted to avoid the difficult paths, but when we take them, we are always glad we did, for the rewards are worth the risks. If we are wise and understand God, we know that the richest life will be found not in getting, but in giving. If we are really willing to do God's will, He will reveal it to us.

There are many who spend time and effort looking for God and claiming that they want to see Him. But if they are not honest with themselves, if their hearts are not pure, they will pretend they have not heard Him, so cleverly, in fact, that they will not consciously hear Him.

We often only pretend to seek God, and we believe our own pretense. We seek a god who will serve us in our own short-sighted and self-centered ways. We will never find that god because he doesn't exist. The true God knows what is best for us, and it is not always to get our own foolish way. God has a bigger and a better plan, but in our ignorance we cannot see the wisdom of His plan. We think that getting our own way is best for us. We do not realize that it is our individual plans clashing with each other that result in the chaos and fighting which mess up our world.

God's plan would unite everyone in peace and love. But we are often too frustrated with the failure of our own personal plans to see or realize that. We want our dreams fulfilled, and we have little time for God's plan. In our preoccupation with finding a god who will do our will, we do not see the God who tries to show us His gracious will, which is the best path. So we all deceive ourselves, and thus we cheat ourselves. God does not deceive or cheat anyone, nor does He hide from anyone. He is right there, if we would open our eyes and look.

Paul says in Romans 1:19, 21-22, "For what can be known about God is plain...Although they knew God they did not honor him as God or give thanks to him, but they became futile in their thinking and their senseless minds were darkened. Claiming to be wise, they became fools."

It is for our own sakes that we must expose the lies we have told ourselves and find the truth. We must examine our hearts and purify them, so we can receive the love and guidance that God so earnestly desires to give us. It is a long, difficult and never ending process. However, it is well worth the effort, for we will more fully feel God's love and acceptance, feeling at peace with ourselves at last. We will also benefit from the wisdom of finding and following God's will.

Then Christ's purpose will be fulfilled in us, for he said, "I came that they may have life, and have it abundantly."(John 10:10)

When we have really seen God and know that He loves and will save everyone, there is no need to hide. Therefore, we can come to God and ourselves honestly, to start seeking and living the best life. The abundant life is found only by following the will of God.

As long as we teach people to fear God, they will only deceive themselves, thinking they are deceiving Him. Because of fear, they will remain lost, not to God's loving and redemptive grace, but to His loving and wise guidance for this life. This beatitude was clearly meant to benefit us in this life. Everyone will see God eventually, but the pure in heart will see Him now and benefit in the present from feeling His love and receiving His helpful guidance for their lives.

The Peacemakers

"BLESSED ARE THE peacemakers, for they shall be called sons of God."(Matthew 5:9)

When we look at this beatitude about peacemakers, we must understand the Hebrew word for "peace," which is *Shalom*. This word and the Hebrew concept of peace do not mean merely the absence of fighting or anxiety. Shalom is not a negative, restrictive term or quality. Shalom means everything that makes for humanity's greatest harmony and well-being.

Shalom may start with inner peace, springing from a sense of contentment and fulfillment. That good feeling should spread to all one's relationships, so they are harmonious and satisfying. Indeed, Shalom refers to the ideal state of every relationship. It is therefore something positive, abundant; to be sought, fostered, to make, as in peacemaker.

Many people misunderstand religion as something that is composed of "Thou Shalt Nots." The idea in their minds is to avoid all evil, to restrict their lives to some straight and narrow path. No wonder such people are jealous of those who are more free and do not follow that straight and narrow path, thus seeming to have a happier, if evil, life. They feel such irreligious people deserve to go to hell, because they have not paid their dues. The truth is that negatively religious people do not really understand Christianity. Christianity is not the avoidance of evil, but the striving for the best and most bountiful life for all. There is no need to envy the destructive lives of the immoral, for their pleasures are often short-lived and end up disastrously.

Looking at it in terms of peace, there are three types of people. First, those who decide that they will fight for what they want, not caring even to obey the narrowest sense of peace as absence of conflict. Fighting is destructive, and they lead destructive lives, bringing grief to others and eventually to themselves. The more frantically they try to fight for what they want, the more they reveal their desperation as they strive in vain for satisfaction.

Then there is the second group. They see peace merely as the absence of fighting or anxiety. They may lead very empty, dull lives. Too much peace in their negative sense can be boring.

Finally, there is the third group, who understand the true meaning of peace as encompassed by the Hebrew word "Shalom." They try to do constructive, nurturing, beautiful things to make life more fulfilling for everyone. They are busy, and have a sense of purpose and accomplishment. Their lives are full of challenges and excitement. Their hearts are full of love.

So take your choice. Would you prefer to lead a life that is destructive and empty, or constructive and full? I presume you would like the constructive, bountiful life of the third group, for then you will be truly blessed and fulfilled.

I know that the days in which I feel that I have done something to make life better for another are the days I go to bed happy and satisfied. Unfortunately, there are too many days when I feel I have accomplished nothing good, and I even fear that I have been destructive. It is not easy to be a peacemaker, either on the international scene or in interpersonal relationships. I will discuss some ways we can try to be better peacemakers.

We might start by at least avoiding fighting. Perhaps we cannot make people happy, but we can try not to make them more miserable. If we realize that fighting will only hurt and not help, we might eliminate it as one of our ways of dealing with others. To help us eliminate fighting, we need to look at why we fight. Perhaps we fight because we do not have something we want and we think we can wrest it away from or out of someone else. Then we are like a child fighting over a toy. In our interpersonal relationships, we should realize that even if we "win," the hurt and hostility created by the battle will prevent us from enjoying our gains.

Perhaps we have been hurt. Taking revenge just hurts the other person, without healing our hurt, and practically assures that they will strike out to hurt us again.

Perhaps we feel threatened. So we threaten the other side. We may think this will frighten them into submission, but they will also feel threatened and increase their threat to us.

Both world wars were preceded by an arms race, on the presumption that strength would bring peace. Instead, only threat and distrust increased. As a result, weapons increased on both sides. Eventually, like a boil, the arms buildup burst into war.

In interpersonal relationships, we only make worse enemies by threatening or fighting with those who threaten us. Fighting always makes situations worse, not better. It is not worthy of the term "solution" to anything. We may be upset about many things in our lives and the world, but be assured that fighting will create more problems than it solves.

Now to proceed to the much more difficult task of making peace in the positive sense of "Shalom," as God intends. There can be no peace, in that sense, unless there is justice and the opportunity for everyone to have a full life.

In the 1960s, people deplored the riots in our inner city ghettos, and condemned violence. What they did not see was the daily violence perpetrated on the inhabitants of those ghettos, in the form of discrimination, poverty and hopelessness. The riots solved nothing, because fighting is never a solution. But there is no real Shalom in the ghettos, even when there are no riots. Therefore, we should not be satisfied just because people are quiet and not responding violently to their daily degradation. If we are to be peacemakers, we must try to bring justice, hope and opportunity for a full life to everyone.

The blessing in this beatitude is on peacemakers, not necessarily peace lovers. When we are merely passive peace lovers, we may choose to ignore an unjust situation, because speaking out may cause dissention. Our refusal to intervene can allow the situation to fester or get worse until it breaks out into violence. By loving peace too much, or in the wrong way, we may allow peace to be destroyed, because we did not act while there was still time. That is the way it is when we let injustice and poverty continue. The anger and despair will someday explode. Then it may be too late to make peace. An ounce of prevention is worth a pound of cure. That old saying really applies in this case.

But how do we bring about change without being violent? Gandhi and Martin Luther King Jr. are two great examples of how to effect nonviolent change. They did not raise up their hands against anyone, yet their refusal to submit to injustice accomplished their goals. They resisted the oppressive system in ways that made the injustice visible.

Usually people submit quietly to the system, in fear of the consequences of resisting. This allows the deprivation to continue silently. When the nonviolent protests begin, it forces the hand of the oppressors. The violence that is part of the system, but not noticed by the outside world, is increased to suppress the protest. When the violence of the system becomes more intense and widespread, it becomes more visible. The protestors may suffer more than before, but if they remain peaceful, sympathy begins to build for their cause. The violence of the oppressors is condemned and pressure to change the whole unjust system eventually brings about change.

Contrast that with the attempt to force the oppressors to change through violence by the oppressed. The violence by the oppressed increases the repression by the more powerful oppressors, who now claim the right of self-defense and proclaim justice on their side. The oppressed earn condemnation rather than sympathy, and no one prevents their destruction. Revenge breeds revenge and the cycle of violence is harder to break.

Even if violent revolution succeeds in overthrowing the oppressor, it is the violent ones who win. They usually become dictators and use the same violent tactics to maintain their power that they used to acquire it. After all, it is their nature to use violence to get their way.

Of course, I do not want to forget the greatest nonviolent force for change who ever lived, which was Jesus Christ Himself. Now some may say that the world is no better since Christ walked this earth about 2000 years ago. I feel that it would be hard to prove that. The world is so large and varied. How would you ever know whether the world was better or not?

On the other hand, it would be easy to prove that some individuals have been changed because Christ lived and taught and died and rose again. Because of Christ, some people have been more loving and have helped others on the path of life. Without their love and compassion, the world would have been a worse place. All the problems of the world are not gone, and they may never be completely solved, but Christ did make a difference to and through individuals. These changed people were more loving and compassionate, because they knew and tried to follow Christ and His teachings. He, more than any, was peaceful to the very end. He, more than any other, was a peacemaker and a Son of God.

Christ was not quiet. He expressed his feelings all too clearly to the Pharisees and other powerful people around Him. He was not violent, but He spoke the truth in the open, where neither the truth nor the speaker could be ignored. He did not change the whole world, but He did change some people around him, and that was a beginning.

Likewise, we do not have to be quiet in interpersonal relationships. Sometimes it is best not to just sit on our unhappiness, thereby allowing it to fester until we explode one day and really fight with those around us. We can state our needs and desires, and we should listen sympathetically to the needs and desires of others. Silence is not always golden, or a sign of peace, as those who have received the famous "Silent Treatment" know. We must learn to talk and listen with love and sympathy, rather than resentment and anger.

We cannot even meet the needs of those we love the most. They cannot satisfy all our needs, either. We can explore together the sad truth that our needs and desires will never be totally met on this earth. And we can continue loving each other, while trying to better meet the needs we can.

Therefore, we should try to understand each other and console each other, instead of fighting and making life more miserable. We need to make ourselves more vulnerable, rather than hiding behind walls in loneliness or sniping at others. I think we will find that in our vulnerability we will come closer to others. They may open up their hearts in tenderness as they see that we are no different than they are and how much we all need each other. Beautiful, tender and loving relationships are one of the greatest blessings of peacemakers. Let us try constructively to make peace, to make life better and richer. We cannot do this when we fight; only when we communicate and console, always in an atmosphere of love.

If we learn to make peace in the full and positive sense, our lives will be happier, more blessed, and we will be called sons of God, which is the Greek phrase for being "like God." Certainly the highest goal in life is to be like God. There can be no doubt that God's life is the best and most beautiful. The closer we get to God's way, the better it will be for everyone. God wants us to be like Him, not to please His whims, or to flatter His ego, but because He knows it is the most beautiful and satisfying way to live and feel. His will is always for what is best for each of us. If we really come to understand and believe that, we might seek and follow His will more eagerly. If we do that, we will be more like God and our lives will be more blessed.

Persecuted for Righteousness Sake

"BLESSED ARE THOSE who are persecuted for righteousness' sake, for theirs is the kingdom of heaven."(Matthew 5:10)

Again we have a beatitude that seems like it can not possibly be fulfilled in the present. How can persecution be a blessing, or blessed? There are many truths in this beatitude, and in the longer one following it in verses 11-12. I will examine some of them.

It seems in some ways to be an irrelevant saying in this land of religious freedom. Persecution on the basis of religious beliefs and actions seems foreign to our experience. In this so-called "Christian" country, it is often assumed that the norms of the general society are synonymous with Christian morality. There seem to be few clashes between the two value systems. So we do not examine what is asked of us, and thus we seldom feel called upon to challenge it.

If we did ask more questions, we might find many subtle forms of coercion or persecution, which would spring up when we followed the will of God. On the job we may be asked to do something that we do not think is right. Maybe no one threatens to fire us, but we have a feeling, or a fear, that following our own conscience, standing up to the boss, will affect our career in some adverse way.

Preachers even feel this when they are writing their sermons. They may be afraid to say some things. I have struggled with this on occasion myself.

The scripture that spoke to me then was Mark 8:36 where Jesus says, "For what does it profit a man, to gain the whole world and forfeit his life? "

Interestingly, this is a scripture which some may use as evidence that not everyone is saved. Those who think that way feel that this scripture is speaking of some future loss of soul, *i. e.*, salvation, after they die. I say that this warning, and I purposely use the word warning rather than threat, is another example of God's loving advice that helps us find a better life in the present.

I do not see this scripture as a threat to my salvation in the future. Instead, I see it as warning me about the loss of my integrity in the present. If I kept my mouth shut to save my job, I could not look into the mirror in the morning. If I have to go into the pulpit every Sunday afraid that what I will say will endanger my job, then I don't want the job.

As they say, "A coward dies a thousand deaths, a brave man dies but once."

The person who chooses to follow his conscience finds more courage each time he surmounts his fears. The person who begins to let fear run his life will find that fears more and more dominate his life. His choices determine whether his life is lived in integrity or fear. A person's life can be run by his sense of what is right or it can be run by fear. Happy is the person who overcomes fear and lives a life of righteousness. Even if persecution is his lot, it is better than the life of one dominated by fear.

The fearful person turns aside at the slightest hint of persecution, and has trouble facing himself in the mirror. Is one of the reasons people have not experienced persecution because they have turned aside at the first hint of it; knuckled under at the slightest threat?

But fear of persecution comes even if you have no boss to threaten you. It comes outside the job. There is the fear of what people will say or think if you do something. There are no guarantees about what people will say or think. Some may think well of you and some may condemn you for the very same thing. Even if you never do anything, people may invent stories about you to fill the void. No matter what you do or say, some people will like you and some will reject you.

Therefore, it is very important that you do what you think is right, so you, in your own integrity, can stand up to the inevitable criticism from some. Happy, or blessed, are you if you follow your conscience when you are criticized. You can stand tall, and weather the criticism through the strength of your convictions. But if you betray yourself, you will be blown over by the slightest negative sentiment.

If I have done something I am proud of, I do not worry who knows or what they say. I wish all the world knew.

If I am a coward and do not follow my conscience, if I am wrong in my own eyes, then I will live in fear of being found out. I will feel guilty even if I receive praise. I will wish I could hide from myself, but I will not be able to escape my own conscience.

We will all receive some criticism in life. We will also receive other forms of persecution, subtle or otherwise. We should rejoice if the criticism is unjust in our eyes, that is if we sincerely feel we followed the will of God as we saw it, because our integrity will shield us.

Peter put it this way in I Peter 3:14-17,"But even if you do suffer for righteousness' sake, you will be blessed. Have no fear of them, nor be troubled, but in your hearts reverence Christ as Lord. Always be prepared to make a defense to anyone who calls you to account for the hope that is in you, yet do it with gentleness and reverence; and keep your conscience clear, so that, when you are abused, those who revile your good behavior in Christ may be put to shame. For it is better to suffer for doing right, if that should be God's will, than for doing wrong."

Notice that the wording at the beginning of this quote from Peter is similar to the beatitude. Also notice that, whereas you may feel more anger when you are unjustly accused of something, it is far better to be unjustly accused, than justly accused. If you have really been wrong, you have no defense at all, even in your own heart, and you will be destroyed. Therefore, whether in danger of persecution or not, it is always best to follow your sense of what is right or righteous.

But what of persecution and the sacrifices sometimes exacted from us for doing what we think is right? Surely no one would welcome sacrifice or persecution. I don't think anyone would welcome such suffering, yet Christ, of his own free will, chose the path of sacrifice and even death for us. Choosing does not mean welcoming, but it is a far cry from running away.

As Christians we should not seek out persecution or martyrdom, but neither should we run away when it threatens, leaving our integrity behind. We might even choose to suffer persecution we could have avoided if sufficient good would be accomplished.

The path that leads to persecution may sometimes be the best path. We see this in Christ's choice. We know that to assure us of our salvation and show us the way to a better life through his teachings, Christ chose a path that He knew would result in His persecution and death. I believe that Christ would always choose the best path.

People frequently choose the path of sacrifice, whether it be parents who choose to have children, or a Mother Teresa who made the homeless children of Calcutta her own. There is something meaningful about sacrificing, if it is chosen voluntarily and for some greater good. Sacrificing for others is the highest and most satisfying goal in life.

Life is not something we can hoard. It slips through our fingers constantly, even as time does. Life is used up daily, no matter what we do. The question is whether it is used for something or someone worthy of the daily expenditure. Each day is spent. We must try to spend each day wisely, if we are to be satisfied with our life. To give our all, as Christ did, is perhaps the ultimate in giving, and thus the ultimate in living.

Someone has said, "We must all die. Happy is the person who can make even death count by dying for something or someone, by accomplishing something even with his death."

This is also true of life. Happy is the person who makes life count. Although no one wants to endure persecution, persecution somehow ennobles the effort. It elevates it in some way. It makes the choices more courageous or cowardly. It is life at high pitch, and hopefully for high purpose.

Studies have shown that as government regulation has made the work place safer, people have pursued riskier hobbies, such as hang gliding, racing, sky diving, etc. People seek thrills, excitement, to give an edge to life. Risks are consequently taken and sometimes suffering results.

Then the questions confront them, "Was that risk worth taking? Why did I do it? "

If the risk was taken in the pursuit of what was right, for the welfare of others, according to our God's loving will, then they can more likely answer, "Yes, the risk was worth taking." Then the wound is a sign of noble sacrifice, rather than shame or foolishness.

So live your life without letting fear of what people will think enslave you. Decide what you think is right and worth doing. If there is risk, it may even add excitement to the endeavor. Walk with integrity, and someday, when you look back, you will be glad you walked as you did. Look to God for your guidance and follow that guidance no matter what threatens.

You walk now on this earth. But if your eyes and your heart and your actions are turned toward God, and you live in His service, you are really a citizen in His kingdom. That is what the beatitude means when it says of those who are persecuted for righteousness sake, "for theirs is the kingdom of heaven."

If you serve the King, you are, in the truest sense, members of His kingdom. This earth is not your real home, but only a pilgrim path. You should act, even on this earth, as a citizen of the kingdom of God, which is your true home. The world may threaten you and persecute you, as it did Christ Himself, but your heart cannot be overcome as long as it looks to God and knows that your real and eternal home is the kingdom of heaven. If you understand, feel, and trust this truth, fear will not be able to sway you. Persecution will only refine you, so you are more prepared for your Lord.

As I grow older and my body begins, all too obviously, to wear out, I realize ever more that I am not immortal on this earth. My time to live and love is limited, and thus more precious. Therefore, I try harder to do what is best with each day that I have remaining. Life becomes richer the more I find and follow the loving advice of my Father in heaven. The ultimate threat of this world is death, and yet death is inevitable. Death I see ever more as release, and a ticket home. It is no threat, but simply a spur to make the most of the life I have left.

Jesus ends the beatitudes with the longest and most exuberant beatitude, which is also about persecution, saying,"Blessed are you when men revile you and persecute you and utter all kinds of evil against you falsely on my account. Rejoice and be glad, for your reward is great in heaven, for so men persecuted the prophets who were before you."(Matthew 5:11-12)

Even on this earth, we give honor to those who take risks and suffer in battle. Surely greater honor will come to those who take risks and suffer in the service of their heavenly King. Perhaps the greatest gift will be the feeling we have when we look back over our life and see that we courageously followed our consciences. The greater the price for following our consciences, the greater is the glory. Fear not persecution. Fear, rather, failing to make the most of life. Once more, Christ, in his teaching, is trying to show us the way to make the most out of our lives on this earth. This beatitude also, is a gift from God and a sign of His love for us.

Chapter 6: Can Anger, Insult and Condemnation be Overcome?

I HAVE BEEN TRYING TO show that the law God gives is an act of love meant to benefit us, not Him. Showing that the beatitudes were meant to be a blessing for us was simple once you understood their spirit. After all, each beatitude starts with the word "Blessed."

The passage I will examine in this chapter speaks of judgement and even hell. How does my view of a loving God who will not punish or condemn us stand up to these threats?

Let's look then at some of the difficult teachings of Christ in the Sermon on the Mount. He seems to make the Old Testament law impossible to fulfill by urging people to fulfill the spirit of the law, instead of just the letter. Those who say that not everyone will be saved, feeling that they will be but the undeserving will not, often base the confidence for their own salvation on their faithful fulfilling of the Old Testament commandments. Can they confidently say that they fulfill all that Christ makes of these laws?

Anger

LET'S LOOK AT the commandment "You shall not kill." (Exodus 20:13)

Christ plunges deeper than the letter of the law to probe the very spirit of it, saying, "You have heard that it was said to the men of old, 'You shall not kill; and whoever kills shall be liable to judgement.' But I say to you that every one who is angry with his brother shall be liable to judgement." (Matthew 5:21-22a)

Most of us can say that we have not physically killed anyone, but how many of us can say that we have never been angry? We might even be a little angry or resentful of God for laying down such a difficult requirement. It is hard enough trying to follow the letter of the law. Now Christ wants our lives to be free of malice.

Must God be so hard on us? Such might be the thinking of one who sees God and His commandments as hard, instead of helpful. I feel God's commandments are gems of wisdom that, if learned and mastered, can make our life better and more beautiful. I think it is good for Christ to want us to have a life free of anger and malice.

Of course, to be restrained from inflicting injury on someone when we feel like it, is really a restriction that we might chafe under. If our heart wants revenge, it will have no peace until it gets it. But then anger will grow into bitterness and fester in our heart, poisoning our soul and staining the beauty of our life. God is well aware of this, but He also knows the solution. The solution is not to take revenge, or to kill someone. God knows the only satisfactory solution is to root out the anger. If we want to find happiness again, we will not find it in anger or revenge. To find happiness again, we must learn to forgive and love the very person we are angry at.

Think about it. You cannot be happy and angry at the same time.

Ralph Waldo Emerson once said, "For every minute you are angry, you lose 60 seconds of happiness."

Revenge does not bring the sweetness imagined or the peace that you seek from it. When you are angry, you destroy your own joy, and thus bring your own judgement upon yourself. Christ, out of love, tries to warn you that anger is as destructive as murder.

Next time you are angry, look into your heart, and see how it has twisted your feelings so that you cannot feel love or happiness. Do you like what you see?

No one wants to be angry. Many people see their hot temper correctly as a curse, and wish they could be rid of it. The problem is how to rid their lives of anger and malice, even after they realize how ugly and destructive it is. That will be a struggle to last their whole lives, but which will make their lives more beautiful for whatever progress they make.

I can only hint at solutions. One has to do with seeing other people in you and yourself in other people, so you realize how fallible we all are. Perhaps then you cannot be angry with them any more than with yourself. But that is still too much to ask, for all too often you are angry with yourself. You need to feel loved and accepted, just as you are, by God and by some others you care about on this earth. If you feel God's love and acceptance for you, just as you are, maybe you can begin to love and accept yourself. Then you might be able to love and accept others as they are.

We are all a mixed bag, and we must learn to accept both good and evil from ourselves and others. Perhaps if we fully realize this, our expectations will conform more nearly to reality. Then we will not be so overwhelmed when things go badly.

When we have been hurt we might cry out, asking, "Why did they do that?"

If we understand human fallibility and have accepted it, we hardly need to ask that question, and we do not expect a satisfactory answer. There can be no satisfactory answer for suffering, no matter how, or by whom, it is inflicted. We must learn to deal with the unpleasant occurrences of life, or they will overwhelm us and deprive us of the joy of the beautiful parts of life. We need to deal with anger for our sake, not God's. It is not something difficult that He demands of us, but something difficult that we need to seek to make our lives better.

When I analyze anger further, I find it to be a secondary emotion. It springs from primary emotions like hurt, fear or unhappiness. To really deal with anger we must figure out the root cause. We must examine what made us angry and why. We need to ask ourselves questions like the following: Has someone caused us pain, either physical or emotional? Has someone threatened us and made us afraid? Has someone prevented us from getting something we feel we need to be happy? Has someone hurt or threatened or adversely affected someone we care about? Always we must look behind the anger to the cause and the primary emotion that is at the root.

If we have been hurt, I think we get angry because it seems to block out the pain as we funnel our feelings into our rage. It would be better to feel the pain and perhaps cry. It is important that we realize and focus on the hurt, rather than turning it into anger and forgetting the cause. If we let anger take over, it rages on without reason and often carries us beyond reason and control. Such anger burns and festers and takes over our life, poisoning and destroying our joy with bitterness. Even if we recognize this, we may still feel justified in our anger and see no reason to do anything about it, not realizing how adversely it is affecting our life.

You might say, "Why shouldn't I be angry? Wouldn't you be angry if someone hurt you?"

I would respond that I would hope not to be angry. If I must find a selfish reason not to be angry, it would be that I don't like pain. As long as I am angry, the pain continues and increases. For example, I know people who are tormented by the possibility of even seeing certain other people on the street, or meeting them at some occasion, because they can not tolerate that person for one reason or another. These people torment themselves because they have not learned to understand and accept those other people. They suffer needlessly when they cannot learn to love and accept others despite their faults. The thought of the person who has offended them gives them pain, and anger springs up worse than at the first. The only way to stop the hurt is to forgive and forget.

People may say, "I can forgive, but I can't forget."

That is usually a sign that they haven't really forgiven. They are still nursing the wound and thus keeping the anger alive.

Maybe you can't really forget. But once you have forgiven, the incident becomes of little consequence, and you seldom think about it. If you do think about it, the situation or the person does not bother you anymore. It becomes a past and no longer a present pain. This person may have caused you pain in the past, but you cause yourself pain in the present by not forgiving. You can perhaps justly blame them for the pain in the past, but you can blame only yourself for the present pain. For your own sake you must learn to deal with this anger and malice. For your own sake, you must learn to forgive. How much beauty you would add to your life if you learned to love the very people who now make you angry. God does not threaten or punish you. You punish yourself. God just tries to warn you that things like anger will cause you much grief.

If we find that it is fear that has sparked our anger because someone has threatened us or someone dear to us, we need to look at that fear and threat. Maybe we are not really in danger. If we are really in danger, the least appropriate and the least effective way of dealing with the threat is to get angry. When we get angry, we lose control, and we do not think straight. Then the person who threatens us will find us an easier mark. In all times of threat and danger we must get our wits together and coolly deal with the threat. So we must cut our anger off at the pass, before it adversely affects our thinking. We must collect ourselves and deal with the threat itself. Anger is dangerous all by itself, and it makes any other danger worse.

If we find that the root cause of our anger is because we did not get our own way, we must examine our expectations. It may be that our expectations are unrealistic. If our expectations are generally out of line, we will find ourselves getting angry often. We might be an adult throwing a temper tantrum. If we recognize this, our anger may go away rather rapidly and we may feel a little sheepish. We might still be unhappy because we did not get what we wanted, but we will have overcome our anger. Then we can look for other ways we can find some fulfillment and satisfaction. Anger tends to keep us focused on the thing we did not get. When we are fixated on what can not be, we cannot move on to a more constructive approach to our unhappiness. If we feel that our expectations are justified, I suggest that we look again. We have no right to expect, more or less demand, anything from anyone or from the world in general. If we look at the world in general, I think we will see many who have so little that we will feel ashamed of our dissatisfaction. The good we receive from another should always be recognized as a gift, not an obligation. When we see good things as free and spontaneous gifts of love, it fills our hearts with joy. When we have realistic expectations, our life is always receiving wonderful surprises. If our expectations are unrealistically high, our days are full of disappointments.

If we are still in the grips of anger after examining and dealing with our own feelings, we need to focus our mind on the person who made us angry. We need to examine why this other person did or did not do the thing that is causing our anger. This may help to break our obsession with our own feelings, and thus lead us out of our anger. It may be that there is no real evidence of any malice on their part. It could have just been a thoughtless word or deed. It might have even been intended to help us. If we realize that they intended to help us, then we might focus on their intentions rather than their actions. This sense of their good intentions may melt our anger. Do not attribute malice to others unless it is proven.

What if it is obvious that they intended to hurt you? Try to imagine why they would do such a cruel thing. Perhaps you were threatening something important to them. Dogs are known as man's best friend. Yet I have often heard that you should never disturb a dog when it is eating. A dog may even turn against its best friend if something as important as its food seems threatened. People can also feel threatened and turn against their best friend or someone they love very much.

In marriage, there is a very loving relationship that is often disturbed by strong disagreements over seemingly little things. This is a sign of how important each person is to the other, and thus how important each thought or word or deed is to the spouse. If one person is very important to another, it is much easier for that individual to disturb the one who cares so much for them. Thus many strong emotions are expressed in the closest and most loving relationships.

Sometimes people are so unhappy that they are filled with bitterness, and it overflows on anyone who comes along. They really cannot help themselves.

An oriental sage once illustrated the reality that we are caught in the current of life and are not as free as we might suppose. He said, "If you are in a boat crossing a river, and an empty boat drifting in the current collides with you, you do not get angry at that boat. But if the boat which hits your boat has a person in it, you get angry at that person."

We imagine that people are in complete control of themselves, and thus we hold them responsible for what they do. Then we feel completely justified in our anger toward them for hurting us. The truth is that people are never in complete control, and they may be as helpless in the powerful currents of life as the empty boat. In their sorrow, they often strike out blindly and wildly at anything or anyone. If you sense that, you might feel sympathy replacing your anger. The best way to deal with anger is always to turn it into concern and hopefully love for the person who made us angry. This can only be done if we take the time to understand the other person and their problems and sorrows.

The hardest person to forgive is the one who is habitually mean, and even seems to take pleasure in lording it over people and hurting them. The person who is often or seemingly always cruel to us, appears to have no redeeming virtues, nothing to care about. Really, that is the one who is most to be pitied. He has long since given up on warm and tender feelings and pleasures, if he ever knew about them at all. He lives in a lonely and cold, cruel world, which he mirrors all too well in his own character and actions. Such a person may hurt and threaten you often. But he, himself, has no light or love in his life.

You, at least, have some people who love you and help heal your hurts, or protect you against threats. There is warmth and goodness in your life, which makes his cruelty seem all the more outrageous. However, that cruel soul lives in such a cold, cruel world that his cruelty doesn't seem out of line to him. He sees it as the way the game must be played in the real world, where he believes there is no love and no giving of quarter. He probably sneers in derision at the sentimental fools who believe that love and kindness are worth anything.

That individual does not get me angry, because I feel sorrier for him than for any of the others. I am not the one to be pitied when he strikes out at me; rather he is the one who needs the sympathy. I feel sad around such a person. I also feel pain around such a person, but the pain and sorrow I feel is as much or more for him, as it is for those he strikes out at. My anger melts when I look into his heart and see how sad and empty his life is. So if I understand even the worst people, I cannot stay angry at them. Love and compassion will fill my heart, displacing my anger.

A heart full of love and compassion is always better and more beautiful than a heart full of anger. For this reason, Christ warns us about how deadly anger can be. The judgement that He speaks of is not something that God puts on us or anything that God would want to befall us. That judgement is something we burden ourselves with when we are angry and allow bitterness to invade our hearts, driving out the love and beauty that God wishes for us. The judgement falls on us when we judge others, for there is always an element of judgement when we are angry. We judge the other person in some way to justify our anger, but we inject poison into our own hearts when we let anger take over. The judgement that Christ speaks of is not a threat. It is a warning, given out of love, to spare us the agony of anger. Because He loves us, God must warn us how dangerous anger is, so His warnings are also gifts of His love.

"Mad" is a word that refers to being angry. Mad is also a word which refers to being crazy.

The Roman poet Horace said, "Anger is a short madness."

God wants us to come to our senses so we can enjoy a sane and satisfying life. To do this we must overcome our anger.

Insult

WHEN WE ARE angry, we inflict suffering upon ourselves. If it is sad that we inflict such suffering upon ourselves, it is worse when we also strike out at others by insulting them.

Christ points this out by saying, "Whoever insults his brother shall be liable to the council," (Matthew 5:22b)

We must go into the background to understand what is being said here. The judgement referred to for anger and killing was before the village elders. The council for insults is the Sanhedrin, which is the highest court of the land. We do not need to fear any punishment from God in the warnings that Jesus gives us in these verses. He is really warning us about the pain and suffering we inflict on ourselves and each other, when we allow ourselves to be angry, and worse yet, to reach out and insult others.

It is bad enough to poison ourselves with our anger and bitterness, thereby destroying our own happiness. It is worse, Christ tries to point out, when we insult others, thus injecting our venom into them and threatening their joy. With words and insults, we inflict wounds on them that hurt more deeply and permanently than physical injuries. While killing is usually condemned in civilized society, it is sometimes condoned and encouraged, as in war. Torture is deplored and condemned at all times, even in war. It is considered inhuman and inexcusable. Yet what torture we can cause with words. Sometimes those wounds never heal. Better to send someone quickly into the arms of his loving Lord, than to inflict such lingering torture, and condemn him to live with the pain for the rest of his life.

We have all said such things. I do not say this to make us feel guilty. Instead, I think of the things I have said, and the pain I have caused. The remorse I feel prevents me from feeling superior to the worst of murderers. I cannot despise another without despising myself more. I can not condemn another without condemning myself. I thank God that He does not condemn me or any other, and I hope I will have the wisdom to accept everyone as God does.

Walt Whitman expressed such sentiments in his poem "Song of Myself."

"What blurt is this about virtue and about vice? Evil propels me and reform of evil propels me, I stand indifferent, my gait is no fault-finder's or rejecter's gait, I moisten the roots of all that has grown."

Hopefully, we will see that we all stand equal, although we express our equality in different ways and through our unique characters. I feel a great warmth and closeness in recognizing that I am no better than anyone else. It is a great relief not to have to try to be better than others, especially since this is impossible for anyone.

Yet all too often false pride and self-righteousness lead to a sense of imagined superiority, which causes us to look down on others with contempt, thus insulting them. When we insult others, we imply that they are inferior to us, and this is quite untrue. It is a shaky subterfuge to try to fool ourselves and others into believing in our nonexistent superiority.

Such supposed superiority is as ridiculous, but not as funny as a camper who joked, "Last year I was conceited, but this year I am perfect."

I imagine it takes a lot of insults to make it appear that others are beneath us. The word translated "insult" is *raca*, which means to despise another with arrogant contempt.

William Barclay tells a rabbinic tale of a Rabbi named Simon ben Eleazer. Returning from the house of his teacher, Simon was feeling quite proud of his knowledge and understanding and goodness. A very ugly man greeted him. In return, Simon told the man how ugly he was. Then he asked the man if all the men in his village were that ugly. The man told him to ask God, who created him, how ugly His creation is.[1]

We are all creatures of that same God. Whenever we despise another, we despise ourselves, and we insult God our Creator. Whatever pretense we have chosen to pretend we are better than others is false.

You may feel that you gain by pretending, even to yourself, that you are better than others, but you really lose. When you set yourself above others, you separate yourself from their fellowship in many subtle and serious ways. One seminary student felt that he was progressing faster than his friends. Increasingly, he would say to them in response to their ideas, "I'm beyond that now." Eventually, he found that he was beyond all his friends. No one bothered to talk to him anymore. He was way out in front, all alone. He had demonstrated not how wise he was, but how foolish.

It is a lonely and dangerous thing to be on a pedestal, whether of your own or other's making. I am always afraid when people put me on a pedestal, because I know that sooner or later I will fall off on my head. That fall is always a very painful experience.

We should hear God's warning against such separation, in this case, caused and maintained by insulting others. It is both dangerous and damaging for individuals, groups or nations. We need to listen to and understand God's loving warning. But to see and feel the truth of that, we must look deep inside and see how much we are like everyone else, and give up the illusion of superiority. This illusion poisons relationships and cuts us off from our fellowship with all of humanity.

Fool!

FINALLY, IF IT is not bad enough to insult a person and thus person-ally inflict harm on him, Christ says it is worse to call him a fool, saying, "Whoever says, 'you fool!' shall be liable to the hell of fire." (Matthew 5:22c)

The hell of fire refers literally to the smoldering garbage dump outside of Jerusalem.

Since one of the major themes of this book is that everyone will be saved, I think I should examine more fully this concept of hell. The Greek word translated here "hell of fire" is *gehenna*. Gehenna really refers to a valley near Jerusalem called Hinnom. It was in this valley that Ahaz had burned children to worship Molech, a false, foreign god.

This fiery sacrifice is referred to in II Chronicles 28:3, "He burned incense in the valley of the son of Hinnom, and burned his sons as an offering."

King Josiah stopped the worship of Molech and cursed the valley forever as a part of his religious reform. It is recorded in II Kings 23:10, "He defiled To'pheth, which is in the valley of the sons of Hinnom, that no one might burn his son or his daughter as an offering to Molech."

Therefore, this valley became a garbage dump for Jerusalem. The burning garbage was always smoldering. This is the "unquenchable fire" Mark 9:44 uses to describe gehenna, which is translated "hell." The garbage was also infested with worms, which shows up in many images of hell. So it is natural that this valley would be seen as a place where useless, filthy things would be destroyed by fire and consumed by worms.

It is more than interesting that the idea of fire and worms found in the garbage dump outside Jerusalem appears in the traditional image of hell. I feel that this is a case of putting into some future, fictional hell, concepts and images that referred to a reality present in the time of Christ. It is absurd to take this image literally. Christ was using a local and dated idiom to convey to his listeners the extreme seriousness of calling someone a fool. To think that the smoldering fires and the loathsome worms from that garbage dump outside of Jerusalem refer literally to some future hell is to seriously misunderstand Christ's message. As in all his teachings and warnings, Christ, because of his love, is trying to keep us from unnecessary suffering on this earth. He is trying to spare us the suffering that can make this life hell.

Another minister once said, "There is enough hell in this life, we don't need any afterward."

God, in His love, would not only save us from some future hell, but also with His good and loving advice would spare us hell in this life. If we feel He threatens us with some future hell, we do not understand His love or His loving will for us either here or in the hereafter.

Each consequence, the judgement, the council and the hell of fire, is seen, in the local idiom, as being worse than the previous one and none are to be taken literally. The ascending order of consequences is referred to in order to make the point that each offense is more serious than the previous one.

I don't think anyone was expected literally to appear before the Sanhedrin for an insult or to be thrown into the garbage dump for calling someone a fool. I am even more confident that none of us is to appear before the Jewish high court, the Sanhedrin, nor are we to be condemned to the smoldering dump infested with worms outside Jerusalem. When we take the words "hell of fire" literally, we are led far astray in thinking we have proof that some people will be consigned to eternal damnation. Even if we are right in thinking such a place would be the eternal fate of some, who would it be? Who has not said, or at least thought, that someone else was a fool?

Christ says it is worse to say, "you fool," because this means, in the Jewish word originally used, to accuse the person of moral evil and thus destroy his good name in the community.

It is interesting that foolishness has here a connotation of evil, since I have been saying that what is called evil is foolishness. I also say that following God's will, which is called good, is wise.

Jesus is saying that this labeling of a person as a fool is clearly worse than even insulting a person. The person who is insulted only has to endure your personal rejection, but the person who is called evil, or a fool, faces the rejection of the whole community. The pain and suffering caused by the malicious tale teller or the gossip over the coffee cups can be the worst injury of all. When they pass judgement on another, as everyone does on occasion, they destroy that person in the eyes of many.

They might also consider that gossip is a two-edged sword. Those who gossip may be lent people's ears, but seldom their respect, and never their trust. Thus they have no real friends or intimate relationships. They must collect gossip and pass it on as their price of admission into people's gatherings and conversations. What they say about others often reveals more about them than those they speak of.

Walt Whitman also gives this warning in his poem "Song of Myself": "Whatever degrades another degrades me, and whatever is done or said returns at last to me."

Our tongue reveals and shapes our character, and thus seals our fate, not in the hands of God, who loves and accepts all of us as we are, but in the hands and opinions of those around us on this earth. The way we live and what we say affects us, more than anyone else. And it is our own doing, not God's, for He bears malice toward none. God warns us to follow His advice for our own sake, not His.

Still, one must recognize that there is a great need to talk about people. After all, people are very important, and they cannot be ignored. I often talk about other people. I wondered what I would talk about if I excluded people from my list of topics. Then it occurred to me that talking about people I love and sharing the good and beautiful things I know about people would be all right. So I tried it. I discovered that thinking and talking about the good and beautiful things I know about people, made my heart fill up even more with love for those people. My heart basked in the beauty of those people. And the people I shared that beauty with, also loved and enjoyed the beauty of those people. I found my heart richer. When I shared those riches with others, they were also richer. I realized then that remembering and sharing good things about others was so much better than criticizing them.

Chapter 7: Turn the Other Cheek?

IN THE LAST CHAPTER, I dealt with the problem of eliminating negative feelings, like anger, from life. In this chapter, I will deal with nurturing some positive responses to life's problems and demands. For this, I look to one of the most familiar passages of the Sermon on the Mount, which is often quoted to illustrate how different and difficult the Christian ethic is.

The scripture is Matthew 5:38-39: "You have heard that it was said, 'An eye for an eye and a tooth for a tooth.' But I say to you, Do not resist one who is evil. But if anyone strikes you on the right cheek, turn to him the other also."

People often talk about "turning the other cheek" as something expected of Christians. I get the sense that they see this turning the other cheek as unreasonable or impractical. There are jokes about it, like, "Turn the other cheek, and if he hits you again, let him have it back."

This implies that they might see their way clear to give someone a second chance to hurt them, but then, watch out. One gets the sense of people trying to bring themselves to obey the letter of the law, and that is their limit. In fact they can hardly manage even that.

But Jesus, in the Sermon on the Mount, is challenging us to struggle with the spirit of the law, until we finally understand what He is asking us to do. Then we may realize that, in some truly amazing way, it is the best and most beautiful way to live.

We must examine this "turning the other cheek" very carefully, if we are even to glimpse what He is pointing us to. To simply take what He says literally, and to think that is all there is, is to be greatly misled, and to miss the pearl of wisdom buried deep within. Christ is not merely talking about what we should do; He is trying to show us the way to become what we should be. Let's look closely then at this scripture.

Most people are right-handed. For a right-handed person who is facing you to strike you on the right cheek, he must very deliberately bring his hand all the way across, and then bring it back, striking you with the back of the hand. In the time of Christ, striking a person with the back of the hand on the cheek was considered extremely insulting. This is because a person suddenly angered would strike you with the more natural motion of the front of the hand. A blow with the back of the hand must be premeditated, and thus fully intended, delivering quite definitely the insult and injury.

So it is not so much any threat of physical injury that Christ is talking about, but a cold, calculating, cruel insult. Therefore I will look at how people react to insults and why. First of all, Christ does not want us to fake our response. He would want us to turn the other cheek, but if we do it just to please Him, we have not understood what He really wants.

What He really wants is for us to achieve a state of mind and heart that will really make us feel like turning the other cheek, rather than retaliating. You see, He wants our life to be so wonderful that an insult does not anger us, and therefore does not generate an urge for revenge. He wants us to be so strong and loving that the cruelest insult simply bounces off leaving us untouched.

We might feel that such an expectation is even more unreasonable and unrealistic than the request that we stifle our anger and turn the other cheek just to please God. But God understands that such pretended meekness, or a religion that demands we stifle our feelings and restrain our actions, will not lead to a full and satisfying life.

God seeks not so much to change our actions as to change our hearts. He wants us to find hearts that freely follow His will because they have learned that His will is the wisest way to live. In this case, He wants us to have such great hearts that they cannot be insulted. Can we imagine being able to go through life never feeling insulted, never getting angry or hurt at the words and actions of others? Wouldn't that be a desirable thing to achieve? It is just such a heart that Christ desires for each of us, because He loves us. So He tells us to turn the other cheek, knowing that those who really struggle with that, have a chance of learning the secret of achieving such a strong and loving heart.

Now, of course, we will never have such a good heart that every insult passes by, leaving us unscathed, but the closer we get to that ideal, the happier we will be. Perhaps we have even known some people who seem able to shrug off insults, with no thought or malice. What is their secret? I think it is self-esteem. A person with a strong, healthy self-esteem is almost impossible to insult. Such a person has a secure self-image and it is not easily threatened. People may say and do terrible things, but this person remains unshaken. The question we must then ask is, "How can we develop a good sense of self-esteem?"

The first problem is that, by yourself, you probably cannot build up your self-esteem. The second problem is that no one else, on his own, can build up your self-esteem either. So there is frustration and failure for the person who tries to build up his own self-esteem and receives no help from others. There is also frustration and failure for anyone who tries to build up someone else's self-esteem and gets no help from that person or from others. Many people must affirm a person if progress is to be made, and one of the people trying, must be the person whose self-esteem is being built up.

At this point, you may be saying, "All right, all ready, tell us what the secret is, and don't keep dragging it out!"

Well, it would be nice if it were so simple. I make it sound complex, because it is complex, not because I do not want you to understand. That is why the teaching in the Sermon on the Mount is so difficult, not because Jesus is trying to hide anything from us, but because finding the best life and living it is difficult. It cannot be made simple.

Now to the ingredients of good self-esteem, or at least the ones I see now. First, a person must feel loved. Of course, you will not be loved by everyone. But you must feel loved by enough people, and they must be important people to you. Feeling loved by only one person is usually not enough. That is why those who think marrying your one true love is the answer to everything are in for a disappointment. One person can never meet all your needs. If enough people who you really care about love you, then the rest of the world can hate you. On the strength of the love from those important people, you can be strong.

This is why it is so important that we express our love for one another. We all need to feel loved, and we need frequent assurances of that love. If enough people express their love for us, it is possible that we can improve our self-esteem enough to feel loved by others, and thus to love ourselves.

Another reason we need frequent assurances that people love us is because the world is always delivering shocks and insults that undermine our self-esteem. And finally, if we know ourselves very well, it is hard to believe that anyone can really love us. That makes it all the more wonderful, even miraculous, that people do love us. The greatest and most precious miracle on this earth is love. Rejoice in it, and share it with others, so they may also rejoice.

Without the assurance of the love of some important others, all of our attempts to build our self-esteem will fail. Everyone needs that love, so seek ways of letting your love flow to others in word and deed. The world is always starved for love. People cannot grow without love, even as plants cannot grow without light. Studies have shown that babies who have all their physical needs cared for, but are not held and loved, may actually die for lack of that love. So let your love shine on others and maybe it will help some of them to grow in self-esteem and love and also in joy and beauty. When their well of love is full, it may overflow and cause them to give some to others.

But everyone does not grow when they are shown love. This is sad, but true. Perhaps they do not grow because they must also work at it. What they must foster in themselves is honesty, integrity and belief. They must, for example, believe in the love that is shown them, or they do not receive it.

We must believe in love to receive it. It can be given, but it cannot make the connection in our hearts, unless we open our hearts up and believe it, thus becoming very vulnerable. It is this vulnerability that causes us to close our hearts and not believe in love.

We would all like to believe we are loved. But if we do open up our hearts to others and lower all our defenses, believing that they love us, we give them the ability to betray us. Betrayal plunges a knife into our hearts and can hurt us terribly. If this happens enough, we may no longer believe in love, because it has hurt us too often and too deeply. We will prefer the loneliness to the pain.

The old saying is, "It is better to have loved and lost than never to have loved at all." There have been times when I thought only the very young could believe that, but those were bad times

119

in my life. I feel now that love is worth any sacrifice and any injury. I hope I will always feel that way.

You cannot really believe anyone loves you unless you are honest with yourself. That may seem a strange statement, but it is true, because one way of trying to bolster self-esteem is by lying to yourself, *i.e.*, by telling yourself that you are better than you are. Such self-pretence, such self-righteousness, is a lie, and you know that deep in your heart. So if people love the good person you are pretending to be, you still cannot feel loved as the person you subconsciously know yourself to be inside. If people love your mask, you will not feel they have loved the real person behind the mask. If you hide that real self, full of good and evil, even from yourself, then no one can love your dark side, because no one, even yourself, knows that dark side. It is the very worst in you that must be revealed and known to yourself, and eventually to some others. All this must be accepted by them and by yourself if you are ever to feel loved completely, just as you are.

Complete honesty is necessary for strong self-esteem. So honesty with yourself and some others, who will love you even with your worst revealed, is necessary to have good self-esteem, and to feel really loved. You must choose carefully those you confess your dark side to, because it will hurt, rather than help you, if you are rejected when you open up.

You should choose people you have found to be very loving and accepting. Then you can slowly build a more honest and intimate relationship with them, until it is all out and loved and accepted. If you are afraid to reveal something, see how they react to the same fault in others, maybe even discussing hypothetical cases with them. It is risky to open up and show the skeletons in your closet. It is even riskier to show them to people who are very close to you. But you must take that risk, to find some people who will love you completely. Their love is needed to enable you to accept yourself as you are, with all the good and bad you are aware of.

Lastly, integrity is needed. As I have pointed out before, integrity can be a help in standing up against insults and criticism. If we do things we really believe in and are proud of what we have done, then criticism will sound like compliments.

Someone told me one day that I was criticized for not preaching about hell. I was glad the word was getting around. I was not in the least offended by what was probably intended as criticism. If I do what I really feel is right, then any criticism of it seems more like a compliment, because the intended criticism describes a deed I consider noble rather than base. If, on the other hand, I have done something of which I am ashamed, any mention of it will probably throw me for a loop. I may be hurt and angry, before I can stop myself. Here, honesty can still help me. If I have already admitted to myself that I have done something shameful or foolish, and dealt with my feelings concerning it, then I will not feel as threatened when it is mentioned. I already know within myself that what they say is not an insult, but the truth.

If I have also reconciled myself to my foolishness, and accepted and forgiven myself, I can stand up against the exposure of my folly. Again, love from others can help. If I have confessed my deed and shame to another, and found they can still accept and love me, I know someone will accept me no matter what others may say. That also makes it easier for me to accept myself as a person who has done this shameful thing. I feel I am a person who is still acceptable and lovable. If all the important people still love and accept me and I have accepted myself, having admitted my folly and knowing that I am not perfect nor will ever be perfect, then I can stand strong and unshaken against any accusation concerning it.

So love, honesty and integrity are things that can build our self-esteem. They can give us a good and secure self-image, so we can stand up against the many insults that life will deal out to each of us. It is such strength that God would wish for us. He encourages us to find that strength by asking us to "turn the other cheek." He hopes this will set us out on a search that, if faithfully and honestly pursued in love, will bring great rewards.

Indeed, one of the rewards is what we can learn, even from insults. Listen carefully to criticism. If we are honest with ourselves and know the insult to be false, we can disregard it.

But sometimes, enemies can teach us more than friends, if they accurately point out our weaknesses. This can help us to know ourselves better, and to understand how others see us.

Then if we turn the other cheek, maybe they will give us more valuable information about ourselves. We can learn from all life's experiences, whether they seem good or bad.

Chapter 8: Love Your Enemies?

WHEN CHRIST CHALLENGES US TO love our enemies, He is setting before us the greatest and most important goal for life. It is probably also the most difficult goal. Why should we undertake this challenge? I have been trying to show that the goals God sets for us are intended to make life better, rather than being something to please a whimsical deity.

So of what value to us is learning to love our enemies? The simplest response I can think of is to ask you this question, "Would you rather be surrounded by people you love, or by people you hate?"

I feel sure we would rather be surrounded by people we love. It is within our power to always be surrounded by people we love. All we have to do is learn to love the people we are surrounded by.

Now that is all very simple and imprecise. We have not defined what we mean by love or looked at how we might learn to love our enemies. But mine is a theology of the heart. My heart seems to lead the way better than my head, and it tells me that loving people is more satisfying than hating them. Later, I reason out why this may be true, but my heart leads the way before I can find the words or concepts to explain it. Even at their best, words and definitions fall far short of explaining the realities of feelings. It is the heart that really moves us, not the head, but words are necessary to convey our discoveries to others.

So I will examine what Christ says about loving your enemies.

In Matthew 5:44-45 Christ says, "Love your enemies and pray for those who persecute you, so that you may be sons of your Father who is in heaven; for he makes his sun rise on the evil and on the good, and sends rain on the just and on the unjust."

First, we must look at this word "love". Love is the most important, yet the least understood, word in the English language and in our Christian faith. I discussed love in the first chapter of this book, but I will refresh our understanding here. The love we usually think of is what I call romantic love. This is love for someone who is desirable and whom we wish to spend time with and make our own.

This is not the love Christ refers to in the statement, "Love your enemies."

He is referring, instead, to the kind of love God feels for us. God's love is constant, unconditional and unending, regardless of what we do or think. It is that quality of love that assures me that everyone will be saved. God, following His own advice to us, loves all His enemies. He cares about us even when we are His worst enemy. We can be God's enemy, but He will never be our enemy. God, in His love, always wishes us the greatest good. That is why He gives us many commandments to help guide us to that greatest good. His commandments are gifts of His love for us.

Christ very clearly states that it is this Godlike love which we are to feel for our enemies. That is what He means when He speaks of our being sons of our Father who is in heaven. Since they did not have many adjectives in the language He spoke, they would refer to being a "son of" in order to indicate that you were "like" that person. Therefore, even if people maliciously mistreat us, we should bear no malice toward them, and, indeed, we should wish them the best. This love does not mean that we necessarily like that person, in the sense that we would desire to spend a lot of time with them and would enjoy their company. It does mean, however, that we care about their welfare, and would help them if they needed it.

Perhaps a good analogy would be that of brothers and sisters. Bothers and sisters often fight, and sometimes they claim not to like each other. They may usually get along like cats and dogs. Still, when the chips are down, they will come to each other's aid. We are all children of our Father who is in heaven, so we are all brothers and sisters. Blood is thicker than water, and we understand that on this earth. What we need to understand is that we are also bound together with everyone by the blood of Christ. Therefore, we should care for each other as we would any brother or sister on this earth.

Perhaps all this makes no sense to us. Why should we care about people who hurt us, who are our professed and proven enemies? We may feel that people should get what they "deserve." We expect people to be punished when they do wrong. Perhaps this is much of the objection to the idea of universal salvation. But Christ points out that God treats both the good and the bad with equanimity on this earth. The rain and the sun come to people regardless of their righteousness.

William Barclay tells a story of a Jewish rabbi who was amazed by the fact that rain fell on the fields of the righteous and the wicked alike. He also was impressed by God's benevolence to all as he noticed that the sun shone on righteous Israel the same as on the Gentiles.[1]

I am reminded of a joke told by my church history professor at Princeton Seminary. Dr. Hope said there was a story from early

Christian times of God making all the cattle of the pagans die, while all the cattle of the Christians remained healthy. "Personally," he quipped in his comical way, "I think that is a bunch of bull."

No matter how people feel about God, He always wishes them well and treats them the same as everyone else. There is nothing we can think or do that will cause God to turn His back on us, or treat us differently. When I examine the real world, I, like the rabbi and Dr. Hope, see no sign of God punishing His enemies on this earth. Some people see this as evidence that God does not care about us. I see it as evidence that He cares about us all equally. It is proof here and now of how God loves and cares, even about His enemies.

I also feel that there are no good or bad people. Everyone is a mixture of good and bad. Christ probably did not put it that way, because people would not understand, and it might only confuse the issue to try to explain it at that point. I know from preaching sermons that I must often oversimplify things to say anything at all. If the bad were to be punished for every misdeed, none of us would survive. Fortunately, God is a God of mercy, and He does not punish us. Instead, God continues to give us the sun and the rain, and also His guidance, to help us on the path of life.

Christ makes it clear that God treats people the same, wishing them all well. Likewise, He would have us treat all people well, no matter how they treat us. Maybe we can understand that intellectually, but emotionally we find it hard to bring ourselves around to loving our enemies. God does not imagine that it will be easy. It is not romantic love, which one falls into without even trying, that He is asking of us. The love that God feels and wishes for us is an act of the will as well as the heart.

The Greek word for this Godlike love is *agape*. Psychologist Erich Fromm portrays agape as being actively concerned about the welfare and growth of those we love.[2] This means that we not only care about the other, but we do what we can to help them become better people. To care for our enemies and return them good for their evil may seem foolish. But this is the only way that holds out any hope of bringing peace and even goodwill between people. Agape does not come naturally or easily. We must make an effort to overcome our tendency for anger or bitterness toward those who threaten or hurt us. Agape means compassion for people we don't even like. This goodwill endures despite the character or actions of our enemy. William Barclay refers to agape as "invincible goodwill."[3]

To achieve this "invincible goodwill," as Barclay defines agape, I think we must also examine our emotions.

Our first and main reaction to being hurt is usually anger and the desire for revenge. We do not want anger to develop into bitterness, which hardens our hearts. Revenge is sometimes seen as a way of settling the issue. Someone has caused us to suffer, and we want to make that person suffer in return. We do not wish our enemies well, but wait for an opportunity to get back at them. This course of action solves nothing. In fact, it makes things worse. Revenge sparks revenge, suffering breeds more suffering, and the situation escalates downward. This way you make more, and worse, enemies.

But there are other reasons why revenge is bad. When I look into my heart, I find I take no pleasure in anyone's suffering, even if they have caused me much suffering. I have seen too much suffering in life. Causing more suffering only makes me feel worse. I cannot help it if someone hurts me. But if I hurt someone else, either on purpose or by accident, I cannot bear it. I agonize over any injury I have caused. So to cause another's suffering, even in revenge, only causes me more grief, plus guilt and remorse. Revenge may seem good on the spur of the moment, but when I regain my senses, I will long lament the suffering I have caused. I grieve at the suffering of others, even if they have caused it themselves. I believe God also grieves whenever any of us suffer, even if it is our own fault.

There is too much suffering in the world and not enough love. So I will strive to love even my enemies. In so far as I succeed in that love, I feel good. I am not responsible for how others respond, whether with good or evil. But I feel better, even if they respond harshly, when I feel that I have not been cruel to them and caused their harsh response. It is my thoughts and words and deeds that cause me joy or anguish, far more than anyone else's.

It is not pleasant to have enemies and to be hurt by them, but I found out long ago that people who deliberately go around hurting others are hurting inside. They are not happy, and their inner pain causes them to inflict pain on others. Happy people mostly share their joy, and sad people, unfortunately, mostly share their sorrow. I feel sorry for those who feel they must hurt me or others; who feel that they must be my enemies. How sad it is that they have chosen to be my enemies. When I see their sadness, I cannot help but care for them. I find my heart growing soft and tender. It is a far better feeling in my heart than anger, which consumes, or bitterness, which poisons a heart. For the sake of my own heart, if for no other reason, I will choose to be their friend, even if they remain my enemies.

Any breach in human relationships is a wound in the hearts involved and in the heart of God. The only real solution is to repair the relationship.

Abraham Lincoln once said, "The only way to eliminate an enemy is to make him a friend."

We may not always succeed in that, but it seems a more positive and hopeful way to relate to people who consider themselves our enemies, than making the animosity mutual. It is sad to have people who do not like you, but the only conceivable method of solving the problem in a happy way is to return goodness for their evil.

Paul says in Romans, "Bless those who persecute you; bless and do not curse them.... Repay no one evil for evil .... Do not be overcome by evil, but overcome evil with good." (Romans 12:14, 17, 21)

It may be difficult, maybe impossible, but it is the path with hope for more love and less hate. No other path makes sense or has any chance of success in healing the broken relationships that cause such sadness and suffering.

We may think that loving our enemies is a nice ideal, but it makes no sense in the real world. So I would like to apply it to a real world problem. In this country, we live pretty secure lives, yet one enemy strikes successfully against all our military might. That enemy is the international terrorist. I look particularly at the terrorists in the Middle East. I will ponder how terrorism might be stopped.

The first response to a terrorist attack is usually anger and the desire for revenge. I have felt this myself. But when I examined the realities, I realized that Israel has followed the policy of retaliation since the very beginning, and terrorism has not stopped. Indeed, retaliation just increases the hatred and desire for revenge on the terrorist side. It should be obvious that revenge does not work.

Maybe retaliation does not work, but how can we love the terrorist? We must understand the meaning of this love we are asked to feel. Remember that Barclay calls it "invincible goodwill." It is invincible if the goodwill can be felt no matter who does what. In this case, I feel that we should have goodwill toward the terrorist, in the sense that we should wish them well. I don't mean that we should wish them success in their terrorist activities. I mean we should wish them true happiness and fulfillment in their lives. Terrorism is the result of the unhappiness, indeed desperation, of the terrorist. Some terrorists even undertake suicide missions. That is a sure sign of how desperate they are. I have found that desperate people do desperate things. If there is a solution to terrorism, it is to relieve the desperation of those who engage in it. We should hope that they find a way out of that desperation to happy, fulfilled lives. That good fortune would be best for them and also for us, because we are the potential victims of terrorism.

When love is understood as wishing the enemy well in his search for true happiness, it is the only thing that can work. True happiness comes from learning to love everyone, in the sense of caring about everyone's happiness. If enemies found that happiness, they would no longer be enemies. What better solution can there be? They will never learn love from hatred or revenge. They may not learn it from love, but it is the only possible way. Love, even for enemies, is the only thing that makes sense or has any chance of success in the real world. Far from being an unworkable ideal, it is the most practical way of living on this earth. God once more shows us the very best way to live, because He cares about our true happiness and fulfillment.

Love is also the path that God always chooses, and chose when He sent His son, Jesus Christ. We are often enemies of God, turning our back on Him and hurting Him, but He always reaches out to us with His love. Christ came and died to bring the message of our sure salvation. He lived to show us the ways to live and love that would lead to the most beautiful life.

When he says in Matthew 5:48, "You, therefore, must be perfect, as your heavenly Father is perfect" he is wishing the very best for us. What more could He wish for us than a perfect life? Everyone would like a perfect life in some sense. Christ tries to tell us that our life will only be perfect if it is lived perfectly in the way God lives His. It may be an impossible dream to completely fulfill on this earth, but it is a great goal. That goal Christ gives us because He loves us.

Conclusion

HIS BOOK IS ABOUT LOVE, especially the love of God. Most Christians would say that God is love, and He loves everyone. But they limit God's love by limiting salvation to Christians. In this book, I state my belief that God's love is without limit, so His salvation is for every person, without exception. This means that all Christians, Jews, Muslims, Buddhists and all other faiths, even agnostics and atheists are surely loved and saved by God. Hopefully, this message will promote peace and reconciliation between all religions, faiths and individuals in this world.

God's love, or agape, is different than the romantic love we often think of when love is mentioned. Agape arises from the very nature of God, so He loves everyone, no matter how desirable or undesirable they are. Agape is an active concern for the welfare of the loved one. God has expressed this concern for each of us by His actions, which are gifts of love.

As His first gift of love, God has tried to assure us of His love and salvation through many messengers. His greatest assurance is found in the sending and sacrifice of His only son, Jesus. God wishes to set our mind at ease concerning our sure salvation, so we can concentrate on the living of our daily life on this earth.

As a second gift of love, God has acted again and again to give us His loving advice for the living of this life. Because He loves us, God gives us guidance through His commandments and the ethical teaching found in scripture. He tries to enrich our lives by leading us into the most meaningful and fulfilling paths. These paths of compassion, peace and love are witnessed to by all the great world religions as the very essence of life's purpose. Only by finding and following God's will can we enjoy the best and most beautiful life on this earth.

When I walk out the door of my country home each morning, I am overwhelmed by the beauty of God's creation, which is another gift of His love. I start the new day fresh, seeking the beauty I am convinced that God, in His love, wishes everyone to experience daily in their lives.

I have written this book about God's limitless love, so we can all rejoice in our certain salvation. I hope we will then eagerly seek God's will and by following that wisdom, find the wonderful life God intends for each of us. It is surely the greatest wisdom to embrace God's love, so it can guide and sustain us, now and forever.

The catechism I learned when I joined the church stated, "Man's chief end is to glorify God and to enjoy him forever."

I have found my greatest fulfillment and joy in seeking God and following His will. In this book, I share some of the insights I discovered in pursuing that end. I pray these thoughts may benefit humanity, as God, in His love, would wish.

It is not my intention that you simply accept my thoughts. Truth is synonymous with reality, and reality can never really be contained in words. I hope you find what I say valuable in your own search for truth and understanding. What is of no value to you, I would advise you to discard.

I wish for you to explore for yourself and find in your heart treasures that are as helpful as these are to me.

If you pursue this important search for meaning, perhaps these words of Walt Whitman in "Song of Myself" will come true for you:

"You shall no longer take things at second or third hand, nor look through the eyes of the dead, nor feed on the spectres in books.

You shall not look through my eyes either, nor take things from me,

You shall listen to all sides and filter them from yourself."

Appendix A More About Salvation

THE FUNDAMENTALIST SEES THE WHOLE Bible as inspired directly, word for word, by God. He interprets it literally, admitting to no contradictions therein. He does not recognize that passages are conditioned by the author and the time in which they were written. There are different currents in scripture which lead interpreters in diverse directions. The most obvious example of failure to find and follow the correct current in scripture is that of the Jewish image of the Messiah prevalent in the time of Jesus.

From the Old Testament prophets, Daniel and the intertestamental apocalyptic literature, came the expectation of a Messiah who would bring an earthly kingdom in which the Jews would rule over the entire world. If the Gentiles were included in this kingdom at all, it was in a clearly subordinate position.

In their zealous study of scripture, the Jews of Christ's day did not notice the suffering servant passages like the ones in Isaiah 53. They misinterpreted these and the many other passages later cited by the New Testament and the Christian church as predicting Jesus.

They missed, and still miss the Messiah, because they cling to the wrong current in the Old Testament.

The Christians saw many Old Testament passages fulfilled by Jesus of Nazareth, thus proving He is the Messiah. They picked out the ripples of the correct current from among the many divergent ones. However, they may have stretched some of the passages to get them to fit Christ. Their use goes from the famous, "Behold, a virgin shall conceive and bear a son, and his name shall be called Emmanuel" in Matthew 1:23, to the blatant allegorical interpretations of Paul. For example, in Galatians 4:21-31, Paul sees the Galatians as children of slavery through Hagar, if they cling to the old covenant under the law.

The "behold, a virgin" passage came from Isaiah 7:14. When the Revised Standard Version of the Bible replaced the word "virgin" with the translation "young woman" in Isaiah, it caused an uproar. It was one of the reasons that many conservative Christians rejected the RSV and stayed with the King James Version of the Bible. This shows how shaky the New Testament's use of the Old sometimes is. The Old Testament did not point clearly, in a single stream, to the type of Messiah to expect. Therefore, it was often necessary to take hints, or glimpses, and show that, in spirit, they fit the Jesus whom the Christians proclaimed as Messiah.

Modern liberal scholars still speculate as to whom Isaiah really referred in his suffering servant passages. They must admit it was probably not the Messiah, and certainly not specifically Jesus of Nazareth, whom Isaiah knowingly foresaw. Still, it is valid to take the spirit of the passages and see them fulfilled by Christ. Some Old Testament passages foreshadow Christ as He appeared. But one needs to go beyond the vision and intentions of the authors of those passages, to really see the Messiah as He actually lived and died and rose again.

In my reasoning so far, I have tried to establish two points. The first is that there are different currents in the scriptures, and we need to pick out the current that best conforms to God's spirit and plan. Otherwise we, like the first century Jews, may miss the Messiah and His message. We must beware of other currents in the Bible suggesting eternal damnation for some. I question the prevalent Christian vision, which sees supremacy, or even the sole salvation, of the New Israel. The New Israel means Christians, however we define them. It smells like the mistake of the Old Israel repeated. The circle of God's love knows no limit, and I believe the circle of the saved is just as all-inclusive.

The second point is that, while there is no full-grown definite teaching of universal salvation in the Bible, there are many glimpses of that spirit. I feel that I have established precedent from the New Testament's use of the Old Testament for expanding these hints beyond the author's specific intent.

How is one to really know which current in scripture comes closest to God's spirit and final intent? It is the Holy Spirit who speaks in the heart and reveals the right interpretation. Hosea discerned God's thoughts and feelings as the result of his own experiences with his unfaithful wife and his feelings about her. So, I will draw from my own heart and experience, which work in me my belief in universal salvation. But even here I will not go unsupported by scripture, which shows the hearts of others who have felt similar feelings. In the testimony of Paul in Romans and the writer of I John, I think I find kindred feelings.

Paul, in Romans 9-11, bares the anguish in his heart over his people Israel. He says in Romans 9:2-3, "That I have great sorrow and unceasing anguish in my heart. For I could wish that I myself were accursed and cut off from Christ for the sake of my brethren, my kinsmen by race."

He struggles, out of love, with the seeming rejection of Israel. He finally concludes in Romans 11:32 with this belief, "For God has consigned all men to disobedience, that he may have mercy upon all."

Paul's heart sees salvation for all his people. We know that what he says here testifies at least to his hope for the universal salvation of Israel. However, in this final verse, it is not clear as to whether he means only the salvation of Israel or of all people everywhere.

While I cannot definitely state that Paul is thinking of salvation for everyone, the same spirit holds for all people. It was his love for Israel that convinced him that God could not reject them in the end. It has been the love in my heart for all people, which has testified within me to the certainty of salvation for all people everywhere, and in every age. If I can love so much that I wish salvation for everyone, surely God's love cannot be less than mine. In fact, we have abundant proof that God's love is far greater. I do not love enough to die for others, but God, in Christ, has already undergone the sacrifice of death on a cross, demonstrating His universal love and salvation for everyone. God's sacrifice has assured us of His love and salvation beyond any reasonable doubt. How can we doubt such a love as that?

That this testimony of love is truly the testimony of the spirit of God is proclaimed by the writer of I John. In I John 4:12-13, we find, "No man has ever seen God; if we love one another, God abides in us and his love is perfected in us. By this we know that we abide in him and he in us, because he has given us of his own Spirit."

In I John 4:8 we read, "He who does not love does not know God; for God is love."

When we love one another, we have God's spirit in us, and we understand the mysterious God to whom scripture alludes. We understand the very essence of His heart. I do not say that God's love is perfected in me, but I have caught a glimpse of it in my heart, in my experience and in scripture. Thus I believe I know God, and His Spirit testifies that all people will be saved.

Still, I am not arrogant enough to imagine that I have convinced all of you of the universal salvation that I have put forth. I am not writing this book to convince anyone that universal salvation is true. I am writing so those who have felt as I do, and want everyone to be saved, can feel free to do so without thinking that idea is heresy. Once I began to openly express my belief in universal salvation I was amazed by how many others agreed with me. This included college religion professors and even a bishop of the Anglican Church. Bishop John A. T. Robinson presented his belief in universal salvation in his book *Honest to God*. Recently a professor of religion from Duke University, now retired, told me that no serious Biblical scholar would consider the contents of my book heretical.

I discovered that as far back as the second century A.D., the great Christian scholar Origen believed God would save everyone.[1] Because it is God's purpose to save people and Satan's purpose to damn them eternally, Origen felt that if hell is not empty in the end, Satan wins against God. The idea that the Devil ultimately triumphs over God is inconceivable.

Is it possible that believing everyone will be saved, if incorrect, will jeopardize our own salvation? Certainly not! Christianity has long preached that if we believe in Christ as our Savior we are saved by that faith. If we believe everyone is saved, that necessarily means we believe we are saved. Whenever we convince someone that they are saved, their salvation is secure. This is true whether everyone is saved or only those who have faith.

That universal salvation is a real possibility cannot be denied. That is the conclusion of the Report of the Commission on Christian Doctrine, appointed by the Archbishops of Canterbury and York, published in 1938.[2]

I agree that universalism goes beyond the explicit New Testament evidence, but Christ goes beyond the clear Old Testament evidence. I have also seen the impossibility of proving which of the biblical currents reveals God's true spirit and intent, just as it is still impossible today to prove to the Jews that Jesus of Nazareth was the Messiah.

The testimony of the Holy Spirit in the heart breeds conviction, and I have written the testimony from my heart in this book. I bring not proof, for that is impossible, but my belief and the basis for it in scripture, as well as my experience and my heart. Indeed, if most parents would really look into their hearts, they would have to admit that they could not utterly reject their children, no matter what they did or became. Then how can we believe that our heavenly Father would reject His children? His love is greater than that of any earthly parent.

Since we are to love everyone and earnestly strive for their salvation, surely we should all rejoice at the possibility that everyone will be saved.

Notes

Chapter 2

  1   Some other scriptures that witness to the salvation of all
are: I Timothy 4:10; Romans 5:18; Romans 11:32; Psalm 130:3-4;
II Peter 3:9; Luke 15:3-7.

  2   *Church Dogmatics, Volume VI, The Doctrine of Reconciliation, Part
One*, by Karl Barth, T&T Clark: Edinburgh, 1985, p. 91-2

  3   *Eternal Life, Life After Death as a Medical, Philosophical and
Theological Problem*, by Hans Küng, Translated by Edward Quinn,
Doubleday & Company Inc: New York, 1984, p. 139.

  4   *The Mind of Christ*, by William Barclay, Harper: San Francisco:
1976, p. 283-4

  5   *Modern Man in Search of a Soul*, by C.G. Jung, Harcourt Brace
and Company: San Diego, 1933, p. 235.

Chapter 3
1   *Modern Man in Search of a Soul,* by Carl Jung, Harcourt Brace and Company: San Diego, 1933, pp. 234-235.

Chapter 4
1   *The Gospel of Matthew, Volume I,* by William Barclay, The Westminster Press: Phila., 1958, pp. 124-125.
2   *Ibid,* p. 125.

Chapter 5
1   *The Gospel of Matthew, Volume I,* by William Barclay, The Westminster Press: Phila., 1958, p. 83.
2   *Ibid,* p. 84.
3   *Ibid,* p. 98

Chapter 6
1   *The Gospel of Matthew, Volume I,* by William Barclay, The Westminster Press: Phila., 1958, pp. 136-137.

Chapter 8
1   *The Gospel of Matthew, Volume I,* by William Barclay, The Westminster Press: Phila., 1958, pp. 174-175.
2   *The Art of Loving,* by Erich Fromm, Harper & Row: NY, 1956, p. 26.
3   *The Gospel of Matthew, Volume I,* by William Barclay, The Westminster Press: Phila., 1958, pp. 172-173

Appendix A
1   *The Judgment of The Dead, The Idea of Life After Death in Major Religions,* by S. G. F. Brandon, Charles Scribners & Sons: NY, 1967, p. 11
2   *Ibid,* p. 134

Scripture Index

Scripture Index

Index

Defense, 71, 73, 89, 94
Demanding, 9, 39, 57, 77, 78
Desperate, 9, 129
Desperation, 59, 87, 129
Despise, 108, 109
Destroyed, 25, 53, 60, 65, 70, 89, 94, 111
Devil, 24, 139
Die, 23, 26, 27, 51, 55, 92, 95, 119, 126, 138, 155
Doubt, 23, 79, 91, 138

E
Earth, 9, 15, 18, 19, 23, 24, 38, 41, 47, 55-57, 61, 64, 68-72, 74, 75, 77, 78, 81, 82, 90, 91, 96, 97, 101, 111, 112, 119, 125, 126, 130, 132
Elect, 20
Emerson, Ralph Waldo, 100
Enemies, 9, 11, 39, 46, 50, 88, 122-130
Enemy, 31, 124, 127-129
Enriched, 28
Envious, 29
Equal, 28, 49, 108, 156
Eros, 17, 19
Eternal, 19, 23, 25, 26, 34, 37, 38, 56, 59, 60, 64, 96, 112, 137, 141
Eternal damnation, 19, 34, 37, 112, 137
Ethical, 11, 34, 39, 43, 46, 48, 132
Ethics, 33, 34, 43
Evil, 9, 23-25, 28, 29, 38, 44,

45, 66, 73, 75, 82, 86, 97, 101, 108, 112, 115, 120, 124, 127, 128, 156
Expectations, 64, 101, 103, 104
Eye, 43, 44, 52, 53, 115

F
Failures, 73
Faith, 33, 34, 37, 45, 47, 59, 60, 66, 124, 139, 155, 156
Faithful, 25, 27, 99
Father, 22, 24, 27, 36, 37, 46, 78, 97, 124, 125, 130, 140, 154
Faults, 7, 9, 30, 79, 103
Fear, 17, 20, 34, 36, 37, 39-41, 44, 45, 51, 82, 83, 85, 87, 89, 92-94, 96, 97, 102, 103, 107
Feelings, 26, 38, 44, 45, 65, 66, 73, 80, 84, 90, 101, 102, 104, 106, 115, 117, 121, 124, 137, 156
Felons, 31
Fight, 69-71, 87, 90, 91, 125
Fighting, 18, 69, 71, 84, 86-88, 91
Fire, 24, 25, 70, 92, 110, 111, 156
Fool, 29, 30, 109-112
Foolish, 34, 38, 45, 66, 67, 74, 75, 84, 109, 121, 127
Foolishly, 29, 66
Forgive, 22, 26, 27, 39, 78-81, 100, 103, 106
Forgiven, 23, 26, 39, 78-81, 103, 121
Forgiveness, 22, 23, 26, 27, 78-81
Forgives, 23, 26, 39, 81
Forgiving, 19, 22, 80, 103

Words From The Author . . . About The Author

I WAS BORN JUNE 7, 1941 in Scranton, Pennsylvania. For the first four years of my life, we lived in a small trailer in a clearing in the woods in West Virginia. When my father abandoned us, my mother took us back to Scranton where we moved in with her parents. Our family became active in the Washburn Street Presbyterian Church.

By the time I reached junior high, the issue of salvation confronted me. A wily adolescent, I decided I would live as I pleased and get into heaven with a deathbed conversion. I was so mischievous that my Sunday School teacher Ted Koch joked to my mother that he would like to demote me. Yet Mr. Koch, who was also our youth fellowship advisor, was an example of a love that was there for me despite the trouble I caused.

We all moved to Middletown, Pennsylvania between ninth and tenth grade. There we attended Middletown Presbyterian Church, where my Sunday School teachers and youth fellowship advisors were Bob and Marge Lebo. Once more they displayed an unlimited patience and love for all of the young people. They really reminded me of Ozzie and Harriet Nelson who were prominent on TV at that time. In school I was the science nerd, but in the church I found a loving fellowship. Still during these years I began to worry that I might die too quickly to get that deathbed conversion in.

I entered Lafayette College, in Easton, Pennsylvania in the fall of 1959. I majored in Physics. While reading a letter by Martin Luther for freshman religion, I suddenly understood Luther's belief that we are saved by faith, as a free gift of God's grace. This was my rebirth experience, which I now realize is simply a flash of insight that is not even necessarily correct. I wanted to share the good news of the gospel with others. Each summer since I graduated from high school I volunteered to counsel at our church camp, Camp Michaux. Between my junior and senior year of college, I decided that I would rather be a minister than a physicist. I graduated from Lafayette College in 1963 with a Bachelor of Science in Physics. That summer I worked with children in wheel chairs at Camp Harmony Hall for the Easter Seal Society.

I enrolled in Princeton Theological Seminary that fall. There I majored in pastoral psychology. I served as student pastor at Irvington Presbyterian Church near Newark, New Jersey in the summer before my last year of seminary. I graduated from seminary in 1966 with a Bachelor of Divinity, which I upgraded to a Master of Divinity in 1970.

The summer of 1966 I took a quarter of clinical training in psychology at Philadelphia State Hospital, living on the hospital grounds for the three months of training.

In the fall I began my work as assistant pastor at First Presbyterian Church in Ambler, Pa., just north of Philadelphia. I chose an assistant pastorate to get more experience before launching out on my own.

In the fall of 1968, I moved to McAlisterville in central Pennsylvania to become the pastor of Lost Creek Presbyterian Church, which had 120 members. Now I was on my own, and I looked around for needs I could meet. I saw that the school district was not transporting children to kindergarten. So I began transporting some of the poor children who would not get there otherwise. Eventually my concerns for a good and equal education led me to serve on the school board for ten years.

I saw that no one was working with young people, so I started a single young adult group. I also started an ecumenical youth fellowship, became scoutmaster and opened a community youth center.

The manse was located close to the Fayette Fire Company and when the siren blew I knew someone needed help. I became a volunteer fireman. I also became an ambulance driver and attendant, eventually certifying as an Emergency Medical Technician. My love of nature led me to also serve as a volunteer Forest Fire Warden.

When I came to McAlisterville, I was a young social activist and anxious to make the church what I thought it should be. The congregation patiently accepted my zeal and naiveté, until I learned from them that loving and accepting people as they are is the best way to minister to people's needs. Love then may inspire people to be more beautiful and loving themselves. Condemnation and pressure inspires judgment and rejection.

From the many youth I worked with, there emerged a small sharing group which met in my house to share faith and other feelings. These teenagers helped me to love and accept even more, as they loved me, and I loved them, as if they were my own children.

Despite my rebirth experience in college, which assured me of my salvation, I was still troubled by my failure to live up to my ideal vision of a Christian life. The sharing group made me want to be worthy of their acceptance, yet I knew I was still a mixture of good and evil. Reading the writings of the psychiatrist, Carl Jung helped me to understand that we are all a mixture of good and evil.

Reading Walt Whitman's poetry helped me to accept all parts of myself and when I had accepted myself, to accept all others.

I had always had trouble with the idea that some people would go to hell, but I did not know of any other way of interpreting the Bible. Reading *Behold the Spirit* by Alan Watts opened my eyes to other possible interpretations. I began to study other religions and other philosophies, I took Walt Whitman's advice to,"Re-examine all you have been told at school or church or in any book, dismiss whatever insults your own soul".

I discovered it was possible to interpret scripture in other ways, and found passages which could mean that God would save everyone.

But if everyone is saved, why obey God's law? I realized that God's law shows us the wisest way to live. To follow it is wisdom and to disobey it is foolishness. The law is God's loving guidance to help us find the best possible life now.

In 1982 I began taking college courses in computer programming. While I was taking courses at Harrisburg Area Community College, I was hired to teach computer courses there. I taught courses to people on public assistance, regular undergraduates and even a course for the prisoners at the state prison in Camp Hill, Pennsylvania.

Unfortunately driving back and forth to teach these courses ruined my back and I had to quit. I did earn an Associate Degree in Data Processing from HACC in 1983.

I continued as pastor of my church until 1987 by which time it was obvious that my back was not going to improve, and I could no longer accept money for a job I could not adequately perform. Laying on people's floors might be all right for visiting members, but it did not work well for prospect calls. During the five years that I could not adequately minister to the needs of my congregation I wrote my book *Love Without Limit*. Some of the book was even typed lying down.

I finally resigned from my pastorate in January 1987. I was placed on the inactive list. After two years on the inactive list Carlisle Presbytery set aside my ordination with the possibility of picking it up again if I could ever serve another church. I retain my ordination in the Universal Life Church. I continued to marry people for a few years, until it became too hard on my health.

My interest in church camping continued throughout my ministry. I served on and chaired the Carlisle Presbytery Camping Committee, counseled, directed, and served as Chaplain at various camps. When Camp Michaux closed I headed the committee that negotiated our merger with two other presbyteries in Camp Krislund. I wrote the "History of Presbytery Camping" for *A Bicentennial History of the Presbytery of Carlisle*, published in 1986. I also wrote a poem entitled "Relationships" at Camp Krislund. I later submitted the poem to a poetry contest where it won honorable mention and was published in *Days of Future's Past* in 1989.

Each summer on vacation I would camp in the National Parks of the U.S. and Canada. Ranger hikes and campfire talks sparked my concern for the environment. I recycled all my waste and started the first newspaper recycling in the county.

In response to the Arab oil boycott of 1972, I insulated the manse and the church, installed storm windows, and constructed solar heating panels on the manse. I also invented some electric socks to keep my feet warm as I turned the thermostat back to 60 degrees. I bought a bicycle and began using it or walking for house calls. I sometimes hitchhiked to hospital calls.

My hobbies were very practical. I did the maintenance and repairs on my vehicles. I did woodworking, plumbing and electrical work, as well as repairing radios and TVs. I was an organic gardener and even saved my own seed from year to year. I studied eatable wild plants and other survival skills in the wild. All these hobbies ended when my back went bad in 1982. I fell back on reading which I had always enjoyed, although this was limited because of my inability to sit long. When I finally invented an infinitely adjustable back rest I was able to sit enough to do more reading.

When I resigned from the church in 1987 I still did not accept the reality of my disability. I thought I might be able to teach school because teachers stand most of the time. I used my certification to teach high school physics and mathematics to work as a substitute teacher. I was tentatively hired to teach Physics full time at John Harris High School in Harrisburg, Pennsylvania, but I failed the physical because of my back problems. I soon found that substitute teaching was also beyond my ability.

That summer I passed a course certifying me to be a District Justice in Pennsylvania and worked two hours a day in that office for a while. I found that even this was too much for my back.

I started walking and swimming when I was able. I suffered a series of other health problems. Finally I was able to crawl out of the hole enough to volunteer at the Juniata County Library for a few hours a week. I had served as secretary of the library board for about six years in the early 1970s.

When some of the people at the library learned I had written a book many years ago, they read it and urged me to get it published. The idea that writing might be a way to continue my ministry, which was cut short by my disability, led me to start writing a weekly religious column in Standard-Journal Newspapers of Milton, Pennsylvania. The column has been well received and I feel heartened that I am able to reach out and help people again.

I hope that my book, *Love Without Limit*, offers some service and guidance to others. The book is only an attempt to pass on some of the blessings and love I have felt from God and other people.

Walter E. Williams
McAlisterville, Pennsylvania 2003

Order Form For *Love Without Limit*

Send this form, a photocopy of this form or a letter containing the information requested below to:

Probe Publishing Company
P. O. Box 395
McAlisterville, PA 17049

Enclose a check or money order for $12.50, payable to Probe Publishing Company. Probe Publishing Company will pay Shipping and Handling and any applicable sales taxes.

Fill in name and address where the book is to be shipped:

Name: _____

Address: _____

City: _____ State: _____ Zip: _____

In case of questions concerning your order, please give your phone number and Email address:

Telephone: _____

Email address: _____

If you have questions, Probe Publishing Company can be reached by calling (717) 463-3878.

If the book is unsatisfactory for any reason you may return it for a full refund.